ILLUSIONS

S. A. Ozment

Dreamspinner Press

Published by
DREAMSPINNER PRESS

5032 Capital Circle SW, Suite 2, PMB# 279, Tallahassee, FL 32305-7886 USA
http://www.dreamspinnerpress.com/

This is a work of fiction. Names, characters, places, and incidents either are the product of author imagination or are used fictitiously, and any resemblance to actual persons, living or dead, business establishments, events, or locales is entirely coincidental.

Illusions
© 2015 S.A. Ozment.

Cover Art
© 2015 Christy Caughie.
Cover content is for illustrative purposes only and any person depicted on the cover is a model.

ISBN: 978-1-63216-488-9
Digital ISBN: 978-1-63216-489-6
Library of Congress Control Number: 2014953478
First Edition February 2015

Printed in the United States of America
∞
This paper meets the requirements of
ANSI/NISO Z39.48-1992 (Permanence of Paper).

Acknowledgments

This is my first novel and I could have never completed it without the encouragement of my friends. Thank you to Patricia, Eve, Teri, Anna, Elisa, Keren, Filippo, and Vicky. And a very special thanks to Dianne and Nicole, who were with me the entire way. And Jo, thank you for always encouraging me to follow my dreams.

To my sweet Courtney and Locksley. I love you both!

ACKNOWLEDGMENTS

CHAPTER 1

THE MORNING sun beamed through the large skylight window, creating a path of solar hell straight into Skylar's throbbing head. *Just whose bright idea was it to put skylights in the bedroom?* he thought as he tried to squeeze his eyes shut. Groaning loudly, he rolled over while pulling the sheets over his face in a lame attempt to block out the annoying sunlight. It took only a microsecond to realize that moving had been a huge mistake. Apparently, rolling over his six foot frame took more skill than he could muster, and he felt puke beginning to rise up in his throat. As dizziness threatened to overtake him, he wondered why in the hell he had drunk so much. Better yet, why had someone *let* him drink so much? Surely someone had to answer for this. But for now, all of that would have to wait. First he had to get himself out of bed.

As he lay there praying for his stomach to calm down and the spinning to cease, he contemplated just staying in bed for the day. Then he felt a tug on the covers he was cradling. *What the hell was that?* His heart pounded loudly as the realization hit him that he was not alone. Slowly he opened his eyes and tried to focus on what—or *who*—was monopolizing his covers. As he blinked his eyes open, a pretty blonde slowly came into view. *Shit! What have you done now?* As he studied her, the pounding in his head intensified. She had petite features and long wavy blonde hair that was spread out on the pillow. From the sound of her soft breathing, he knew she was still asleep. Leaning in a little to take a closer look, he saw that she was naked from the waist up, and though the rest of her was hidden underneath his extremely old, worn-out duvet, he was willing to bet she was naked from the waist down as well. *He* really *needed to stop drinking.*

Groaning, he lay back on his pillow, closing his eyes again in hope that it would all go away. *Who was she?* As he strained his throbbing brain to remember who was sharing his bed, pieces of the previous night slowly began to come back to him....

It had been the premiere party for his new television show. It was a special night, because normally television shows didn't get this type of promotion. However, *The Executives* aired on an American premium cable network, and the powers that be had invested a lot of time, money, and energy in hopes that this publicity stunt would give it an extra push to success.

The entire cast had been expected to be at the theater in West Hollywood at seven sharp. Apparently not trusting him to make a timely appearance, the network had sent a car to his house to collect him and to make sure he was walking the red carpet with his costars. As he arrived at the theater, he could see that there were fans already draped around the entire venue, hoping for a glimpse of the cast and a quick photo.

As Skylar stepped out of the car, he immediately heard his name being shouted from all around him. Nervously he stuck his hands in his pockets. He was glad he had decided to go casual. He was wearing his favorite jeans, high-top black leather Converses, and a tight T-shirt layered beneath his red-and-blue checked Indian Falls shirt, which he had scored during his recent Abercrombie modeling campaign.

He might have achieved the "cool" look, but his anxiety was on overload. All this attention was the one part of acting that he didn't like. He forced a smile and waved to a group of people standing over to the side, trying to get his attention. Then he headed to the red carpet as quickly as he could. As he walked toward his other cast mates, he looked around the crowd. He noticed that the fans were being held back by ropes while every magazine, newspaper, and online news source in Los Angeles was allowed to line the red carpet. This ticked him off. As much as he disliked the attention, if he had to talk to anyone, he much preferred talking to the fans. He hated the questions that were constantly yelled at him by the photographers. Each of them with their cameras poised, just hoping for the money shot of the night.

Fortunately he wasn't the main star, and therefore not their main focus. That honor went to the beautiful Kelly Bane, the "It" girl from the '70s. She played his Christian conservative right-winged mother in the show, but at night, she often played the role of his lover.

Skylar could see why she had been on the bedroom walls of every red-blooded teenage boy in the '70s. As she played to the media, he couldn't help but appreciate her beauty. She was tall, sexy, and had amazing curves in all the right places. The fact that she was older than him wasn't a concern to Skylar. Thanks to all the Beverly Hills plastic surgeons on her payroll, Kelly was superhot.

The off-screen connection between Skylar and Kelly was not public knowledge. Both actors realized that fans would not accept the "angst-filled mother/son dynamic" if they learned that the fifty-year-old mother and twenty-eight-year-old son team on The Executives were, in reality, banging in Kelly's pool house on a regular basis. Therefore, Kelly and Skylar kept quiet, arriving at venues at different times, careful to never be seen alone. And that was perfectly fine with them.

Glancing back down at the blonde in his bed, with her angelic face and incredibly long eyelashes, Skylar remembered that Kelly was the reason for the beauty lying next to him.

There had been some insanely hot women—and, for that matter, hot men—at the premiere party. Skylar wasn't particular when it came to sexual partners. He usually ended up with females, but he had no problem having sex with a man if he was attracted to him. Sometimes if he was in the right state of mind, he liked both—at the same time. Sex was something Skylar enjoyed, and he saw no reason to limit himself in any way. Not committing to any particular sex partner was how he liked it. Easy, no strings, and commitment free.

As he thought about the fact that he was attracted to both sexes, he thought about his mom and dad. Deep down he knew they were the real reason behind his inability to commit to anything or anyone. When Skylar was seven, his dad had left and never looked back. From that point forward, Skylar had no choice but to grow up very quickly. Living with a mother who went through the next "love of her life" like a box of tissues was not something that led to a very stable lifestyle. When she was in love, she was at her happiest. However, when she was heartbroken, which always happened sooner or later, she found solace in her bedroom, and Skylar was left to fend for himself. This constant back and forth of emotion, based solely on whether she had a man in her life, was a weakness in Skylar's eyes. A weakness he would never allow for himself. When he was with a partner, it was because he wanted to be, and as soon as he was bored with them, he moved on to the next one. Life was much simpler that way. No strings, no attachments, no hurt, no pain. Just the way he liked it.

The summer Skylar turned sixteen, his mother finally met *"the"* love of her life. Quinton lived in New York City, and it wasn't long before Skylar and his mother lived there as well. Because Quinton came from money, it was decided that Skylar would attend a private school. Skylar didn't mind the idea of a private school because he thought he could hide from the world and figure out just what he wanted to do with his life. However with his strong jawline, high cheekbones, jet black hair, and bright blue eyes, he couldn't hide for long. Being tall, good-looking, and having family money made Skylar one of the most sought-after guys in the school.

Glancing over at the blonde again, he was puzzled. Now, not only was he struggling to remember how he had met her, but it baffled him that he would bring a stranger into his home. He must have really been wasted. Skylar never brought anyone home, especially someone he'd obviously just met. Usually he had to totally trust them before handing out that type of information.

Another pain shot through his head as he attempted to remember more. He vaguely recalled searching for Kelly during the night to try to convince her to meet him at her pool house. Kelly, being in her element, wanted nothing more than to stay as long as possible and bask in what she considered her well-deserved glory. The premiere had been a huge success, and the press loved the show. It appeared to be on track to becoming a critic's choice, and Kelly wasn't going anywhere until she had milked every ounce of attention. On the other hand, Skylar, after six gin and tonics, had suddenly developed an urge to go home and have sex until he passed out. He was over all the press, the interviews, the nice talk. He wanted hard-core sex, and he wanted it right then.

After being rejected by Kelly, Skylar remembered taking in all his options. There was the guy who had been serving champagne during the party. He was fucking gorgeous! He had been about Skylar's height, blond, lean, and muscular. Definitely everything Skylar liked in a sex partner. He remembered thinking that he would be perfect for a night of hard-core sex, but that idea was quickly nixed when Skylar determined that the guy was a fan.

What a disappointment that had been. Skylar had few rules in life, but one that he tried to always stick to was his self-imposed rule to never date fans. He had learned long ago that dating and/or sleeping with fans led to nothing but trouble. Nine times out of ten they had him on a pedestal so high that he couldn't possibly live up to the image in their minds, not that he would bother to try. Most had already decided they loved him and therefore had preconceived notions that might or might not be true. Or worse, they fell in "love" with his television character and upon learning he was nothing like the character, were devastated. No, it was a definite deal-breaker when Skylar discovered his latest object of lust was a fan. He stuck to others in the industry because chances were they were as self-absorbed as Skylar, and that worked for him.

So the hot, sexy champagne man was off-limits. And if he remembered correctly, he was off-limits with a vengeance. Not only did he wear the "fan" label, he reeked of "long-term relationship," and Skylar was as noncommittal as they came. He had no intention of ever falling in love. Hell, he never intended to live in a house long enough to hang pictures. He was lucky he owned furniture. No, he wanted a good one-night stand who, with any luck, would be gone by the time he opened his eyes. Glancing once again at the blonde in his bed, he realized he had failed miserably at that. As he watched her sleeping, images of bare breasts, long legs, and hot kissing flashed in his mind. He lifted the duvet and sure enough, she was completely naked. *Great.* This was not looking good. He might not be particular about the gender of his lover, but he was damn well picky about *who* that lover was. Why did he have the distinct feeling that he was going to be sorry? And why could he clearly remember the blond dude but he couldn't remember having sex last night? Damn! Frustrated again, he continued struggling to figure out how she'd managed to make it in his house, into his bed, and still be here with the morning light.

As Skylar sat there trying to piece together the previous night and contemplating ways to remove her from his bed, she began to stir a little. The movement startled him, and Skylar backed up to his side of the bed. He waited it out while she rubbed her eyes and stretched and took even more of his covers. She looked over at him and smiled. Then she said, "Good morning, sweetheart," with a hint of southern twang.

Skylar's head started spinning as he felt the dizziness coming back. Now he was certain: getting her out of his bed wasn't going to be easy.

CHAPTER 2

SOPHIE STARTED her morning on the wrong foot. After last night's premiere party, she was lucky to be able to crawl out of bed, much less on the right foot. She had overslept by thirty minutes, so she had less than an hour to pick up Skylar's coffee and his script for the following week, and get to his house in the Hollywood Hills. She had been his assistant for all of two weeks, and at this rate, she would not be making it to three.

"Darce… where are my gray pants?" she yelled down the hall to her roommate as she continued to toss clothes around her room in her search for the elusive gray pants.

"How should I know? You're the one who took them off," Darcy yelled back.

Crap! Every second she spent looking for those lost pants was yet another second for Skylar to add to his "you're late again" speech. It's a good thing she thought he was hotter than Hades or she would have quit already. Seriously, was there another personal assistant in town that had to be at her boss's house at the crack of dawn on a *Sunday*? He could be so demanding, yet she kept hoping there was another side to him and he could be sweet as well. Rethinking that, she reminded herself, *Who am I kidding? He can be a royal pain in the ass.*

As she searched around her room that now had the appearance of being hit by a category five hurricane, she spotted something gray over in the corner. "There you are!" She reached over and grabbed her gray pants, which were hanging halfway out of the hamper. After giving them the once-over and shaking them out, she decided they could pass as clean and unwrinkled. After slipping into them, she headed for the stairs.

She raced down the stairs and into the kitchen, stopped long enough to sip the coffee Darcy had brewed, grabbed Skylar's copy of the script, and ran out the door, yelling, "See ya later!"

As she settled into her car and headed to the coffee shop, she thought about last night's after-party. Skylar had been so drunk; he had practically broadcast to the press about his and Kelly's affair. He was not very smooth with his "come on, babe; it's been a week" comment to Kelly. She had first ignored him, then patted him on the butt and pointed him in the opposite direction. Then she proceeded to blow off the situation by saying in a loud voice, "Skylar is *such* a tease, how can you not love him?" Skylar, who was too drunk to realize he had just been dismissed, didn't get angry but instead immediately set his sights on the next hottest thing. Sophie had watched as Skylar walked toward the extremely hot waiter, who had been serving champagne.

Everyone involved with the production of the show knew about Kelly and Skylar's affair. The truth was they didn't try to hide it very well. The constant ass-patting and hot, frantic kisses in the dressing rooms had everyone tuned in to that May-December lovefest. However, the team also knew to look the other way and never breathe a word of it. After all, what happened in production stayed in production. The network's bigwigs would see to that.

"Half caff double latté with skim milk," Sophie said into the microphone at the drive-thru of Java Joe. Then, remembering the number of drinks Skylar had over the course of the night, she changed her mind. "Wait! Make that a double espresso with a hint of skim milk."

Within three minutes Sophie had her coffee and was on Mulholland heading toward Skylar's house. It was a beautiful Los Angeles morning. The sun was shining brightly, and it softened Sophie's mood. Slowly her thoughts drifted back to the party. At the point she had seen Skylar talking to the hot server, she had assumed from his body language that Skylar was looking to hook up. However, the last time she had seen the highly intoxicated actor, he was stumbling out of the party, being held up by a pretty blonde girl she did not recognize. *So much for the sexy waiter.* As she started to turn into Skylar's driveway, she could only hope that the girl was already gone. The last thing Sophie wanted to do was walk in on her boss during morning sex.

CHAPTER 3

HE IS so beautiful. That was Emma's first thought as she woke up to see Skylar Murphy staring at her. From his dark hair falling softly over his face to his rock-hard chest, which was lightly covered in soft silky hair, he was simply the most beautiful man she had ever encountered.

"Good morning, sweetheart," she said with a smile. She had never felt so happy. She wanted to pinch herself to make sure it wasn't a dream. To be in Skylar Murphy's bedroom, curled up under his comforter, waking up next to him, was more than she had ever allowed herself to imagine. As she gazed into his bright blue eyes, which were now slightly shaded red from the alcohol, she knew that this must be how heaven felt.

"Uh… mornin'," he slowly responded, followed by a clearing of his throat. As Skylar began to shuffle around, trying to pull the excess cover over him, Emma noticed that he was looking at her strangely.

Hesitantly, she asked, "How are you feeling this morning?" She knew he'd had several drinks at the party, and she had personally mixed two more before they left. And just as she suspected, judging by the distasteful look on his face, the answer was not going to be good. "I bet you're not feeling so great after last night," Emma said as she reached over to rub his arm.

Skylar, still a bit shell-shocked at finding someone in his bed and not remembering her at all, just sat there, staring, not saying a word.

Emma was so happy that even the strange vibe she was getting from Skylar could not bring her down. Calmly Emma took his hand and held it up to her cheek. "We had such an amazing time last night. I'll never forget it."

Okay, time to go, thought Skylar as his nerves started to tingle from panic. This was not good. Red flags were flying, and every alarm in his pounding head was going off. Still managing to not speak, he pulled his hand away and turned so that he was sitting on the edge of the bed, with his back to Emma. His mind was zooming as he tried to come up with an escape plan.

Watching Skylar sit there with his back to her, Emma didn't know what to think. Worried, she asked, "Did I say something wrong?"

Just about everything, thought Skylar.

"Didn't you have fun last night?"

When Skylar still didn't answer, Emma continued, "Don't you *remember* last night?" Even as she asked the question, Emma wasn't sure she wanted to know the answer.

Not a damn thing, he thought as he rubbed his forehead, turned, and looked at her blankly. That was partly due to his head continuing to pound like a drum and partly because he had no idea what to say. *How on earth did I get into this mess?*

As she began to realize that Skylar didn't remember her, or their night together, Emma felt tightness forming in her chest. Suddenly feeling very uncomfortable and *very* naked, Emma reached over and grabbed her bra and panties from the armchair beside the bed. After turning away from Skylar in a moment of modesty, she quickly put on her underwear. Waiting a moment, she took a deep breath and then turned to face Skylar. "You really don't remember last night, do you?" Her voice was barely above a whisper as she tried to calm herself.

"Not really." Then, realizing how bad that sounded, he added, "I mean, it's all very vague." Skylar nervously ran his fingers through his hair. But now that he had found his voice, he continued speaking as if trying to rush all his words out at once. "Okay, this is going to sound really rude, but please tell me, who *are* you?"

Emma felt like a knife was piercing her heart as the tightness in her chest grew heavier. She reached for her blouse and started putting it on. As she buttoned her shirt, devastation began to overtake her. This was not how the morning was supposed to go. Skylar was going to wake her up with kisses and realize that he couldn't wait to make love to her again. At least that was what he promised last night as they lay on this very bed, kissing so intensely Emma thought she might die from the passion.

The thought of kissing him again reminded her of the beautiful night they had spent together. After they had left the party, Skylar had given her his address, and she'd typed it into her GPS. As she drove to his home in the hills, Emma knew her dreams had finally come true. Weaving through the winding roads, she knew she was headed to her destiny. Looking over at him as his head lay against the window, she had chosen to ignore the fact that Skylar was completely wasted. She knew she only needed a chance to show Skylar how much she loved him. And he would love her too, once he got to know her.

As they pulled into the driveway of Skylar's Hollywood Hill's home, Emma couldn't help but be a bit disappointed. Skylar didn't live in a mansion, or even a mini mansion. No, he lived in just a plain brown—ugly—house. This was not what she had expected. While it was obviously well landscaped and taken care of, it backed up to a dark forest and wasn't at all glamorous. Never having been to a TV star's home, she wasn't sure what she'd been expecting, but Emma had seen enough reality shows to know that the rich and famous usually lived in expensive, grand-looking homes.

Hearing a bang she saw that Skylar was about to fall out of the car, so she ran around to help him, forgetting her disappointment in Skylar's house. Together, they stumbled to the door. Skylar pointed to a little ceramic frog and said, "There... just grab the extra key." Emma picked up the key and opened the door, and together they made their way into the house. Emma was disappointed again as she took everything in. The inside of the house was no more glamorous than the outside. She tried to hide her disappointment as she glanced around. There were boxes sitting around all over the floor and nothing personal to be seen. Not one photo, not one flower. He obviously needed a woman's touch, and she made a mental note to help him with that.

As Skylar continued to weave down the hallway, Emma caught up with him and followed him into a bedroom. Skylar headed straight toward the big oak bed and immediately fell onto it.

"Normally, I don't get this wasted," he slurred.

"Really, it's okay. Tonight was a special night, and you deserved to have fun," Emma responded as she leaned down and kissed him gently on the mouth.

Sitting back up Emma took a moment to glance around the room. His bedroom looked almost the same as the living room. It was basically bare other than the bed, which sat in the middle of the room with its headboard against one wall. There were two french doors that seemed to lead out onto some sort of terrace, a television on a plain wooden stand, and a chair that she could only assume he used as a closet. There wasn't a single picture hanging on the wall, and there were more of those taped-up boxes pushed against one wall.

As she felt Skylar reach up and pull her face down to meet his, Emma forgot all about refurnishing his house. After years of following Skylar through his television shows, on Facebook and Twitter, idolizing every word he said, she was here in his house, in his bed, and he was kissing her with all the passion she had seen him display numerous times on television.

His soft full lips captured hers, and she immediately responded. The touch of his tongue in her mouth sent her reeling. She felt feelings that she didn't know existed and had to remind herself to breathe. After all, Emma had decided a long time ago that Skylar would be her lover, and now she was well on her way.

That was, until this morning, and now everything had suddenly changed.

Looking over at him, and receiving a blank look in return, she began to feel desperate. This wasn't fair! Emma had planned this moment for so long, and it was falling apart right in front of her. She had taken the job with the catering service because she knew they catered the large Hollywood parties. She had practically begged her supervisor to please let her work *The Executives* premiere party because she'd known Skylar would be there. Of course, all the workers had strict instructions to be professional and not engage in conversation with the actors, but Emma had no intention of letting that stop her.

All night she had tried to get his attention, but he'd only had eyes for the lead actress, who could have been his real-life mother, and then his focus shifted to her coworker, Aiden. Finally at the very end of the night, to her good luck, the "mother" went off with a producer, and Skylar seemed to lose interest in Aiden. Thank God! Skylar being gay was not in her plans at all. She had taken that moment of Skylar's disinterest in Aiden to make her move. She offered him a couple more gin and tonics and played it cool. Once she had him interested, she pressed forward and asked if he needed a ride home. Skylar told her he had a car waiting for him, but after looking over at Aiden and then back again, he smiled and said, "Okay, a ride home it is."

And now, the morning after, all Skylar could do was sit there, running his fingers through his thick beautiful hair. She gathered her courage and asked another question. "Do you remember meeting me at the party?" she stammered.

Oh dear God, *just leave already, my head is* pounding! Sighing, Skylar responded, "Not really," as he rubbed his head.

Emma felt like she had been kicked in the gut. As tears began to well up in her eyes, she took a deep breath, telling herself again that she could still salvage this. Maybe if she reintroduced herself and started over, that would make things better. "Well, my name is Emma, and I work with the catering service from the party, and I'm a huge fan."

That explains it. As this new knowledge slowly sank into Skylar's still throbbing head, he asked, "So how did you get here... in my house?"

"I asked if you wanted a ride, and you accepted, so I brought you home last night."

Things were becoming increasingly clear to Skylar, and the most obvious was that he'd had about six gin and tonics too many. Judging from the fact that they were both naked, Skylar knew the answer but had to ask anyway. As he glanced around the bed and then back to her, he mumbled, "Did we...?"

"Yes, we made love," a tearful Emma replied before he could finish his sentence.

Made love? Seriously? Who says that? Skylar could barely keep from rolling his eyes and probably would have if his head wasn't *pounding.*

"Several times," Emma continued.

Anddd... things just keep getting better! Skylar groaned inwardly.

Emma was close to tears. "Don't you remember what we talked about? How we went to sleep in each other's arms?"

With that last sentence, Skylar had taken all he could. Regret didn't begin to describe how he felt at the moment. Slowly, and choosing each word with care, Skylar said, "Okay, listen. I really need you to leave now. This should not have happened. And I'm sorry that you had other expectations." Skylar grabbed his jeans and began putting them on. He had to get her out of here.

At that, Emma realized she was fighting a losing battle. Tearfully she finished putting on her clothes, gathered the rest of her things, and walked to the bedroom doorway. As she opened the door, she looked at

Skylar with her eyes shining bright with tears. "I just want you to know that last night was like a dream come true for me." She could barely speak. She took a deep breath and continued in a quivering voice, "I've loved you for a long time, and I knew that being with you would be amazing." She looked at him with pleading eyes, looking for a sign, any sign, that he still wanted her. At the sight of his beautiful face, his hair flopping down in his eyes, her heart ached at the thought of never seeing him again. Looking down at the ground, she whispered to herself, "I realize now that I approached our relationship in the wrong way." Looking back up to face him, she continued, "Do you think that maybe it's possible we could start over?"

Not in this lifetime, Skylar thought the second he heard the word "relationship." But not wanting to create any more drama than it appeared was happening at the moment, Skylar walked over to Emma. "Let's just chalk last night up to too much alcohol and bad judgment on both our parts." Pulling the door all the way open, Skylar motioned her out.

Emma looked at him, her eyes filled with hurt, before walking out of the bedroom. Skylar followed her all the way to the back door to make sure she found her way out. She looked at him one last time as the tears spilled completely over and started pouring down her face. The moment the door shut behind her, Skylar all but collapsed against the doorframe. His head was throbbing, he was feeling a slight pang of guilt about the girl, and this was all just too much to take. He had to go back to bed. Sophie would be there soon, and he just wanted to be left alone. But one thing was for sure: no more gin and tonics for him.

CHAPTER 4

IT WAS Aiden's turn to make breakfast for the firehouse crew. Although it had been two days since his part-time gig as a waiter for *The Executives* network premiere, he was still trying to catch up on his sleep. He had already worked half of his twenty-four-hour shift, and now he was beginning the second half by making breakfast for the crew. Tired and a bit grumpy, Aiden was juggling tasks as he fried bacon and flipped pancakes.

He got interrupted by the ringing of his cell phone. He looked down to see the face of his best friend Ryan smiling up from his phone. Wondering what had taken Ryan so long, he answered, knowing exactly the reason for the call.

Without saying hello, Ryan practically shouted, "Okay, I gave it a day but I couldn't stand it any longer! So tell me, who all was there? Don't you dare leave out a single detail." Without taking a breath, he continued, "Did you meet any of my faves?"

As Aiden winced at the use of the word "faves," he said, "I was wondering why it took you so long to call. But to answer your question, I didn't know anyone. Therefore, I couldn't possibly tell you if I met any of your *faves*."

Aiden could picture Ryan's face as he heard the gasp.

"Seriously? You can't honestly say you didn't recognize Skylar Murphy. He would have only been *the* hottest guy there! I know you know him. He was on *Royal Life* for a couple of seasons." When Aiden still didn't hint that he knew who Ryan was referring to, Ryan continued in frustration, "Oh, come on! The man is a Greek god! Tall, dark hair, full, kissable lips, and crystal blue eyes that could make you want to drop down to your knees and—"

"Okay, stop, I saw him," laughed Aiden, stopping Ryan before he could take this conversation into the gutter. Now he definitely remembered who this Skylar Murphy was. And not because he had ever watched one single episode of *Royal Life*, but because he was incredibly hot, and Aiden remembered the eyes that could "make you want to drop to your knees."

And then like a bad taste creeping in after an amazing meal, he also remembered how Skylar had behaved at the party. Skylar had flirted with him for a long time, and truthfully, it had been fun until Skylar started asking for another drink. When Aiden refused, due to Skylar's inability to stand up, Skylar had developed an attitude.

"Come on, one more drink," Skylar had demanded.

Aiden pulled the drink tray away, saying, "I'm sorry, but I don't think that's a good idea."

"You know what? Fuck it, I need to get away from you anyway." And with those words, Skylar had disappeared.

What an asshole. Typical Hollywood celebrity—flirting, fawning when they want something and then gone when it's not given. And just what did he mean by "I need to get away from you anyway?" What the hell? Annoyed, Aiden kept working. After a few minutes, Aiden decided not to let it bother him. He also decided that this Skylar guy had way too much to drink and couldn't focus on one thing or one man for very long. Later, as Aiden was doing a final sweep of the bar area, he saw Skylar leaving with Emma, his coworker, who was a bit of a flake. *Oh well. They belong together*, he had thought and moved on. Until now.

Aiden continued to flip his pancakes and talk to Ryan. However, Ryan was making it increasingly harder for Aiden to "move on" because he wouldn't stop telling him Skylar's life story. Although by the time Ryan had slowed down for a breath, Aiden had decided that he would never work another Hollywood party. *Thank you, Ryan! Geez!*

"He's so good at playing gay, although I hear he's straight," rambled Ryan. "You should've seen him in *Royal Life*. He was the best friend of the prince. Oh my God! His character was in love with the prince, and it was pure torture to watch every week and see how they yearned for each other but could never be together. *Broke my heart.*" Ryan's voice rose as he continued with his high praise of Skylar.

Shoot me now, thought Aiden, holding the phone out to the side as Ryan continued to talk aimlessly of his love for Skylar. "I still watch YouTube clips of that show and just cry because it's sooooo beautiful," Ryan whispered into the phone.

Only Ben, the station's chief, and the other guys wandering into the kitchen saved Aiden.

"Got to run, Ryan. I'll see you Wednesday at the gym."

"Later, love, but don't think you're getting away with just that little bit of info on that hot man. I *will* find out more," promised Ryan.

"Okay, later," Aiden said as he hung up the phone, thankful for the interruption.

"Early riser, aren't you, Lieutenant?" Ben asked as he reached around Aiden to grab a handful of bacon.

"Hey, you know me—can't sleep past 6:00 a.m.," replied Aiden.

"We need to clean all the apparatus gear today, and if we get to it, Truck 15 needs an overhaul due to that fire at the homeless shelter," Ben reminded him as he found a seat at the table, coffee in one hand and strips of bacon in the other.

"Sounds good. I'll meet you guys out there after we eat and I get the kitchen in shape," responded Aiden. He turned and poured himself a cup of coffee and then went over to sit down and read the morning paper.

"Hey, you never said how that swanky Hollywood party turned out the other night," said Ben, his mouth full of bacon.

Aiden knew that Ben had no interest in "swanky Hollywood parties," but Ben was a good guy, and he was only trying to show some interest in Aiden's off-duty life.

"It was different," said Aiden. "Of course, my night consisted of serving champagne and wine to the Hollywood elite. However, I did have a good time just watching all the celebrities soak in the praise as the network guys played them like violins. Not sure I'm into the Hollywood types," Aiden continued thoughtfully as Skylar Murphy, and his gorgeous blue eyes, popped into his head. "Some seem a bit fake, and you know me—I like my guys real," Aiden pointed out.

"So no love for the lieutenant that night," said Paul as he wandered in on the last part of the conversation.

"No. No love for me that night. I guess I'll have to find my man in less extravagant circumstances," said Aiden.

The whole firehouse crew knew Aiden was gay, and most of the guys were all right with that fact. Every once in a while, a new crew member would come aboard and Aiden would feel an awkward coldness from him, but for the most part, the current crew of Hollywood's Fire Station 11 was cool with his sexuality.

Even if they had not been cool with it, Aiden made no apologies for being gay. He had known he was gay from an early age. He was also one of the lucky ones: he had understanding and supportive parents who helped him accept who he was from the beginning, unlike many of his gay friends.

He had also known very early on that he wanted to be a firefighter. When he was ten years old, he stood by and watched the LAFD save his next-door neighbor from a raging fire that had swept through her house. He was mesmerized as he watched them become heroes right in front of his eyes. After that night he never wanted to be anything else. And here he was, a lieutenant at Fire Station 11, living his dream. And because his dream didn't cover the costs of living in Hollywood, he worked as a private waiter on occasion to make extra money. He could not ask for a better life. Being gay was just a part of who he was, and he was more than okay with that.

"Well, from what I've seen from *The Executives*, that Kelly Bane is one hot mama. Tell me, is she as hot in person as she is on that show?" asked Paul.

"Don't tell me that you're going to actually *watch* that show?" Ben said, laughing.

"Sure I will. It's—" Paul was cut off by the sound of the alarm.

Everyone jumped up and started running toward the truck bay. Aiden checked the stove before following the others. They ran into the engine room and pulled on their bunker gear in record time. As they hopped into the truck, they heard the voice from the command center saying, "Smoke detected at Monumental Studios on Highland Ave. Soundstage 4. Respond immediately."

CHAPTER 5

"I'M JUST telling you what I saw. The scene felt a little flat," said Kevin Hall, the director for the latest episode of *The Executives*, as he roamed around Skylar's trailer on Lot A of Monumental Studios.

Toying with an old camera and trying not to look Kevin directly in the eye, Skylar protested, "I'm trying, but I don't feel Toby would be that distraught." Turning to Kevin he was greeted with a stare of skepticism. Then he tried reasoning with him. "Okay, so his mother *almost* found out he's gay. I understand that's a big deal, but come on... distraught? Maybe a bit worried, scared of what could have happened, but not distraught."

Skylar knew the director was basing his thoughts on the fact that his character's mother, played by Kelly, would go over the edge if she found out her sweet, wonderful, soon-to-be-married son was actually gay. To be more direct, she would be more concerned with how it would affect her work in politics. But still Skylar couldn't see it in his character to be *that* upset.

Taking a sip of his coffee, Kevin looked directly at Skylar, and said, "Regardless, that's how I want the scene played, so come back to set with that frame of mind, and we'll get this shot in one take." Kevin was not about to back down.

Putting down the camera, Skylar sighed, looked at Kevin, and said, "Fine, whatever you say. I don't like it, but I'll do it the way you want. I'll meet you on set in a sec. I need to clear my head."

Realizing he was being politely dismissed, Kevin walked over to the door, opened it to go out, then suddenly paused to look directly at Skylar. "You're brilliant, you know. I've seen you pull off scenes that were way more difficult than this. It's an easy take. Tears, a little shaking. Terrified—that's what I want. You have to remember, not only did his mother almost find out he was gay, but she almost walked in on him having sex with a man. I want to believe that Toby was terrified to think that his world, as he knows it, almost came crashing down. *Make* me believe it," Kevin said with all seriousness.

Skylar looked at him, his retort sitting on the edge of his tongue, when the sound of approaching sirens took precedence over their conversation.

"What the hell?" said Kevin as he ran down the steps, heading in the direction of the soundstages. Skylar was close behind him.

The wailing of the sirens became louder as the large fire truck pulled through the guard gates at the front of the studio. The fire truck was followed by a unit from the LAPD and an EMS truck bringing up the rear. Kevin, Skylar, and the three emergency vehicles raced toward Soundstage 4, where they could see smoke billowing out the side door.

People started pouring out of Soundstage 5, which housed the *The Executives* sets, to see what was happening, as the fire truck rolled up to Soundstage 4. Firemen jumped out from all sides of the truck, grabbed masks and tanks and started putting them on over their uniforms. Skylar and Kevin arrived just as the one of the firemen, whom Skylar assumed was the fire chief, took out a clipboard and ran up to a group of men standing in front of the soundstage to size up the situation. Skylar could hear a man shouting to the fire chief.

"It started out small, and we tried to put it out ourselves, but it just kept growing. We couldn't get it out," shouted one of the men, whom Skylar recognized as a grip on the show *Mallard's Fortune*. Pointing to the smoke-filled area behind him, he continued, "However, we did manage to keep it contained to one area, behind this wall."

"Anyone in the building?" asked the fire chief.

"No. The show is on hiatus, so unless someone broke in, there shouldn't be anyone inside," stated the grip.

Using a megaphone, the fire chief started giving orders. "Fire appears to be contained behind this wall. Structure was closed, no one reported in the building, but be sure to take a good look around." Turning to the largest fireman, who was standing nearby, the chief continued, "Collins, use the main hose and start pouring water from the top. Meanwhile, the rest of the men can pump water inside the building. Let's stop that fire from spreading." Turning to the gathering of people who had wandered out of the adjoining studios, he instructed, "People, I need you to step back," as he motioned to an area farther away from the fire.

Skylar did as instructed and stepped back, away from the main action, but continued to watch in amazement as Collins and another firefighter started climbing the aerial ladder to the top of the building. As they climbed, someone else was advancing the hose to them from the top of the truck. Once they were at the top of the building, it took both Collins and the other guy to hold the hose still as water started gushing out in an attempt to extinguish the fire.

Meanwhile, on the ground, the remaining firemen had located a water hydrant and connected the hose to it, and were already dragging the hose inside the building. Skylar was amazed at the coordination among all the firemen. Skylar watched as the firemen disappeared inside the smoky building.

Suddenly, Skylar realized that he had not seen Kelly outside. He knew she was on set because he had seen her running lines with her assistant, Cary, before Skylar had left for his break. He pulled out his cell phone and found her number.

On the second ring, Kelly answered. "Skylar! Where are you?" she shouted into the phone.

Skylar was relieved to hear her voice. "I'm here outside of Soundstage 4, watching all the action. Are you okay?" he asked anxiously.

"I'm fine. I'm on the other side of Soundstage 5. I stepped out the back door to work with Cary. We heard the sirens and walked over, but when we saw all the people we decided to come back here to be out of the way."

The mention of Cary's name reminded Skylar of his own assistant, Sophie. *Where is she?* he thought as he looked around. Not seeing Sophie, he focused back on Kelly. "Okay, cool, just making sure you are okay. I'll see you inside." And with that, he hung up the cell.

Skylar called Sophie's number. It barely rang once before she answered.

"Sophie! Where are you?"

"Why? What's wrong?" she responded.

"There's a fire here in Soundstage 4, and I wanted to make sure you're okay."

Immediately Sophie panicked. "What? Oh my God! Are you okay?" she asked.

"I'm fine," responded Skylar. "As I said, it's Soundstage 4, and no one was in the building. The firemen are here, and they're working on it." He glanced over to where the firemen were diligently working to put out the fire.

"I'm at the commissary picking up lunch for Kelly. Apparently, her assistant was too busy, so Kelly grabbed me. I looked but couldn't find you. I'm sorry I just left like that," explained Sophie.

"No... no... it's fine. I'll see you when you get back," said Skylar, and then he hung up.

At this point the smoke was not billowing as much, so it appeared that the fire was under control and being contained. After about ten minutes, the firemen could be seen backing out of the building. Having never been this close to a fire, Skylar was curious about what had started it. He decided to walk down a little closer to the fire chief.

One of the firemen walked up to the chief and said, "It's under control, but we should do some overhauling to make sure there isn't a hot spot in the wall."

"Did it spread anywhere besides the wall?" asked the chief.

Until now the fireman had his back to Skylar, but as he removed his helmet, Skylar noticed that there was something familiar about him.

"No, it appears to have been a very small fire that created more smoke than actual flames," responded the fireman. Suddenly the fireman turned toward Skylar, and their gazes met. Skylar took a step back as a shock went through his system. *Holy hell,* he thought. It was Mr. Champagne from the premiere party.

CHAPTER 6

IT COULDN'T be… could it? Skylar looked again to make sure he was not mistaken. This time Skylar saw the flicker of recognition in Mr. Champagne's eyes before he turned back to continue talking to his chief. As Skylar stood there, trying to decide his next move, he watched Mr. Champagne grab an ax from the side of the truck, put on his helmet, and disappear into the building. That was it. Maybe it was the sheer hotness of that guy just grabbing his ax and walking into a smoke-filled building, or maybe it was the memory of that rock-hard body, but Skylar knew he had to know more about him, fan or not.

He walked over to Kevin and asked, "Can we take a few minutes before returning to set?"

"That's fine, but I'll need to regroup with everyone before we continue. Thirty minutes, we'll all meet on set," responded Kevin as he walked away toward Soundstage 5.

Now that the action had died down, most of the onlookers had started to wander back to their original locations. Skylar, not sure what to do, just stood there in his same spot, hands in his pockets, shuffling his feet. It was times like this that he wished he smoked so he would at least have a reason to be lurking outside like some kind of paparazzi wannabe.

He heard the crunching of gravel and looked over to see Sophie standing beside him. Sophie was a pretty girl. She had long red hair that she often pulled back in a ponytail. Skylar couldn't help noticing that her hair was the same color as the fire he had just witnessed.

"Do they know how it started?" she asked as she handed him a coffee.

Looking back at the soundstage, Skylar saw the smoke was beginning to disperse.

"I haven't heard, but it seems to have been a small fire. More smoke than flames, which is good," Skylar said, then sipped his coffee. "By the way, thanks for the coffee."

"Sure! When do you have to get back to set?" asked Sophie, wondering why Skylar was still standing outside.

"In a few. I saw someone that I think I know. I wanted to say hello to him."

"Out here, near the fire?"

"He's one of the firemen. I think I met him at the premiere party the other night," replied Skylar.

"Really? A fireman who came to the premiere? Who is he?" asked Sophie, her curiosity piqued. She looked down toward the soundstage to see if she recognized anyone.

Catching her scoping out the firemen, Skylar tried to downplay it. "Not anyone you would know. He was one of the servers from the party, and I recognized him a few minutes ago. Nothing major—just wanted to say hello. Why don't I meet you back on set in a few?" He really didn't want Sophie hanging around if he decided to speak to the firefighter.

Sophie had a hard time believing that Skylar would wait on anyone, much less a man who worked as a fireman by day and server by night. There had to be more to this story.

About that time, Mr. Champagne walked out of the building, which was now almost smoke free, and headed toward the fire engine. As he removed his helmet to wipe the sweat off his face, Sophie knew immediately why Skylar was so interested. It was the hot serving guy she had seen him flirting with at the party.

"Is that the guy?" asked Sophie, motioning toward the firefighter.

Skylar moved to block her from Mr. Champagne's view. "Yes, that's him, and would you please stop being so obvious?"

"Are you going to talk to him?" she asked.

Getting annoyed at the constant string of questions, Skylar just glared at Sophie and said, "I might. I haven't decided yet." Then, motioning toward the soundstage, he said, "But will you please meet me on set? I'll be there in a second."

"Okay, fine, but I really think you should talk to him." At Skylar's second glare, she said, "I'm leaving, I'm leaving. See you in a few." Sophie walked off down to Soundstage 5.

Skylar was a bit surprised at Sophie encouraging him to talk to the firefighter. Maybe his preference for women *and* men was more common knowledge than he was aware of. If so, he had to correct that. But first, he had a hot fireman he wanted to meet, even if it meant breaking his rule about dating fans.

Turning back to Mr. Champagne, who looked slightly busy trying to get the hose latched onto the truck, Skylar tried to be patient. But after a few more minutes, Skylar felt he had waited long enough. *It's now or never*, he thought as he started toward the fire truck and the sexy fireman.

"Hey," said Skylar as he walked up behind Mr. Champagne.

Mr. Champagne turned around. Upon seeing it was Skylar, he said, "Hey," and then he immediately turned back to his truck to finish tying in the hose. He had no time for the disappearing actor.

Okay, what the fuck? Not sure exactly how to take that reaction, but not wanting to back down, Skylar continued, "I saw you a few minutes ago, talking to your fire chief, and I thought that I recognized you. Didn't you work *The Executives* premiere party the other night?"

Aiden paused for a second, then turned back and replied, "Yeah, that was me." And then, unable to stop himself, Aiden said, "Although, I must say, I'm surprised you remembered me. If I'm not mistaken, you were more than wasted that night."

"You can say that again," Skylar agreed, as he remembered waking up in bed with Emma, naked, with barely any memory of the previous night. However, wanting to salvage his reputation, Skylar continued, "Yet, I do remember you, so I believe that proves that I did have some clarity that night. But I have to admit, if you introduced yourself to me, your name was lost someplace between six and eight gin and tonics."

Aiden looked at him for a second before responding, "Actually, I didn't find it necessary to introduce myself. I was just serving champagne to the party guests."

Well, damn! Skylar, a bit taken back by the chill in the fireman's voice, said, "Okay. I only thought that you might have because in my experience, most fans introduce themselves right away. Forgive me, I didn't mean to assume something so simple."

Aiden turned all the way around, looked Skylar straight in the eye, and said, "Actually you're still assuming, if you think I'm a fan. Truth is, until that night, I didn't know who you were." He paused before finishing with, "Sorry about that."

Skylar, a bit insulted yet somehow intrigued, stood there for a moment, taking all this new information in. Then he smiled, held out his hand, and quietly said, "No apology needed. Let me introduce myself. My name is Skylar Murphy." *And you are certainly going to know me now.*

As Aiden looked directly into those blue eyes, he felt an overwhelming sensation. Maybe he had been a bit rude. After all, the guy was trying to be nice. Hesitantly, he took Skylar's hand and shook it. "I'm Aiden Moore, your neighborhood firefighter-slash-champagne-server."

Skylar laughed. And as he saw Aiden's eyes light up as he grinned, Skylar knew he wanted to know more about this man. Feeling more confident now that he had Aiden's attention, Skylar continued the conversation. "So how did you manage to combine those two jobs? They seem to be quite different."

Aiden smiled and said, "It's called the necessity of having a part-time job to survive in this city. And if there is one thing I'm good at, it's serving at parties. I did it while I was completing all the certification requirements to be a firefighter."

"Well, I'm certainly glad you have those serving skills or I would have never met you," teased Skylar.

Suddenly realizing Skylar was flirting *again*, Aiden decided a change in topic was needed as this was a road leading to nowhere. As Aiden recalled, the last time they had tried this flirting thing, it had ended badly. Plus, the last thing he needed was some hot actor flirting with him, getting him stirred up and excited, only to find out he was straight and not available.

"So, is this where you film your new series? What's it called again?" asked Aiden.

"*The Executives.* Actually, we film on Soundstage 5. I was in my trailer with the director when we heard the sirens, so we came out to see what was going on. Fortunately, it looks like our studio was spared." After a pause, Skylar continued thoughtfully, "Strange to have a fire like that on a studio lot. Can't imagine what started it."

"Could have been anything," said Aiden. "It wasn't a very big fire, so maybe just a short in the wiring or something. The fire investigators are here now, trying to locate the point of origin. They should know something soon, I hope." He pointed to the two men now wandering around the building.

"Point of origin?" Skylar asked.

"It's the starting point of the fire. Normally, it will tell us how the fire was started."

"Hmm… pretty interesting line of work you have there, Aiden," said Skylar.

"Your line of work is just as fascinating, I would think," said Aiden.

"It has its moments." Skylar thought about all the fun he had on set and how much he loved creating new characters. "Actually, I can't think of anything I would rather be doing."

"Tell me about this show, *The Executives*," Aiden said.

"It's basically about a family led by a domineering mother whose life is immersed in politics. She only has time for that and, occasionally, her family." Seeing that he held Aiden's attention, Skylar went on to say, "The dramatics come into play with my character and how he interacts with her character. I play her closeted gay son who is getting married. So there's lots of drama and angst-ridden scenes, mixed a bit with intrigue and mystery in the world of politics."

"You play gay a lot, huh?" asked Aiden. "Does that make you uncomfortable?"

"I thought you didn't know anything about me," teased Skylar.

"Don't get too excited. My friend Ryan is a big fan, and he filled me in." Now was the moment of truth. Aiden waited for Skylar to come back with the overused expression "I'm just an actor playing a role."

"Well, to answer your question, yes, I've had the opportunity to play several gay roles, but I'm cool with that. Kiss a man, kiss a woman. It's pretty much the same for me. I actually quite like it," replied Skylar with a wink in his tone.

Okay, sounds like he is either a player or he's playing with me. Either way, time to move on, thought Aiden. "I guess I'd better get going. I really should be helping the guys clear up the place," Aiden said while attempting to move away.

Impulsively, Skylar reached out and grabbed Aiden's arm. Something about this guy was getting under his skin. Maybe it was the fact that he didn't have a clue who Skylar was. That alone was very intriguing. However, knowing himself rather well, Skylar knew it was most likely the usual "wanting what he can't have." Regardless of the reason, Skylar was willing to risk the wrath of his manager and ask this guy out.

Not wanting to create attention, Skylar kept his voice low as he said, "Hey, wait… would you like to have coffee or just get together sometime, maybe hang out?"

Aiden felt Skylar's touch on his arm all the way to his toes. Damn, what was this man doing to him? Regardless, it didn't matter what he was doing to him; it was a bad idea to go down this road. "No, I don't think that is such a good idea," responded Aiden.

"Why not?"

As Aiden looked into those crystal blue eyes and felt tingling down his spine, he forced himself to say the only thing that came to his mind. "I make it a point not to date actors."

Are you fucking kidding me? Skylar stepped back and looked at him with disbelief. "Okay, seriously, that sounds a lot like bullshit to me. That's like me saying I don't date firefighters-slash-champagne-servers. Why does it matter what I do for a living?" Skylar asked. He didn't get turned down much, if at all, and this was more than annoying. It was one thing if there wasn't any attraction there, but Skylar had *felt* the sparks between them when he grabbed Aiden's arm. So what was this guy's problem?

Before Aiden could respond, Skylar continued, "Dude, we're talking coffee, not a date to the Emmys."

Yeah, first coffee. Next thing I know, my heart gets broken. No, thank you. "I still say it's not a good idea. But it was nice meeting you." Turning his back to Skylar, Aiden walked away.

Skylar just stood there, wondering just where and how the conversation had gone south.

CHAPTER 7

AS HE looked around the crowded café, Aiden wondered what had possessed him to agree to meet Ryan for dinner. He knew that Ryan would drill him about Skylar, and truth be told, all Aiden wanted to do was go home and crash. He had worked his twenty-four-hour shift, and now he was off duty for forty-eight hours. And he really needed this break. Besides the fire at the studio, a raging house fire had almost taken the life of a woman and her twin girls.

However, luck had been on their side, and Aiden had been able to get inside the house and bring them out. It had been such an emotionally charged moment, but it was exhausting. And as if that wasn't enough, he had not been able to stop the vivid thoughts swirling around in his head about a certain blue-eyed, gorgeous television actor.

No matter how much Aiden tried, he couldn't stop thinking about Skylar. Part of him wanted to hunt Skylar down and retract his "no" to coffee. The other part of him wanted to just keep running as fast and far as he could. Skylar Murphy was nothing but trouble. And that was trouble Aiden did not need.

As he made his way across the restaurant, Ryan was already standing up at the table, motioning for him to hurry. Aiden had barely sat when Ryan started in with the questions about Skylar.

"So tell me. I'm dying to know. Is he as hot in person as he is on television?"

He's freaking gorgeous, thought Aiden. "I suppose." Aiden thought about Skylar's handsome face and big blue eyes, "Yeah, he was kind of hot. Maybe a bit on the arrogant side, but he seemed nice enough." After hesitating for a moment for Ryan to mentally catch up, he said, "But wait! I haven't told you the strangest part. There was a fire at Monumental Studios this morning, and you will never guess who was there."

"If you tell me that you saved that beautiful man from a burning fire, I may kiss you right here in this overcrowded yet well decorated café," Ryan said, and he waved his hand around.

Aiden laughed. "No need for that. I didn't have to save him, and besides, he seemed fairly capable of saving himself."

"I just bet he could. Do you have any idea of the dreams I've had about this man? However, now that I think about how hot that would be, I may have just found a new fantasy." Ryan practically groaned as he rubbed his lips at the very idea of rushing in to save Skylar from a fire.

The waiter walked over to take their order as Ryan continued to daydream.

Aiden spoke up first. "I'll have the cheeseburger—hold the onions—with fries and a draft beer."

The waiter turned to Ryan, who sat there with a stupid grin on his face. After a moment of silence, Aiden threw a napkin at him to get his attention.

"Oh... oh... sorry, my mind was someplace else." Ryan scrambled to place his order. "I'll have the BLT with light mayo. And a beer... just make sure it's in a bottle." As the waiter turned to walk away, Ryan grabbed his arm. "Please make sure it's 'lite.'"

As the waiter walked off, Ryan was nonstop questions. "Okay, so what happened? Was my beautiful man hurt? Did he require mouth-to-mouth? Because if he did and you didn't call me to help... well, darling, I may have to disown you as my best friend. As everyone knows, I am very good with my mouth."

Ignoring that last comment, Aiden told Ryan about the fire in the soundstage and how Skylar had recognized him from the premiere party. He stopped talking as the waiter came back to the table with their beers. After taking a sip of his beer, Aiden then made the colossal mistake of telling Ryan that Skylar asked him out.

At that point, Ryan could barely contain himself. "What?" Ryan threw up his hands. "And why was this not the *first* thing you told me? When are you going?"

"We're not. I told him that it wasn't such a good idea," said Aiden.

"*You turned him down?*" Ryan said loud enough that the couple at the table next to them looked over to see what the excitement was about.

"Shushhhh…. Can you keep it down?" Aiden asked Ryan as he glanced over to the couple and gave them a slight smile of apology.

"Have you lost your mind?" Ryan asked incredulously. "Do you know what I would *give* to meet that guy, much less go out with him?" Then shaking his head, his tone became very serious. "Really, I fear that there is something wrong with you, 'cause sweetie, no one in their right mind would turn down that man." Not missing a beat, Ryan continued, "Have you seen him without a shirt? I could drown in that six-pack."

"There is nothing wrong with me," Aiden said defensively. "But trust me, I know his type. Egos as big as Texas, and they don't care about anyone or anything as much as they care about themselves. So, I'm not going to be just a notch on that guy's belt. And believe me, that's all he's looking for."

"You don't know that, and besides, just think about the notch in *your* belt. 'Cause sleeping with Skylar Murphy would be one hell of a notch," Ryan countered. "One great big *giant* notch."

"There isn't going to be a notch in anyone's belt because the date, the coffee, or whatever you want to call it, is *not* happening."

Ryan just sat back in his chair. This was a lot for him to take in. Finally he said, "Well, did you at least give him your number?"

"Are you not hearing a single word I'm saying? I am *not* going out with him."

"Fine, then give him my number," said Ryan bluntly.

"I will not. I'm not giving him anyone's number. Forget it, Ryan," said Aiden.

"Okay, whatever, but when that hot hunk of man is snatched up by Hollywood's latest flavor of the month, don't complain to me that you missed out."

"Believe me, I won't," said Aiden. "Besides, how do we know that he's not a straight guy doing a bit of gay research for his character?"

Ryan had to think about that for a second. "Truthfully, I did think he was straight. There are rumors that he and Kelly Bane, his *mother* on the show, are hitting it pretty regularly on the side. So maybe he's bi?" Ryan suggested.

Thinking back to Skylar's remark about kissing both men and women and liking it, Aiden had to think that this might be true. But he quickly shrugged that off and said, "Who knows, who cares. I am 100 percent not interested." And with that, he chugged the rest of his beer. He was finished discussing Skylar Murphy.

Ryan tried to bring up Skylar several times during the meal, but each time Aiden was able to stop the conversation before it was started. As they paid their check and left, Aiden told Ryan that he just needed to go home and sleep. In reality, he could think of nothing except Skylar, and he just wanted to be alone. Ryan gave him a hug and left to go to the LGBT shelter where he volunteered several nights a week.

As Aiden walked to his car, he thought about how gorgeous Skylar had looked when he smiled. *How did celebrities have such perfect teeth? And those eyes... they could light up a room.* Aiden rubbed his arm as he recalled Skylar's touch. *Why is life so complicated?* Once he was home, Aiden started channel surfing before finally ending up on Netflix watching *Royal Family* and countless scenes of one Skylar Murphy.

CHAPTER 8

IT WAS close to midnight when Skylar finally pulled into his driveway. It had been an especially hard day at the studio. He had screwed up his lines more times than he cared to admit, and all he wanted to do was just go home and get some sleep. Hopefully things would improve by the morning.

As he neared the front of his house, he saw a car parked in his usual spot. What the hell? He certainly wasn't expecting anyone at this hour. As he slowly got out of his car, he noticed that the little yellow Volkswagen bug appeared to be empty. He walked up to the window and looked in. There was nothing to be seen other than an oversized yellow flower sitting on the dashboard. He shook the door handle only to find that it was locked. Realizing the driver could be outside, he quickly looked around to make sure no one was standing there ready to bash his head in. He could hear the news promo now: "Television star murdered in his driveway. Suspect is a flower-wielding gypsy who was last seen driving a bright yellow bug."

Deciding that he had better be more alert, Skylar carefully inched his way back to his car and reached in the backseat for the baseball bat that he had left in there since last spring.

Walking up to his house with the bat in his grip, he kept looking around and behind him. There was nothing he could see; all seemed quiet and still. When he got to his front door, he reached for the handle, and the door pushed in, creaking as it opened. Okay, this was starting to freak him out. Was someone in the house? Had he been robbed? The thought occurred to him that he should call the police, but with the mood he was in, he was ready to kick some ass.

Slowly he crept into the kitchen, through the doorway, and into the dining room. There was no one to be seen. He looked down the hall toward his bedroom. Light was shining from his room. Not sure what to think, he slowly made his way down the hall. As he got closer to the room, he could hear the television. Had he left it on this morning? With his heart in his throat, he slowly walked up beside the door and peeked inside. Sitting up in his bed was Emma in of those tiny little sexy outfits. Normally, this sight might have sparked his interest, but all he could feel at this moment was intense anger.

"What in the *hell* are you doing here?" Skylar yelled as he stalked into the bedroom.

Emma jumped at the sound of his voice. "Skylar! Gosh, you scared me!" she stammered as she pulled the covers over her.

"I scared *you*? Are you out of your fucking mind? What are you doing here?"

"I… I… was hoping to surprise you," she stammered. "I thought we could spend some time together, kind of start over after our misunderstanding the other night."

Skylar couldn't believe he had heard her correctly. Normally, he would try to watch what he said, but right at this moment, he honestly couldn't care less if he hurt her feelings. Looking at her with disbelief, he said, "Misunderstanding? Are you kidding me? The only misunderstanding was yours. I was drunk, Emma! In fact, I was so drunk you had to bring me home!"

"But…," Emma started to protest.

Holding up his hand to stop her, he said forcefully, "*Wait*. I'm not finished! Okay, so we had sex—sex, by the way, that I don't even remember—and now you think you can just come into my house anytime you damn well please without asking me?" Skylar was so angry his heart rate was through the roof. Then it occurred to him. "And *exactly how* did you get in? Break one of my windows?"

"No," Emma said, shaking. "I would never do something like that."

"Oh, but breaking into my house is something that you would do?"

"*No*! I used the key that you keep under the ceramic frog outside," she said defensively.

"How did you know about my key?" Now Skylar was shaking with anger. All he wanted to do was throw her out the door… on her ass.

"You showed it to me. The other night, after the party, when we were coming up to your door, you told me where to find the key. I thought that since you told me where to find the key, you were okay with me using it."

"Well, you thought wrong! Listen to me, and listen closely." Skylar lowered his voice to a threatening level. "We had sex one night. *One* night. That is all it will ever be. Do you understand me? I've had one hell of a bad day, and you have succeeded in making it ten times worse. Now get your stuff, and get out of my house."

At this point Emma was starting to look a bit scared. "I'm sorry, Skylar, I really thought you would be happy to see me."

Shaking his head in disbelief, he answered, "I'm not happy. Not one damn bit. You basically broke into my house. What were you thinking? No... don't answer that. Just go. You're lucky that I'm not calling the police. I should... but I won't." At seeing her hesitation, he continued, "However, you have about one minute to disappear before I change my mind."

Emma was devastated. Why couldn't she do anything right when it came to Skylar? She loved him—couldn't he see that?

Skylar watched her. She appeared to be conflicted about something. "You're still here," said Skylar in a threatening tone as he walked around to the side of the bed toward her.

"I'm leaving. But at least let me cook you some dinner, you know, to make up for... for this," Emma said with a bit of hopefulness.

With a death tone that would have made Darth Vader proud, Skylar bit each word out: "Emma. Leave. *Now.*"

With that, Emma grabbed her coat and ran out the door. Skylar didn't follow. Surely she wouldn't be stupid enough to hang around. Damn, what was wrong with that girl? Was he going to have to get a restraining order against her? Deep down he knew she was harmless, but she was annoying as hell. And now he was going to have to change his locks or find a better hiding place for his key.

He sat down on the bed with a sigh and put his face in his hands. Rubbing his face, he wondered why his life was suddenly full of drama. *Because you have the hots for some guy who won't give you the time of day, and you slept with a crazy fan. Couldn't pick a sane one, could you?* Skylar sighed heavily and stood up to start changing his clothes.

On the television in the background, a reporter was interviewing someone about a house fire. A voice caught his attention. As he turned to look at the screen, he saw Aiden talking to the reporter. *Him again.* Skylar turned up the volume as the reporter was saying that Aiden had gone into a burning house and had managed to locate a mother, who was hiding in a back room with her two little girls. He was able to bring them out of the house, thus saving their lives.

Skylar watched the story unfold, and all he could think was how amazing Aiden looked. Even with all that soot and sweat, he was gorgeous. And how brave was he to run into a burning house, risking his life? Skylar couldn't remember the last time he'd felt so much respect for someone. He wanted nothing more than to get to know this guy. It wasn't often he wanted anyone this badly, if ever, but something about Aiden made Skylar crazy. And the fact that he was now some kind of hero only made Skylar want him more.

Frustrated and disappointed, Skylar pulled out his computer and signed on to Twitter. *Hello Twitterworld*, he wrote in his first tweet. *Tell me something good.*

With any luck maybe someone would reply and cheer him up. Sure enough it wasn't long before fans discovered he was online and started pouring out the love. As Skylar read their messages, then answered a few, it occurred to him that it was ironic that he had all these people wanting to be with him, yet the only person he had any interest in didn't want him. Life sure could suck at times.

CHAPTER 9

EMMA WAS devastated. Sobbing uncontrollably, she drove through the Hollywood Hills and away from Skylar's house. She didn't understand why Skylar had been so angry. Remembering his face when he saw her in his bed, she shivered. So maybe she shouldn't have just "let herself in," but she'd thought it would be the perfect way to surprise him. All she wanted to do was make things right between them. She wanted to make love to him and show him how much she loved him. There was absolutely no reason for him to get so angry and out of control.

She had spent all afternoon shopping for the perfect outfit. She had chosen his favorite color, which she knew was red. Not only had she spent an enormous amount of time and energy finding the perfect outfit, she had used most of her paycheck to buy it. And he hadn't even noticed it! All he had noticed was that she had borrowed the key and let herself in. Was she ever going to do anything right in his eyes?

As she drove toward her house in Studio City, she was at a loss for what to do. Part of her wanted to turn around and drive right back to Skylar's house and demand that he apologize. Another part of her was afraid of making him angrier than he already was. She had never seen him so mad. Of course, she had seen him behave that way on television, in various roles, but that was television. This was real life. She had never imagined that "her" Skylar would behave in such a way.

But yet, she couldn't stand the thought of him being mad at her. Her heart felt as if it was literally breaking. She didn't want him angry with her. She just wanted to start all over again. There had to be a way to make him understand how much she loved him, and when he did, she was sure he would fall in love with her.

But sex was not the answer; at least it didn't appear to be high on his list. So what could she do to make him love her as much as she loved him? There had to be a way, and if it was the last thing she did, she would make Skylar Murphy love her.

CHAPTER 10

KELLY BANE felt like she owned the world. Everything was falling into place. The premiere of *The Executives* had won the timeslot for the night, and now she had talk-show hosts begging her to make a guest appearance. It was about time she found her glory days again—it was long overdue.

Lounging on her sofa in her trailer, she watched as her assistant Cary sorted through her wardrobe for the show.

Cary was the quiet type, never having much to say. He wasn't bad-looking, just small and slender. And if he would get rid of those old-fashioned glasses, it would improve his appearance greatly. As she watched him, Kelly wondered if he had ever had a girlfriend.

"Are you going to the party at Gray Hudson's house this Saturday night?" he asked. He was furious at the wardrobe department. They were supposed to lay out Kelly's outfits prior to every scene but they had yet to show up. Dammit, he would just do it himself.

"Oh, of course I am," Kelly responded as she sat up. "So please make sure you put that on my schedule. I certainly don't want to miss an opportunity like that. I heard that there will be quite a few A-listers there."

"Probably. But you'll be the most important one."

That made Kelly smile. "You know very well that I'm not an A-lister—at least not anymore—but it is all about who you're photographed with and how often. There are celebrities you want to be seen with, and, well… those you stay far away from. It's all about association in this town. You know my motto: 'Make every photo count.'"

Then stay away from that troublemaking kid. Cary frowned at the thought. But to Kelly, he said, "Of course, you're right. I'll put it on the schedule immediately."

"Oh, and also, let's make sure to find time to shop before then. I really need a new dress. Something blue that brings out my eyes, yet is figure fitting enough to show all my curves and make me look twenty years younger," Kelly ordered as she ran her hands down her hips. Turning to Cary, she changed her tone of voice. "Oh and speaking of younger, have you seen Skylar today?"

Cary had his back to Kelly, so she didn't notice the eye roll. "Not since early this morning. I saw him at the craft table grabbing breakfast before that first scene between Toby and his fiancée." Turning to face Kelly, he continued, "I would try his usual hangouts—his lot trailer or the community dressing room." Cary was referring to the dressing rooms housed within the soundstage area that the cast used off and on during the day if they didn't want to go to their own trailers.

"Great! I need to see him," purred Kelly. She applied fresh lipstick, straightened her skirt, and headed down the hall toward the community dressing rooms.

You mean you need to screw him, Cary thought angrily. Of course, he would never say that out loud; he needed this job too much.

Halfway down the hall, Kelly turned back to Cary. "I'll be back in a little while. If anyone needs me, you don't know where to find me. I'm not due on set for at least an hour."

Cary was too preoccupied in his own thoughts to respond.

As Kelly approached the community dressing rooms, she heard Skylar inside, talking to someone. "Are you serious? They want me? Excellent! I needed some good news! ... Yes, definitely talk to them and see what I need to do. If I need to audition, I will. Just let me know the time and place."

Kelly tapped lightly on the brown wooden door. Within moments she heard Skylar walking over. He opened the door and smiled when he saw that it was Kelly. Motioning her in, he continued talking to the person on the telephone. "Yes, great! I'll be anxious to hear what they have to say. ... Okay, cool. ... Later."

As he hung up the phone, Kelly immediately wanted to know what was going on. "That sounded like great news," she stated.

"Fuck yeah! You know that franchise, *King's Pawn*?" he asked as he turned to greet her.

"Yes, of course." Kelly knew all about the franchise, which had sparked two major motion pictures that had been huge successes domestically and internationally.

"Well, that was my manager, Nick. They're very interested in having me play the lead in their next film, which has the working title of... wait for it... *Checkmate!*"

Kelly couldn't remember the last time she'd seen Skylar this excited. Laughing, she said, "That's amazing, my darling." She walked over to him and gave him a hug. "You deserve such recognition. I knew it was only a matter of time before you hit the big time, my little A-lister," she purred.

Skylar, lost in his thoughts, didn't seem to notice that she was continuing to rub his arm.

"This is fucking cool. This franchise is on the verge of topping the Bond films. This and *Illusions*, which I don't stand a chance for, are *the* films to be in this year. It would set my career," he mused as he moved away from her and went over to the counter to pour a cup of coffee. "Definitely have to get this role."

Kelly, who had already planned to seduce Skylar, was even more turned on by this news. Feeling confident by her very successful week, Kelly moved around until she was behind Skylar. Putting her arms around his waist, she kissed his back as she began using her fingertips to trail up his stomach. How she loved the feel of his flat hard stomach. She became more excited as her fingers lingered over each abdominal muscle.

Skylar, finally realizing what Kelly was up to, just stood there and let her continue to touch and massage him.

"*Illusions*. Isn't that the book about a couple whose relationship is built on lie after lie and how they have to untangle the lies before one of them is killed?" Kelly purred into his ear.

He moaned as she began to circle his nipples through his shirt. He whispered, "Yes, that's the one. Everything is an illusion." He leaned his head back, closed his eyes, and continued, "The book sold thirty million copies, and the studios have practically killed themselves over who would get the movie rights." He felt her tongue run up over his ear. He shivered at the sensation. "And I would give anything to have that lead," he said through a moan as he turned around to kiss her.

Her mouth opened immediately when his lips touched hers. She reached up and wrapped her arms around his neck as Skylar ran his hands up her sides. Reaching her breasts, Skylar cupped them while rubbing his thumb over her nipples. She gasped. He lightly squeezed while gently twisting each nipple. Kelly moaned out loud. *She's really hot today*, Skylar thought. He felt their fullness, and as he continued to massage her breasts, she moaned into his mouth.

Feeling dizzy with excitement, Kelly continued to ravish the inside of his mouth as his tongue fought hers for dominance.

She wanted him so much her knees were feeling weak. Skylar kept kissing her and fondling her breasts before slowly beginning to unbutton her shirt. She moaned and reached down to rub his cock through his pants. Feeling his hardness created more excitement within her.

Kelly continued rubbing her hand up and down the length of his cock. *Ah... yeah, mmmm, just like that*, thought Skylar. He continued to kiss her as he proceeded to grind his cock into her hand. As he felt his mind fogging up and lust-filled emotions taking over, an image of Aiden popped into his head. Feeling like a cup of ice water had been thrown in his face, Skylar stopped kissing Kelly. *What the fuck?* He had seen Aiden's face as he told him no, he didn't think it was a good idea to go out with him. The memory sent Skylar into a tailspin, and when he felt Kelly's lips seeking his, Skylar took a deep breath and desperately tried to find his momentum again.

Okay, just focus, he told himself. Trying to bring himself back and maintain his erection, he continued to massage her breasts before bending down to nip at them through her bra. Kelly moaned louder. *Okay, better*, he thought. He tried to concentrate on the feel of her hand on his cock, stroking up and down and gently tugging at it. He imagined her wet, hot mouth on him. He felt his erection harden. He was back.

Moving his hands down, he cupped her ass in his hands. He began to kiss her neck, flicking his tongue up and around her ear, gently sucking at her earlobe as he walked her backward over to the couch. She hadn't stopped moaning, and her breathing was becoming erratic. She started to unbutton his jeans as he laid her down on the couch. Skylar bent over and started removing her blouse. Once he had the blouse off, it was mere seconds before he was practically on top of her. He unsnapped her bra, shoved it up under her neck, and began assaulting her waiting nipple with his mouth.

Kelly was on fire. She couldn't get enough of him. Her hands were inside his jeans, continuing to rub and tease him. Skylar was trying to keep up with her level of energy and abandonment when he thought of Aiden again. *Seriously, dude, get your act together*, he chastised himself. As images of Aiden continued to flutter through his mind, he struggled to keep his thoughts on Kelly—her mouth, her body—but it was not working. Fighting to keep his erection, he worked his way back up to her face and began to kiss her on the mouth.

Kelly kissed him back with an urgency that couldn't be denied. With a searing building sensation gathering in the pit of her stomach, she started pushing his head back down to her breasts and lower. She wanted to feel his mouth on her, as it was the only thing that would quench this fire within her.

As she continued gently pushing his head lower, Skylar fought for some clarity. He stopped at her breasts to suck and tease them a bit more. As he sucked and licked, he tried to pull her skirt up so that he could taste her all over. *You don't really want to do that.* And at that thought, Skylar realized that maybe he didn't want this. In between kissing her, rubbing her breasts, running his hand up the inside of her thighs, all he could see was Aiden standing with the reporter outside the burned-out house. What the fuck was wrong with him? He had one of the hottest women in Hollywood writhing beneath him and all he could think about was Aiden and how he wanted it to be Aiden underneath him. Skylar could feel his erection shrinking. His mind was too jumbled to focus.

Kelly was rubbing his cock and fighting to keep it hard. What the hell was wrong with him? He was losing the momentum for some reason. She tried to unzip his jeans, but all at once, with a force from out of nowhere, he just pushed himself up off her and off the couch.

"What's wrong?" she asked, panting as she tried to pull him back on top of her.

"I don't know. I can't... I... I... I'm just not in the mood. Can we do this another time?" Skylar stammered, almost in a panic.

"Another time? What the fuck? I want you right now, not another time." Kelly was having difficulty breathing as she was still incredibly turned on.

Seeing her and realizing the state she was in, Skylar contemplated just finishing her off with his mouth, but he just didn't have it in him. The feeling was gone. This was pathetic, not to mention bullshit. And definitely not his style.

"Really, Kel, I'm sorry. My mind is just all over the place. Besides I need to grab a quick shower before I go back on set. Maybe later I can meet you at your guest house." *Or maybe not, especially if I can't get this man out of my head*, he thought.

"Skylar, get your ass back on this couch. You can't just roll off me like I'm some whore that you're paying by the hour and now the time is up." Kelly was really irritated now. She had been so close to orgasm, and for Skylar to decide he wasn't in the mood was completely unacceptable.

"Come on, Kel, don't be pissed. I just have way too much on my mind right now. It's not you, I promise."

On that note, Kelly jumped up, grabbed her blouse, and put it on. Skylar watched her in surprise as he was sure she would not give up that easily. Kelly adjusted her hair and her clothes, and as she stalked by him on her way out the door, she said, "I never thought for a moment it was me."

CHAPTER 11

THE HALLWAY was empty, just the way it had been planned. Everyone except for Skylar was on set taping a scene. It was a short scene; therefore, quickness was of the essence.

Arriving at the dressing room door, he tapped lightly. He waited for an answer. No one came to the door. Trying to be patient, he tapped again. Once he was positive no one was going to answer the door, he pushed it open. His heart was pounding with excitement as he walked into the dressing room. This was half the fun—getting inside. If he got caught, he had already devised his story, so he wasn't worried.

Being careful to not make a sound, he looked around for the perfect spot. The room was a disaster, but one that created endless possibilities. He could hear the shower running in the bathroom. The leather jacket thrown over the chair confirmed it was Skylar in the shower. Great! Knowing he only had a few minutes, he walked over to the window. Bending down to the ground, he took out his lighter and lit the corner of the curtain. At first, the fire wouldn't stay lit, so he added paper that was lying around on the floor and lit several more areas of the curtain. Finally the fire slowly took hold and started moving up the side of the curtain in a beautiful blaze of orange and black. He stood there with a smile on his face. Finally. Payback time!

He moved closer to the door, and just before walking out, he pulled a metal bar out of his coat pocket and dropped it near the entranceway. Before closing the door, he looked back to make sure you could see the big *L* written in paint on the metal bar. He disappeared down the hallway as the fire continued to move from the curtain over to the papers on the nearby desk.

CHAPTER 12

AIDEN COULDN'T quite figure it out and it was annoying the hell out of him. He had gone to the investigator's office and asked for a copy of the report from the soundstage fire. But now that he had been studying it for a while, he couldn't shake the feeling that he was missing something.

The fire had been ruled intentional, but there were no leads as to who might be the arsonist. All they really knew was someone had started the fire by lighting a big pile of gas-filled rags and had left them in the corner of the room. It was overkill, which suggested it was a male, but at the moment, they did not have any solid leads. The investigator's report also mentioned that they had found a metal bar with the letter *A* painted on it. It had been placed outside the room as if it was meant to be found. The investigator had also noted that he wasn't sure if the metal bar had anything to do with the fire; however, he felt it should be mentioned. Thinking the letters might mean more, Aiden made himself a copy of the investigator's report and placed it in his shoulder bag.

So far it had been a quiet day, and all the guys were taking it easy. Ben was outside in the parking lot washing his car. Paul and Dave were reading, and Aiden was studying the investigator's report. The alarm startled them all. Dispatch could be heard loudly across the intercom: "Structural fire with possible entrapment. Monumental Studios. Soundstage 5. Melrose Avenue, Hollywood."

Aiden felt his heart skip a beat as he listened to the address. Again? What was going on over there at the studios? And wait, wasn't that Skylar's soundstage?

Aiden joined the other guys as they ran into the bay and threw on their gear as quickly as they could. They were on the truck in less than a minute.

Barreling down Melrose Ave, the truck turned again, for the second time in two weeks, into the gates of Monumental Studios.

Aiden could see the smoke from the gates as they came in, dodging onlookers as they drove to the scene of the fire. The soundstage was being evacuated, and as the fire engine rounded the corner, Aiden could see a crowd gathered around someone lying on the ground. He was off the truck before it had come to a complete stop. As he pushed his way through the crowd to get to the victim, he saw that it was Skylar. His heart racing, Aiden bent down to try to evaluate the situation. Behind him he could hear his coworkers pulling out the hoses to work on the fire. Meanwhile, Ben was pushing everyone back behind an imaginary line.

Judging from the amount of coughing that Skylar was doing, Aiden knew that he had inhaled smoke—it was just a question of how much. Was his throat burned? Had he inhaled a large amount of smoke? Aiden needed to know. Looking him over carefully, he appeared to be all right. When their gazes met, Skylar gave him a small smile, quietly saying, "It's you."

Aiden smiled back as he asked, "Are you having any trouble breathing?"

"No," Skylar responded, "I'm fine."

"Is your throat sore, feel burned in any way?"

"No, not at all."

Aiden felt a wave of relief wash over him as he realized that Skylar was most likely okay.

Remembering his first job, Aiden yelled to his coworker, "Paul! Do you all need my help?"

"No! You take care of him. We have it under control. The paramedics will be pulling in any second."

"What happened?" Aiden asked the crowd lingering near Skylar.

A short red-haired girl, who had been standing over Skylar, was wiping away tears as she attempted to explain what had just happened.

Looking down at Aiden, she said, "I'm Skylar's assistant. I was coming down to the dressing rooms to get him for his next scene. I saw the smoke coming out from under the door and I ran over to it. But before I could get there, Skylar was coming out. He was coughing and choking, so we brought him outside for air." She stopped talking long enough to wipe more tears. "Is he going to be all right?"

"I think so," Aiden responded. "But just to be on the safe side, let's have the paramedics check him out."

"Seriously, guys, stop talking over me as if I'm not here. I'm fine," Skylar said from his lying position on the ground. "Just need to clear some of this smoke out of my lungs." Skylar started coughing, as if to prove his point.

The smartass is back. He must be okay. "Can you sit up?" Aiden asked Skylar.

"I think so," Skylar responded as he sat up. That movement led to more coughing. As Aiden watched him closely, he noted that Skylar seemed to be able to breathe more easily.

"What happened in there?" Aiden asked him.

"No idea. I was in the shower, I got out to dry off, and that's when I saw the smoke coming in under the bathroom door. I opened it, saw the fire covering the entire side of the room, and I ran out the door as fast as I could," Skylar said.

"Okay, that explains why you're lying here in only a towel," Aiden said quietly.

Skylar smiled as he thought, *This might turn out to be a good thing.*

"The guys almost have the fire out. Hopefully we'll know soon how it started. But for now, at least you're safe," Aiden said with relief in his voice.

Noting the relieved sound, Skylar looked up at Aiden, gave him a lazy smile, and said so that only Aiden could hear, "Hey, aren't you supposed to be giving me mouth-to-mouth or something?"

Ahh... the boy is definitely all right. "Not unless you're dying, and you look like you have a few good years left," Aiden said.

"It was worth a try," Skylar said with a small laugh in between his coughs.

"Okay, everyone move out of the way," the paramedic said as she made her way to Skylar. "Let me check him over."

Aiden stood up, a little disappointed that their conversation had been interrupted, but there was still a fire to contend with.

"I'm just leaving to go and help the crew." Looking at Skylar, he said, "You take care of yourself. This is becoming a common occurrence with you."

Skylar managed to smile at him before the paramedic took over and started giving orders.

"Let's get you up and over to the ambulance so I can check you out properly. Do you feel you need to go to the hospital?" she asked.

"No, I'm fine. I'm barely coughing now." Glancing at the soundstage that was still blowing out black smoke, he said somberly, "Damn. I could have died in there."

The paramedic looked over at the soundstage and said, "Well, it appears the firemen are getting it under control. Good thing for you that you were able to get out in time."

She helped Skylar get up off the ground and supported him as they walked over to the ambulance to get him checked out.

Aiden was watching from across the way. He was surprised at how concerned he had been when he'd seen Skylar lying on the ground. Why on earth did this guy keep getting under his skin? He kept telling himself that he would feel the same about anyone, but he knew that wasn't true. Maybe he should do something about it. But for now, that would have to wait.

He heard a commotion and saw a woman rushing over toward Skylar, a man trailing behind her.

"Oh my God! Skylar! Are you okay? What on earth happened?" the woman asked.

Aiden saw that it was the woman from the premiere party, Kelly Bane.

Skylar, who was over at the ambulance, held up his hand, indicating that he was fine. Sophie proceeded to fill her in on what had happened.

"He was really lucky that he got out in time," said Cary. Kelly just shook her head and stood there watching Skylar.

"I was just there. It's the strangest thing," she said quietly. "I couldn't have been gone more than twenty minutes. I don't remember seeing anything unusual." But then again, she'd been focused on her lack of sexual satisfaction and therefore would have most likely missed the fire itself.

"I'm sure it was something simple, maybe faulty wiring, or maybe he was smoking in his trailer," suggested Cary.

"He doesn't smoke. That's only for the show. You know that!" Dammit, Kelly hated it when Cary said something stupid.

"Then it must have been something else. I'm sure they will figure it out," Cary said as he pointed to the firefighters.

Kelly shook her head. "I certainly hope so. This is getting to the point of being ridiculous." Looking over at Skylar, who was still with the paramedic, Kelly realized this was the second fire in two weeks. Maybe she would suggest that they have more security around the actors. Either way, they were all going to have to be more careful.

CHAPTER 13

"IT CERTAINLY appeared to be intentional," said Paul, stroking his beard as he rolled back and forth in his chair. "It reeked of gasoline over on that one side of the room. I'm willing to bet my next paycheck that it was started by something as simple as gas and a lighter, just like the last fire at the soundstage."

It was late afternoon, and the firefighters had arrived back at the firehouse and were now sitting around in the kitchen trying to make sense of the two fires.

Looking around at the group gathered in the fire-station kitchen, Ben asked, "So, do we think the fires are related?"

As he waited for a response, Ben reached for the investigator's report of the first fire. Aiden had taken it out of his shoulder bag, and it was now sitting on the table for everyone to read.

"I think so. It's just too coincidental, the fact that it's the same studio and they both appear to be intentionally set by someone," said Aiden. "Yeah, I definitely think they're related."

"Okay, so let's think about that for a minute. Why would someone want to set a fire in an empty soundstage and then turn around and set another fire in a community dressing room in a different soundstage?" asked Ben.

"Someone who doesn't like the show?" said Paul.

Aiden sent him a warning glance in response.

"Maybe, but that doesn't explain the fire at the empty soundstage," said Ben, continuing to look over the investigator's report.

"Perhaps they didn't know it was empty," said Paul. Turning to Aiden, he continued, "What about that actor in the dressing room? Is there any reason to think someone is targeting Steve... Sam... what was his name again?"

"His name is Skylar Murphy, and I have no idea. He didn't act like he was worried someone might be after him, but I do think the investigators should check into it," answered Aiden.

"Yeah, there could be a connection there," Paul said.

"Okay, so let's think access," said Ben, continuing on the same train of thought as before. "Who would have access to both the soundstage and the cast dressing rooms?"

"I believe it would have to be someone who belonged there, at the studio. Don't they issue badges to people who are allowed to be on the property and in the building?" asked Paul.

Aiden shook his head as he said, "I'm sure they do, but that could be hundreds of people. Monumental Studios houses ten different soundstages, with most of them employing dozens of crew members. Not to mention the actors, directors, and extras."

"Someone's been studying up on the history of Monumental," Paul said with raised eyebrows.

"Just doing my job," Aiden fired back.

They all sat there in silence. No one had any more answers to the situation. Aiden felt his cell phone vibrating in his pocket. "Excuse me, guys, for a sec," he said as he headed outside to take the call.

"Aiden Moore," he said into the cell phone.

"Hello, Aiden. It's Jamie." Jamie was the manager at the catering service that Aiden moonlighted for on his off days.

"Hi, Jamie," he answered.

"I hope I'm not disturbing you, but I needed to confirm something with you. I have a party in Bel Air booked for this upcoming Saturday. I thought you told me you were free, but I wanted to make sure you were available to work it for me."

"Sure, I'm off this weekend. Just e-mail me the details, and I'll be there. Just serving… no bartending?" Aiden asked, because he preferred walking around among the partygoers rather than being stuck behind a bar.

"Yes, it's an informal get-together at Gray Hudson's house, the producer of that new television show *The Executives*."

Aiden could have sworn his heart skipped a beat. *Get a grip, Moore. What are you, thirteen?*

"Count me in. I wouldn't miss it for the world," he assured her. "I'll look for the e-mail and see you on Saturday."

"Thanks, Aiden. I'll see you then."

After hanging up his cell, Aiden walked back into the other room. The others were still discussing possible motives for the fire in the dressing room.

"He's back," Paul said, motioning with his head toward Aiden.

"Did y'all figure out something?" Aiden asked with hope.

"I think so. I was just reading in the report that a metal bar was found at the first fire scene, with a letter on it." Ben said, looking again for the part of the investigator's report mentioning the metal bar. Finding it, he motioned to Aiden. "Come here... look at this.... There was a bar with the letter *A* marked on it," he said, pointing to a small paragraph near the bottom of the page.

"I saw that too. I thought it was a bit strange, but I wasn't sure if it was relevant or not," Aiden answered as he walked over to look at the report with Ben.

"Oh, I definitely think it's relevant," Ben said with excitement. "As I was leaving the scene today, I saw a metal bar near the doorway of the dressing room with the letter *L* on it. Boys, I think we have a serial arsonist on our hands who wants to play a little crossword puzzle game with all of us."

CHAPTER 14

SKYLAR FELT the best he had felt in days. It was a good thing he had gotten out of the dressing room when he did, because just the tiny bit of smoke he had inhaled had bothered him way more than he thought it would. He was only now feeling 100 percent again.

He left his car with the valet and walked up to Gray's Bel Air home. Gray was one of the executives for Monumental Studios. He was a very amiable man from the South, and Skylar had always had a soft spot for him. And the feeling was mutual, judging from the casting opportunities Gray continued to pass along.

This was going to be a huge party, and from the numerous elongated windows on each side of the front entrance, Skylar could clearly see that there was a crowd of people already there. Shit! Seeing that certainly didn't help his nerves. In the old days, he'd loved surrounding himself with a lot of people, but these days, not so much. He was okay with small parties, but when it came to hanging out with the Hollywood crowd, he became really uncomfortable.

Taking a deep breath, he walked up to the door and hesitantly rang the doorbell. Gray's housekeeper, Amanda, answered the door.

"Mr. Murphy! It's very nice to see you again," she said with a welcoming smile. "Please come in." She reached for his coat.

"Good evening, Amanda." Skylar thanked her as he handed over his coat and walked into the foyer. From there, the place came alive with music and decorations. Floral arrangements lined the foyer, beautifully accented by the elegant mirrors hanging above them. Upon reaching the doorway leading into the main living room, Skylar stopped to do a quick glance around the room to see if he recognized anyone.

Standing alone in the center of the room was Kelly. Great! He would stand with her and hopefully not get cornered into a conversation with someone he didn't know.

As he walked through the living room, he was greeted by a few of the guests who recognized him.

"Hello, Skylar, great job you're doing on the show this year." Skylar smiled at the small, balding man. Sam Newman was head of publicity at Monumental Studios and a very pleasant guy.

Shaking Sam's hand, Skylar responded, "Thank you, Sam. Hope you are having a great evening."

"It's a lovely party. I'm enjoying myself quite a bit." And as if to prove it, he cheered the air with his very large glass of wine.

"Gray definitely knows how to throw a party," Skylar said with a smile. He turned as he heard his name being called. He looked up to see Kelly motioning for him to come over.

He turned back to Sam and said, "I'll catch up with you later. Kelly seems to need me."

"Sure, Skylar. Looking forward to it."

Skylar continued moving in Kelly's direction. He had barely reached her when she grabbed him in a big hug.

"*Darling*! You really scared me during that awful situation over at the studio. My heart literally froze when Cary told me he thought it was you that they had carried out of the building. I couldn't get to you fast enough. Are you all right now?" Kelly pushed him away so she could look straight into his face, checking for any signs that he had been hurt.

"I'm fine, Kelly," Skylar said as he pulled her back into the hug. "Don't worry about me. Takes more than a fire to wipe me out," he said teasingly.

She pulled him closer and put her mouth up to his ear. "I'm just so sorry about how I acted before all that happened. I was quite frustrated, as you were well aware, and I let my emotions get the better of me."

Skylar whispered in her ear, "It's okay, Kel. I was having a weird moment myself, so I can understand your frustration with me."

"Well, you owe me a night, so I shall be collecting soon," Kelly murmured in his ear while squeezing his arm.

"Sounds good," Skylar said halfheartedly. Lately, he was having a hard time thinking of anyone... other than Aiden. *However*, maybe a good lay would do him some good and put things back into perspective. "Maybe we'll find Gray's pool house later," he teased in a low whisper.

"If only he had a pool house. I think we're out of luck with that one, darling," Kelly cooed. "But I did notice he had a gazebo off by itself back behind the west wing of the house. I saw it when he was giving me the grand tour."

As Skylar smiled at the thought, she continued, "Maybe later we can meet there. Come find me before you leave tonight."

Skylar leaned in again and whispered so low that only she could hear, "It's a date."

"Could I offer you both something to eat?" a familiar voice said from behind them.

Skylar turned to see Aiden standing there in his waiter's uniform, looking absolutely gorgeous, holding a tray of hors d'oeuvres, with a huge smile on his face. Seeing Aiden without the weight of his fireman's gear, Skylar could now fully appreciate how attractive Aiden was, and he liked it.

Skylar's entire outlook of the night changed immediately. *Now things have a chance at getting interesting*, he thought as he looked back at Aiden with a smile that matched Aiden's in size. "Well, damn, look who it is!" Turning to Kelly, he continued, "Kelly, meet the firefighter who saved me from that terrible fire."

Kelly looked puzzled as Aiden said, "Don't listen to him—he's exaggerating. I arrived after he was safely out of the fire and just lying around in a towel."

Skylar laughed. "True, but still, you would have been there to save me, if I had needed it."

"It's a good thing you didn't. How are you feeling now?" Aiden's voice changed as it filled with concern.

"Oh, I'm fine. I was just telling Kelly that it would take more than a fire to take me out."

"Well, it's a good thing you saw it when you did. This fire was a bit nastier than the one at Soundstage 4."

Hearing this made Kelly realized that the young, very good-looking waiter really was a firefighter. "Oh! I thought he was kidding about you being a firefighter."

"No, he's not kidding. I'm a firefighter in my other life," Aiden said with a smile. "This is my side job that I do on my days off from the fire station."

Skylar recognized that look of interest in Kelly's eyes. *Oh no, we're not going there*, he thought as he casually moved to try to block Kelly's view of Aiden.

"Kelly, could I bother you a moment? They need you over here," Cary said as he walked up.

Kelly glanced over at Cary and frowned. "Who needs me?"

Ignoring her look, Cary continued, "The LA affiliate wants to get a quick photo with you and Gray."

"Fine, I suppose." Taking an hors d'oeuvre from Aiden's tray, she muttered, "Excuse me, but I'll have to catch up with you young men later." Blowing them both kisses, Kelly walked off with Cary.

Skylar couldn't help feeling pleased that she had left. He had been hoping for a few minutes of alone time with Aiden. "It's great to see you here," he said.

"Yeah, when Jamie called me about working the party, I was hoping you would be here."

"You were?" *This is getting better and better....*

"I wanted to see for myself that you were okay after the fire incident the other day," Aiden explained.

A visibly disappointed Skylar shook his head. "And here I thought you were going to reconsider going out with me."

"Actually, I have reconsidered." Aiden smiled to himself as he watched Skylar's face light up.

"And...?" Skylar said, feeling strangely excited.

"I would love to have coffee with you sometime," declared Aiden.

"Excellent! How about tomorrow night?" Realizing he was sounding too excited, Skylar cut the enthusiasm in half and continued, "Unless of course, you have to work."

"No, actually, I'm free tomorrow night."

Before Aiden could change his mind, Skylar took out his cell phone. "What's your number?"

"It's 312-555-7482. Give me a call in the morning, and we'll make plans about where to meet."

"Or I could just pick you up." Skylar was not letting this opportunity get away.

Aiden smiled as he looked at the actor with amazement. Maybe he really did have a gallant side to him. "That would be great."

"Don't you want my number?" Skylar asked coyly as he tucked his cell phone back in his pocket.

Okay, he was really beginning to like this side of Skylar. "You don't mind giving it out?" Skylar's offer surprised Aiden. He thought most celebrities kept their cell numbers private, so he hadn't dared ask for it.

"Not to people that I want to have it."

Aiden sat down the tray and took out his cell phone. He didn't want to give Skylar time to change his mind. He had barely gotten the phone out of his jacket when Skylar said, "Let me." After taking the phone from Aiden's hand, Skylar began searching it to figure out how to add his private number. As Aiden stood there, watching him in surprise, Skylar added his number and saved it into Aiden's contacts within a minute. Noticing the look on Aiden's face, he said point blank, "Didn't want you to type the wrong number."

Their fingers touched as Aiden took back his cell phone, and electricity shot through both of them. "I don't think there was much chance in that," Aiden said quietly. As their hands separated, the two men looked at each other with gazes that could set a room on fire.

Bringing himself back into the moment, Aiden realized that he had not been doing his job. "As much as I don't want to leave, I really have to keep moving." Then he looked at Skylar, his bright eyes full of questions. "Maybe I'll run into you later?"

"Count on it," Skylar said as he tried not to show the aching that filled him. He didn't understand this intense longing he had for Aiden, but for the moment, he was just going with it.

Aiden moved away from Skylar and headed back into the kitchen. Skylar watched him leave and then remembered where he was and that he was supposed to be mingling. *Okay, so mingling it is.*

"I saw you with Mr. Champagne." Skylar heard Sophie before he saw her. Laughing, she said, "You really should go out with that guy." Skylar, not sure he wanted Sophie to know his personal business, responded with "Why would you say that?"

"Because it's obvious you want to," she replied.

"Really? And you know all of this from… what? Your view across the room?" Skylar said as he tried not to grin.

"Okay, I get it. You don't want to talk about it. But I still say you and Champagne Boy would make a good couple."

A server walked by carrying a tray of wine. Sophie took two glasses and handed one to Skylar.

"Enjoying your night so far?" she asked, deciding she had better change the subject.

"Yes, I must admit, it's been both surprising and very pleasant." Skylar felt like his mood had jumped up ten notches since speaking with Aiden. He knew they would be great together. It had been a long time since he had been this excited about going out with someone, if ever.

"Did you find out any more about the movie deal?" Sophie asked, referring to the movie role that Nick, Skylar's manager, had told him about earlier in the week.

"They're definitely interested in me. But I need to audition with the lead actress. Check for chemistry, that kind of thing," explained Skylar.

"That's fantastic! I've always thought you were excellent, therefore I'm not really surprised. It's about time Hollywood recognized that mega talent of yours."

"Thanks," he said grinning. Skylar felt great, like the world was his for the taking. Nothing was going to ruin his good mood. Then, like a punch in the gut, he saw her. Shit! Over on the other side of the room, dressed in a tight white serving outfit was *Emma*! *What the hell is that crazy woman doing here?*

Emma looked up at him, and as their gazes met, Skylar quickly looked away. Dammit! Now what was he going to do?

"What's wrong?" Sophie asked.

Skylar leaned over to Sophie. "See that girl over there? The one with the long blonde hair in the serving outfit," he muttered under his breath.

Sophie looked over to see Emma watching them.

"Isn't that the girl that you left the premiere party with?"

"Unfortunately, yes. And by the way, why didn't you stop me?" Skylar asked as he remembered wanting to accuse someone of that.

"I didn't know that saving you from crazy women was part of my job description," Sophie said defensively.

"Crap! She's coming over here. Whatever you do, don't you dare leave me with her, okay?" Skylar ordered as he waited to see what Emma had in store for him this time.

Emma approached the two of them slowly. "Hi, Skylar," she said, looking directly at him.

"Emma, what on earth are you doing here?" he responded in exasperation.

"I'm working the party. It's my job," she stated.

Well, that's just fucking perfect. Skylar was beginning to think he would be stuck with her hanging around him forever.

Realizing that Skylar was not happy to see her, Emma hung her head and mumbled, "Don't worry; I'm not going to bother you again. I just wanted to say hello and apologize again for the other night."

Sophie perked up at this information. So, he had been with her again?

Noticing the curious look on Sophie's face, Skylar clarified, "Emma showed up at my house unannounced the other night. But we quickly set that straight," he said, turning to look at Emma, "and it won't be happening again."

Emma, apparently realizing that Skylar was still angry with her, quickly looked down and said, "I'm sorry. I have to go." And then she ran off.

Sophie turned to Skylar, but before she could say anything, he warned, "Let it go. That's history... history that won't be repeating itself."

Taking a hint, Sophie dropped the subject. "Well, I guess I'd better mingle some more. My main reason for finding you was actually to tell you that Gray wanted to speak to you about the fire. I think he's concerned for your safety."

And my night was going so well.... Skylar sighed and turned to look for Gray. Spotting him across the room, Skylar said good-bye to Sophie and started walking in that direction. As he approached Gray, he thought about what Sophie had said. *My safety. What the hell is that supposed to mean?*

"You wanted to see me?" Skylar asked Gray as he walked up to him.

"Skylar! Hey, son! Yes, I did want to see you. I would like to talk some more about this on Monday, but I wanted to let you know that I'm going to assign extra security on set for a while. And I wanted to ask you if you felt a need for a personal bodyguard? At least until they figure out who or what is causing these fires."

"Me? Why? Because I was in the dressing room when the fire started?" Skylar asked.

"That, and I had the fire investigators call me this afternoon with some interesting information," Gray continued.

"What type of information?" This didn't sound very good to Skylar.

"Apparently, at each of the two fires they found a metal bar. They each had a letter painted on it."

"Letters? Is someone playing games?" asked Skylar.

"We don't know, but to be on the safe side, I'm beefing up security at the soundstage, and yes, because you were actually in the fire, I want to make sure you're not some sort of target," said Gray.

"I really don't think so. No one could have possibly known I was in that shower at the time," Skylar said. Remembering the letters, he asked, "And what do you mean there were letters painted on a metal bar?"

"The authorities are not sure it means anything, but apparently on one there was an *A* and on another one there was an *L*. At least that is what I think he said," Gray replied as he tried to remember.

"LA? Someone from LA, maybe?"

"No idea. But I just wanted you to have a heads-up. Lots of crazies out there, and as you become more popular and more well known, the crazies will come out of the woodwork."

Isn't that the damn truth! Skylar thought as he looked over at Emma standing across the room. At least she wasn't staring at him this time.

"Okay, thanks for letting me know," said Skylar. "I'll come see you first thing Monday morning. After shaking Gray's hand, Skylar walked off in search of a drink.

A few minutes later, drink in hand, Skylar decided he'd had enough of this party. When he walked outside to the patio, he saw that the path led off into the dark. Anxious to get away from Emma and all the people who seemed to think they knew what was best for him, Skylar started down the path.

As he walked farther from the house, the lights grew dimmer, and the music started to fade. However, he could still see the path thanks to the gorgeous full moon in the sky. Pausing for a second, he saw the gazebo down near the lake. He decided to walk down and enjoy his drink.

As Skylar neared the gazebo, he heard something behind him. Immediately thinking it was Emma following him, he said, "I *swear to God*, if that's you, Emma, I may...."

"May what?"

Skylar swung around at the sound of Aiden's voice.

Smiling, he said, "May... nothing... never mind. There's a fan who insists on following me around. I thought you were her."

"Nope, not a fan. And definitely not a 'her,'" Aiden teased.

"Hmm... wonder if I could change that?" Skylar said with a smile.

"What? The fact that I'm not a fan or the fact I'm not a 'her'?" Aiden asked.

"A fan," laughed Skylar.

"Keep it up. You are definitely headed in the right direction," Aiden said as he walked closer to Skylar.

Skylar, whose heart rate started skyrocketing, tried to make himself chill out as he asked, "Want to have a seat in the gazebo or do you have to get back?" He looked toward the house.

"No, I'm on break. I saw you walk off down the path and thought I'd take the chance to follow you."

"I'm glad you did," Skylar said with his heart in his throat. *Okay, this crap needs to stop. Since when do I get nervous over a little flirting?*

Aiden and Skylar walked over to the gazebo. They managed to stay a good distance from each other, as if they were afraid to touch in any way. Once inside the gazebo, Skylar went to stand against one of the beams, setting his drink down on the railing.

"It's sure is beautiful out here tonight," Skylar said as he looked up at the moon.

"It sure is," Aiden whispered as he gazed at Skylar.

Noticing the tone change in Aiden's voice, Skylar turned to see Aiden walking closer to him. Within a second Aiden was standing directly in front of him. The closeness was intoxicating as the ache inside him magnified and began settling in his groin. Skylar reached out to touch Aiden's cheek. Very tenderly he began running his finger down the side of Aiden's jawline. Both men held each other's gazes and tried to steady their breathing.

Skylar continued to draw Aiden's face with his fingers as if he wanted to memorize it forever. His finger reached Aiden's lips and lingered there as the touch of his lips sent jolts through Skylar's body. Aiden opened his mouth slightly to capture just the tip of his finger in his mouth.

Skylar gasped. He had a hard-on so rigid, he felt like it might burst out of his jeans. Groaning slightly, Skylar leaned down and replaced his finger with his mouth. Grabbing Aiden's upper lip with his mouth, Skylar moved his lips around until he had completely covered Aiden's mouth. Instantly, Aiden opened his mouth, and Skylar pushed his tongue inside.

Taking their time, the kiss was slow and deliberate. Skylar pulled Aiden closer to him as he worshipped his mouth with an intoxicating, slow movement that drove both of them crazy. Gasping and straining against each other, the kiss deepened. Aiden moaned as he pushed Skylar back against the pole, the kisses becoming more desperate. Lost in the passion of the kiss, Skylar reached down and hesitantly touched Aiden through his pants. He was equally hard. And judging from what Skylar could feel, he was a perfect size, and Skylar wanted him more than he had ever wanted anyone.

In response Aiden reached down and found Skylar's cock: nice, hard, long, thick. He stroked him through his jeans. His heart was pounding out of his chest, and he wanted desperately to take Skylar's cock in his mouth.

Then they heard a rustle in the trees. Jumping away from each other, they looked out into the darkness. After waiting a second and not seeing anyone, they slowly looked back at each other.

"Damn, who knew?" Skylar said, rubbing his mouth.

"My thoughts exactly." Aiden responded the best he could with his mind jumbled from feelings of lust and desire.

They'd started to move back toward each other, their mouths nearly touching again, when they heard the sound again. Someone was definitely out there.

"Who's there?" Skylar called out into the darkness.

Upon receiving no response, Aiden said, "Maybe we should go and pick this back up tomorrow night."

Smiling at the thought, Skylar said, "I agree. But it'll be hard to wait that long."

"But it'll be worth it. And no worries of anyone watching," Aiden promised.

Skylar decided to take the risk and leaned down and slowly placed his lips on Aiden's in a soft kiss. "It's a date." As he said the words, he remembered his promise to Kelly. *I'll have to deal with her later*, he thought as he squeezed Aiden's hand.

As they walked off together toward the house, they didn't see the figure standing behind the tree, tears streaming down her face.

CHAPTER 15

"WHAT ARE you doing here?" Aiden asked as he opened the front door to a very excited Ryan. He had just gotten out of the shower, and Ryan was the last person he expected to see on his doorstep.

"Where else would I be? I'm here to make you *gorgeous* for your date with that smokin' hot man," he responded with a big smile.

As Ryan pushed his way into the house, Aiden turned and said, "I think I'm more than capable of making myself presentable for a date."

"Oh, honey, this isn't just any date. This is a date with the hottest guy this side of the Mississippi, and that, my darling, takes precise planning. Therefore, I took it upon myself to bring you a few items you might need." As Ryan waved the bag around, Aiden couldn't help but laugh.

"I'm really afraid to ask what's in that bag."

Ryan twirled around and said, "Then don't ask. Come now, let's go to your room and get this party started," as he wandered down the hall to Aiden's bedroom, continuing to swing his bag of goodies.

Aiden knew better than to protest and obediently followed him down the hall.

As Aiden walked into his room, he could see Ryan tossing things out of his closet, the goodie bag now sitting on the bed. "Wait a second! What are you doing?"

"Seriously, sweets, who buys your clothes?" asked Ryan, who was a self-admitted clothes snob.

"Uh... that would be me," confessed Aiden. Then, realizing he had just been slammed, he asked, "What's wrong with my clothes?"

Ryan looked at the clothes that were now sitting in a pile on Aiden's bed, turned up his nose, and said, "I think the question is what's *right* with your clothes."

Annoyed, Aiden handed Ryan his goodie bag and said, "No one asked you to come over and critique my clothes. Why don't you bounce on out of here so I can get ready?"

"I'm not going anywhere until I have turned you into the man of Skylar's dreams," Ryan said as he placed the goodie bag back down on the bed.

"Ryan, really, it's just a date. Most likely just coffee. Nothing special, nothing to get this excited about."

Ignoring Aiden, Ryan kept digging through the closet. "*Ah!* Okay, this might actually work." Ryan pulled out a baby-blue long-sleeved tight-fitting V-neck sweater. "Now, to find some pants." As Ryan continued to dig through Aiden's closet, Aiden sat down on the edge of the bed.

Glancing over at the bag Ryan had brought, he asked, "What's in the bag?"

"Just a few things to make sure your date ends up on a happy note."

Curious, Aiden pulled the bag over to him. As he looked in the bag, he was immediately sorry he had bothered to open it. Inside were colorful condoms, lube, and something that resembled handcuffs. "You know, this isn't a casting call for *Fifty Shades of Grey*," he said in frustration. "It's *coffee*."

"Yeah, yeah… first coffee, a couple of goofy stares into one another's eyes, then you're signing consensual letters regarding bondage and having fan fiction written about your sex life." Rolling his eyes, Ryan continued, "Really, darling, you should have watched *Royal Life*. Just so you know, that boy can be a smokin' hot love machine."

"When are you going to remember he's an *actor*, not the prince from *Royal Life*?"

Ryan shook his head in disbelief. Exasperated, he corrected Aiden, "Uhhhhh… first off, he is not the *prince*; he's the best friend of the prince. And secondly, yes, he's a great actor, but I'll bet my next three paychecks that he rocked that man's world from a real-life experience.

Ryan was really starting to annoy him. "If you say so." Having had enough of Ryan and his snob attitude, Aiden stood up to lead Ryan out of the room. "Okay, you've found my so-called fashionable clothes. Now you can leave."

Ryan stopped dead in his tracks and looked at him in disbelief. "But I can't leave. I want to meet him."

"Ahhhh, so this is the *real* reason you're here. I should've known," said Aiden with a hint of amusement in his voice. "It's all about you."

"Of course it is," Ryan said, as if he couldn't believe that Aiden would think otherwise. "If the beautiful Skylar is going to be my new best friend, don't you think he should meet me?"

"You're really something else, you know that?" Aiden said.

"And don't you forget it. Now, let's get these clothes on and see how great you look," Ryan said, tossing Aiden a pair of jeans.

A few minutes later, as Aiden looked in the mirror, he had to admit that Ryan definitely knew what clothes looked great together.

Ryan stood there, rubbing his jaw as he said, "Doll, you look fantastic. Skylar Murphy won't be able to resist you. It'll be like that time on *Royal Life*, when the prince invited his best friend to eat with the royal family. Throughout the entire dinner, they only had eyes for each other. Skylar was simply *fabulous* in this one scene. He walked over to the prince and leaned down to say something in his ear, and you could just *feel* the hotness between the two. I think I got a hard-on just watching."

"That was television, this is real life," said Aiden.

"Same thing, if you ask me," said Ryan. "Wait and see, Skylar will be whispering sweet nothings in your ear by dessert."

They both jumped as the doorbell rang. Looking at the clock, Aiden realized that it had to be Skylar. They had spoken earlier and decided on eight o'clock.

"Oh my God.... *Oh. My. God!*" Ryan said in glee as he practically jumped up and down. Then he dramatically took a deep breath and said, "Let me get it."

Aiden fully expected to hear Ryan's head hitting the floor as he passed out, but wonder of wonders, when Aiden walked into the living room, Ryan was still standing. Granted, he was standing like a statue with his mouth hanging open, but he was standing.

Skylar stood on the other side of the door, waiting for Ryan to either let him in or slam the door shut.

"Ryan, can you let him in?" Aiden suggested.

Ryan, coming out of his dream stance, said, "Oh yes… yes… I'm sorry," as he looked directly into Skylar's eyes.

Skylar didn't meet fans this infatuated very often but when he did, it always made him feel good.

"Hi, I'm Skylar. And you are…?" Skylar said as he extended his hand to Ryan.

Ryan took his hand and said, "Ryan… my name is Ryan. And holy hell, you are hotter in person than I imagined."

"*Ryan*!" Aiden couldn't believe Ryan had said that. Walking over to Ryan, Aiden tapped him on the shoulder. "You can let go of his hand now." Looking past Ryan to Skylar standing on the porch, he smiled and said, "Skylar, come on inside, if you can make it past Ryan without getting accosted."

Skylar laughed as he withdrew his hand. "It's nice to meet you, Ryan."

Aiden led Skylar over to the couch. They both sat down for a second, neither of them knowing how to start the conversation.

"How was your day?" Skylar asked Aiden.

"It was fine. I didn't have to work today, so that was nice."

"Yeah, me neither. As far as I know, I work tomorrow morning, but my producer is so freaked out about the second fire that he may be hiring his own investigation team. I'm not sure how that will affect production this week."

At the mention of the fire, Ryan came running over to join the conversation. As he sat down on the arm of the sofa, facing both men, he said with a dramatic wave of his hand, "Speaking of the fires… I'm all over this. I've been studying the two fires, and, Skylar, I think you need a bodyguard. And I'm the perfect person for the job."

Aiden laughed. "Ryan, don't you need to be someplace?"

"Nope… no place to be but here," responded Ryan. Looking directly at Skylar, he said, "I'm serious. Aren't you the least bit concerned that you were in close proximity of both of those fires? Hell, you were *in* the second one."

Good heavens, thought Aiden. "Ryan…," Aiden began, in an attempt to rein him in.

"No, it's okay," said Skylar. Turning to Ryan, he said, "I did wonder about it, but with the first fire, I was in another building. And truthfully, there were way too many people around to think it was directed at me."

"But—" Ryan interrupted.

Holding up his hand to stop him, Skylar continued, "And in the second case, I was taking a shower in a community dressing room. Anyone could have been using that shower. Therefore, I have to believe whoever started that fire didn't know I was in the room."

"I'm not so sure about that," Ryan said. "Maybe it's someone who's holding a grudge against you. Broken up any marriages lately?" he asked in all seriousness.

"Ryan, for God's sake… let it go," said Aiden.

Skylar was becoming amused at the two of them. It was obvious they were great friends, and if he could get past the overwhelming fan love gush, Ryan might also be fun to hang out with. "Not to my knowledge," he said as he laughed.

"Well, I'm one phone call away if you decide you need that bodyguard." As Ryan looked Skylar up and down, he continued, "And we do *not* want anything happening to that body."

"Okay, time to go! Skylar, are you ready?" Aiden jumped to his feet, and Skylar stood up to join him. Ryan, still sitting on the arm of the couch, said, "Okay, boys, don't believe me. But if something happens to Handsome, here, don't say I didn't warn you."

In his rush to get out of the house, Aiden practically pushed Skylar out the door. Turning back to Ryan, he called, "Make sure you're not here when I return." Closing the door behind them, Aiden and Skylar left for their date.

CHAPTER 16

"THIS IS a nice cozy place," Aiden murmured to Skylar. The restaurant Skylar had chosen was a quaint little Italian place in Santa Monica, up from the pier. The candlelight from sconces on the wall mingled with the glowing candle in the center of the table. Together, they bathed the men in radiant light.

Looking around, Aiden could see that it was not very crowded, but the few patrons who were there only had eyes for each other. Aiden looked at Skylar through the soft light of the candle, and his blue eyes were shining brightly. Aiden thought he looked incredibly handsome in his loose-fitting white shirt. He had that bohemian look going on and was totally rocking it. Skylar noticed Aiden gazing at him and smiled.

"So what do you think of the place?" Skylar asked Aiden.

"It's very cool. How did you find it?"

Skylar leaned over and poured Aiden a glass of wine as he said, "Sometimes, I want to be alone and have no one bothering me. Therefore, I am always on the lookout for a dimly lit restaurant."

"And here I thought you might be trying to hide me from the world."

"Oh, I am, but only because I want this to be a special date and not have any interruptions," Skylar confessed.

Aiden could feel the blush rising in his cheeks as he smiled at Skylar's words.

The waiter chose that exact moment to walk up and take their order. Once the waiter had walked off, Aiden lifted his glass and said, "Let's make a toast."

"Only if I can make the first one," Skylar said, smiling.

Aiden nodded his consent.

Lifting his glass Skylar looked directly into Aiden's eyes as he said, "To the bravest, most inspiring man I've had the pleasure of meeting in a very long time."

Aiden felt his heart skip a beat as they clinked their glasses and took a sip of their wine. "My turn," Aiden said as he raised his wine glass again. Looking into Skylar's eyes, he said, "To the most persistent man I've met in a long time. May you always be so persistent." Both men gazed into each other's eyes as they toasted each other once again.

"I forgot to tell you that I saw you on television the other night," Skylar said as he continued to sip his wine.

"Me? Shouldn't that be my line to you?" Aiden asked.

"Yes, you. That reporter was interviewing you after you saved that lady and her two children," responded Skylar.

"Ah… okay. I'd forgotten she was a reporter from television."

"I have to say that you interviewed well. Maybe you should look into a job in television."

"No, thank you, I'll leave that kind of work to you."

Skylar laughed as he reached for the homemade bread in the center of the table. "It's actually quite fun. It can be exciting, but it can also be tiring hanging around the set all day if something isn't working properly."

"Does that happen a lot?"

"Depends. I've spent all day sitting around in my dressing room waiting to film because something wasn't working on set. Those are long boring days. But for the most part, it's a lot of fun, and I like playing the different characters."

"Ever thought of going into movies or are you strictly into television?"

"I've definitely thought about it. As a matter of fact, I'm up for a part now that could really make my career," said Skylar.

"That sounds exciting. Are you allowed to talk about it?"

"Not yet, but once I can, you'll be the first to know," Skylar said.

"Then good luck with that. I hope you get the part."

"If my luck continues, as it has been so far this week, the part will definitely be mine."

Aiden looked up at Skylar and said, "I couldn't agree with you more."

CHAPTER 17

CAUGHT UP in each other's eyes, Aiden and Skylar didn't notice the person watching them from the tiny spot over in the corner. Alone, with a hat pulled down over his face, he went unnoticed by the two men. All was quiet as the waitress approached the lone person, who simply ordered a coffee while continuing to watch the two men totally engrossed in each other, oblivious to anyone else in the room.

CHAPTER 18

AS SKYLAR and Aiden wandered along the boardwalk, the bright lights from the Ferris wheel on the Santa Monica Pier creating a romantic atmosphere, it occurred to Skylar that he hadn't been this relaxed in a very long time. What was it about Aiden that made him feel like he had known him forever?

"What are you thinking about?" asked Aiden as he artfully dodged a skateboarder who obviously felt he owned the boardwalk.

"Just thinking how nice it is to be outside, walking, talking, and generally enjoying myself. It's been a long time since I've felt this comfortable with someone."

Aiden smiled as they kept walking. He was beginning to really like Skylar despite that nagging voice in the back of his mind that was sending out warning signals. But for now Aiden wanted to ignore it. *Just have fun. Enjoy the moment*, he thought to himself. "So how did you become an actor?"

"It just kind of happened. After my dad left, my mom raised me alone. She met her current husband while he was here on a scouting trip from New York. He was, or I should say is, the owner of a talent agency back in New York. They fell in love, and he ended up taking the two of us back with him. I remember the first time I saw Times Square. I had never seen anything more exciting and amazing. Man! I love that city." Skylar was lost in thought as he recalled seeing the big city for the first time and how it took his breath away.

They kept walking along, and Skylar continued, "Anyway, as I was saying, I was placed in a private school, and somehow I discovered their theater department. I was cast in a play immediately and fell in love with acting. My stepdad came to see the show, and he told me that he thought I had real talent and I should give professional acting a try. I worked with him for a while in New York, but then I decided I really wanted to be in Los Angeles. I came out during pilot season and auditioned for everything. I was here maybe six weeks when I booked a modeling gig. And then I booked my first guest appearance. From that, they hired me for *Royal Life* and now, here I am on *The Executives*."

"Sounds like you were really lucky. But then again, I've seen some of your work, and you definitely have a lot of talent. So I'm not surprised you were picked up so quickly."

Skylar smiled and said, "And what was this you told me about never seeing my work and not knowing who I was?"

"Ah, that…. The truth is, the night I met you, I honestly had no idea who you were," Aiden admitted. "But after I met you, I have to confess that I watched a few episodes of *Royal Life*." *Actually the entire first season*, he thought to himself.

"What did you think?" asked Skylar, surprising even himself that he was interested in Aiden's answer.

Aiden stopped walking and turned to face Skylar. "I thought you were amazing." There was a dead silence as the two men just gazed at each other before almost being run down by another skateboarder.

Feeling the excitement between them building, Skylar reached for Aiden's hand and said, "Let's get out of here. Let me take you home."

Aiden responded by giving Skylar his hand, and they walked off toward the parking lot.

As they drove to Aiden's house, they were both lost in thought about the evening and the promise of the night.

I can't believe how relaxing this night has been, thought Skylar. *Damn, I want him so much, but would sleeping with him ruin everything?* As Skylar glanced over at Aiden, who was gazing out his window, he felt the familiar tingle in his groin start to cause an ache. *Oh hell, who am I kidding? I want that man more than I've wanted anyone in a long time.*

Aiden, reflecting over the evening, started thinking about what would happen if he spent the night with Skylar. *I really want him, but how should I handle this? He is probably used to having anyone he wants. Do I really want to be another notch on his bedpost?* He looked over at Skylar, who had now turned and was watching the road, his hair softly blowing in the breeze. As Aiden felt butterflies starting to flutter in his stomach, he thought, *Hell yeah, I do. As Ryan would say, I want that really big notch.*

Skylar parked the car, and they got out and walked to the front door. Aiden had his key out, so he reached down to put it in the lock. He had not turned the key yet when Skylar touched him on the shoulder and said in a raspy voice, "Aiden...."

Aiden turned around, and suddenly Skylar had him in his arms, hungrily seeking solace in Aiden's mouth.

He felt Skylar's strong hands grip him by the neck, his fingers digging into his skin and holding him in place, and he started giving back as hard as he could. Their mouths tangled in a raging, passionate kiss that made all their senses come alive, and the only noises audible in the night were their mingling breaths. Skylar sucked on Aiden's lower lip, and Aiden thought he might come undone right there on the front porch. He reached behind his back and turned the key in the lock, and the door flew open, causing both men to fall into the hallway while never letting their mouths separate. Skylar pushed Aiden up against the wall as he kicked the door shut with his foot and tortured Aiden with his tongue as they both gasped for breath. They clung to each other as their hot, wet mouths moved in time. Neither wanted to pause long enough to move away from the main hallway.

Skylar became more dominant. He licked and sucked at Aiden's lips and then down the sides of his long, slender neck, feeling the strong pulse under his exploring tongue while he ran his hand down the front of Aiden's jeans.

Aiden jerked, releasing his mouth for a moment, forcing much needed air into his lungs as he pushed his groin into Skylar's firm hand.

"Oh God, Sky...."

Skylar could feel Aiden's hardness under his hand and began rubbing and massaging him through his jeans as he continued to torture him with his mouth. The mere thought of knowing that Aiden was just as excited as he was caused the butterflies in Skylar's stomach to come alive. He let his hand creep up to the bottom of Aiden's shirt, and the first slight brush of his fingertips against warm skin forced Aiden to inhale deeply, followed by a low groan. In one swift movement, he pulled Aiden's shirt over his head, messing up his blond, finger-combed hair in the process and stepped back just long enough to gaze at the gloriousness of that rock-hard body.

A small whimper escaped Aiden while Skylar simply stood before him, gazing at him through half-closed eyes. His head dropped back against the wall with too much force when Skylar started kissing and licking his way down his tight chest, but he neither cared nor felt any pain, his brain too befuddled with pent-up lust.

Skylar paused only long enough to suck and nip at each nipple until he could hear Aiden panting above him. He kept moving down, leaving a trail of moist kisses in his wake, the musky-fresh fragrance of warm skin almost making him dizzy, until he reached Aiden's waist. He slowly started to feather-lick around the waistband of Aiden's jeans as he worked to unbutton them. Skylar fell to his knees, and he could feel Aiden's hands in his hair, pulling and pushing at the same time, causing his own painfully hard erection to push against the inside of his pants. He mouthed Aiden through the denim, and he could hear Aiden moaning softly over his head while his hips involuntarily moved closer to Skylar's lips, seeking contact. This was unusual for Skylar. Normally, he was the one being serviced, but he didn't want that tonight. He wanted to make Aiden feel good.

Aiden could barely breathe. He ran his fingers through Skylar's hair, the soft strands caressing his fingertips as he kept pushing Skylar's head farther down his body. As Skylar mouthed him through his jeans, his cock ached to be touched. Within moments Skylar had unbuttoned Aiden's jeans, and the second his cock sprang out, Skylar had it in his mouth. Aiden almost came right then, his legs beginning to shake. *Damn, oh my God, this is... so... fucking... good.*

It was all Aiden could do to hold himself back when all he wanted to do was let loose and pour himself down Skylar's throat. Skylar continued to worship him with his mouth, running his wet hot tongue underneath his cock before taking him deep again. *Oh damn, oh shit, damn... damn...* was all Aiden could think while squeezing his eyes shut tight, all his concentration now on the unbelievable feeling Skylar was providing. Skylar was sucking him hard, his teasing tongue stopping long enough to lick around the head. His firm grip followed his lips while he began squeezing Aiden's balls with his other hand. When a deep pleasurable groan escaped Skylar's throat, the sensation could be felt down to Aiden's toes, and he couldn't take it anymore.

"Stop... babe, stop. I'm... oh fuck, I'm... going to come," he pleaded with Skylar.

But Skylar had no intention of stopping. He wanted Aiden to come for him and come hard, his own raging erection almost forgotten for the time being. Skylar took him as deep as he could, letting the back of his throat massage Aiden's cock while his finger barely brushed up against Aiden's entrance, and that was it. Without further warning Aiden roared and came with a force that nearly dropped him to his knees. His body jack-knifed from the strength of his orgasm, his hands gripping Skylar's shoulders—the only thing holding him up—as if holding on for dear life. Skylar took every bit and swallowed without thinking twice. He could hear Aiden groaning and gasping as Skylar continued to milk out every drop. Aiden slid down the wall and dropped to the floor, Skylar right along beside him. Both sat there for a minute, Aiden gasping for air and Skylar waiting for the dizziness in his head to subside.

Aiden looked at Skylar, whose head was leaning against the wall, his eyes closed, his face flushed red and covered with sweat, and he couldn't remember ever having seen a sexier picture of a man. Skylar's full lips were swollen and begging to be kissed again, and Aiden thought he must be the most beautiful man he had ever seen.

"Wow, I… I don't even know… what to say." Aiden gasped out each word while he wiped his sweaty forehead with his arm. He was having a hard time catching his breath.

Skylar slowly moved his head to the side to look deep into Aiden's eyes. After a few silent seconds, he smiled, and before leaning his head back again, he responded, "Don't say anything. Just relax for a minute and enjoy the feeling."

Aiden followed his lead, in hopes of getting his breathing back to normal. After several more minutes of repose, his breath evened out, and he glanced over to see that Skylar was still semihard. He reached over to place his hand on Skylar's thigh and softly began caressing him while he slowly moved his fingertips up. Skylar's eyes narrowed to mere slits as he watched the long, lean fingers, and he shivered as Aiden gently started to massage him through his jeans.

"You don't have to do that," Skylar said as he looked at Aiden with genuine affection.

"I don't have to, but I want to," Aiden responded.

He continued to stroke Skylar through his jeans as Skylar leaned back against the wall and closed his eyes, inhaling deeply.

By the time Aiden moved closer to unbutton his jeans, Skylar was hard again, his erection straining visibly against the inside of his zipper.

That was fast, Aiden thought, a smile crossing his face. After carefully unzipping his pants, Aiden tenderly ran one finger from top to bottom of Skylar's cock, enjoying the hot, velvety feel against his skin. He watched as a drop of precum escaped, and he moved to catch it with his fingertip. His gaze moved up Skylar's torso, and as their eyes met, he realized that Skylar had been watching him, lust written all over his face. Aiden raised one eyebrow, and with a mischievous grin, he teasingly licked his fingertip, never breaking eye contact with Skylar. As Skylar witnessed Aiden's bold yet teasing gesture, a moan escaped him from deep within, followed by a husky "Aiden…. Please…."

"Sit back and enjoy the ride, babe."

With those last words, Aiden motioned Skylar to lift his hips so he could pull down his pants a bit, which caused Skylar's cock to spring up into full view. Aiden took only a moment to fully appreciate Skylar's large size before bending down and lovingly kissing the flushed head. He ran his tongue up and down, licking, teasing, stopping to swirl his tongue around the top while inhaling the musky masculine scent mixed with remnants of Skylar's cologne on his skin.

Skylar began moving with him, following him as he watched Aiden in fascination. Never in his life had he ever been this turned on, with man or woman, and he had to remember not to thrust into Aiden's throat and possibly hurt him.

Aiden could taste the precum and that made him want more. He slowly took Skylar's cock all the way into his mouth, inch by inch, careful not to let his gag reflex kick in.

Skylar moaned softly and reached out to rub Aiden's hair, then ran his fingers down his smooth back before finally reaching around to play with Aiden's nipple, which immediately became hard as a pebble and made Aiden groan out loud. *Ohhhhh my…. Damn*, he thought as Aiden's moan vibrated throughout his entire body, leaving a tingling feeling in his balls. He heard Aiden take a deep breath through his nose as he took him even deeper in his mouth, his tongue teasing the underside of his cock relentlessly. *Holy fuck!* He knew he wouldn't last long as Aiden started moving up and down, taking him in as far as he could, then pulling almost all the way off, just to swallow him whole again. Aiden reached down and held Skylar's balls tight, bringing him back from the edge just to tease some more by pulling his mouth off completely and blowing hot air over his moistened erection.

In a hopeless attempt to keep himself from shooting down Aiden's throat so soon, Skylar covered Aiden's hand with his and squeezed his balls even tighter, but watching Aiden sucking him off, giving him the best blowjob he had ever known, made any attempt useless.

Fuck, fuck, fuck, thought Skylar as he placed both his hands on the floor on either side of his hips and began to lift his hips off the ground to meet Aiden's mouth, frantically trying to chase the tantalizing warmth. Aiden's tongue was all over and under Skylar's cock, and when he took one of Skylar's balls into his mouth while using his hand to continue to rub up and down his cock, Skylar thought he might go insane. Pearls of sweat were dripping down the side of his face now, getting lost in the dark stubble covering his cheeks, and his breathing became erratic. "Okay, A… Aiden…. Aiden, I'm close, I… I think I'm going to—" As Aiden lifted his eyes to look directly into Skylar's, his full, glistening lips again covering most of his cock, Skylar's words got stuck in his throat. He held his breath, thrust one more time, and then froze. His head hit the back of the wall, and white streaks like lightning passed behind his closed eyelids as an orgasm hit him so hard he was certain his heart skipped a beat or two while his legs began to shake uncontrollably.

Aiden licked and sucked until even the last bit of cum had made it down his throat. The bittersweet taste was almost addictive, and Aiden savored every last drop.

After endless minutes, they fell away from each other and again tried to catch their breath, neither saying anything. Would this be the awkward moment after? But as their breathing began to slow down, their gazes met again. Grins spread over both their faces, and as their hands found each other, they held on tight and knew there would never be an awkward moment after for them.

"I can't believe we didn't make it out of the hallway," Aiden said, laughing.

"Well, at least we managed to shut the front door," Skylar said with a grin.

Both laughed for a moment, until Skylar got quiet and said, "That was really amazing. Thank you."

Aiden wasn't sure whether to be insulted or not. "Don't thank me. I enjoyed it."

"That's what I meant. I knew we would be great together, but really… this was unbelievable," Skylar clarified as he ran a tired hand down his face.

Carefully standing up, Aiden held out his hand for Skylar to use, who, in turn, grabbed hold and pulled himself off the floor.

They stood there for a moment, staring at each other, before Skylar slowly reached out and cupped Aiden's face. Gently, he drew him close and kissed him lightly, tasting himself on Aiden's lips. Using his tongue he delved inside Aiden's mouth for just a second, before finishing the kiss with a soft pull at his lips.

Aiden was in a trance. He opened his eyes and looked into Skylar's crystal blue eyes. He leaned forward and kissed him again but with slightly more passion. Their tongues tangled for a moment before Skylar felt that familiar anxious feeling, pulled away, and said, "Aiden, I really want to stay with you tonight, but I had better go. Unless I hear otherwise, I'm shooting a promo tomorrow, so it's an early morning for me. But can we get together again?"

"Sure we can. I would like that." Hesitantly, he added, "I really would."

After playfully helping each other adjust their clothing, they walked to the front door, their fingers laced together. Aiden opened the door for Skylar, and with a smile he said, "Thank you for the great dinner. For… everything."

Skylar turned around and smiled. "You're welcome. Let's do this again next weekend. Sound good?"

"Definitely."

Skylar grabbed Aiden by the neck and leaned in once more to tenderly kiss him. "Night, baby." His whispered words left a warm mist across Aiden's swollen lips, making him shiver once again.

"Good night, Sky," Aiden responded as Skylar turned and walked out the door.

CHAPTER 19

THE EXECUTIVES had now been on the air for several weeks, and it was already receiving a huge amount of buzz from industry peers and fans. Because it had premiered in the spring, it was eligible for this year's Emmy's, set to air in a few weeks. The producers had already submitted the show for consideration, and now it was up to the members of the Academy of Television Arts and Science to decide whether *The Executives* or its cast would garner any nominations. It was Wednesday afternoon and Skylar was in his trailer trying to wipe off the excess makeup from spending the majority of the morning in front of the camera. Today's scenes had been incredibly hard. He had been filming intense emotional moments, and his eyes felt like sandpaper. He didn't want to use the eye-watering stimulants, so he had developed his own way to make himself cry on cue. It had been handy in his career, as he was prone to play broken and damaged characters. Today was no exception, beginning with the first scene of the day: the confrontation between Toby and his mother after she discovered Toby in a hot embrace with his lover. It had been painful to film, but Kelly's performance today surely would secure her a win at the Emmys. In fact, if she didn't win, Skylar would have to stand up and protest. She was an amazing actress, and he loved working with her.

As for his own performance, he had struggled with the more emotional moments. His usual recipe for bringing tears to his eyes hadn't seemed to work. Normally, he would take himself down to a low place within his mind using memories of the day his dad walked out or the days his mother threatened to kill herself. Those memories usually did the trick for him. However, thanks to a certain very hot firefighter, Skylar was genuinely happy for the first time in a long while.

They had spent almost two hours on the telephone the night after their date, and he couldn't wait to see him again on Saturday. *I'm such a fucking girl*, he chastised himself in the mirror as he saw himself grinning at the thought. But at the moment he didn't care. He was enjoying it for as long as possible. Skylar knew himself well enough to know his limits, and he had no doubt he would reach those same limits with Aiden. But until then, he was going to relish every minute.

Skylar turned as he heard someone open the trailer door.

"Can I come in?" There was no denying the booming voice of Skylar's manager, Nick McPherson.

"Sure, come on in," responded Skylar.

"I come bearing good news." Nick grinned as he came inside the trailer, waving a small stack of paper. Nick, who was well over six feet and packing around 250 pounds, looked like a linebacker for the Oakland Raiders, so to watch him waltzing around waving paper was comical.

"Okay, what might that be?" Skylar asked as he laughed at Nick's antics.

"You, sir, have been requested to screen-test with the leading lady for *Checkmate*, and I have here your sides to study," Nick proudly announced.

As he took the papers from Nick's hand, Skylar felt like jumping through the roof. Feeling like the world was finally aligning in his direction, he glanced over the sides—the part of the script he would need to memorize and rehearse—for the audition.

"This is fucking awesome! When do they want me to come in?"

"They are looking at next Monday. Will that work? I told them it would have to be after your responsibilities here," explained Nick.

"I think the afternoon will work. Let me grab my schedule." Skylar walked over to the makeshift desk he had created in the corner of his trailer. Quickly rifling through the stack of papers, he said, "I don't know what the hell Sophie does, but organizing my crap isn't one of her top priorities."

"I thought you liked your assistant."

"I like her just fine as long as I don't have to depend on her for scheduling, thinking ahead, or anything that might require initiative on her part," Skylar complained.

"We can get you a new one," offered Nick as he walked over to help Skylar find his schedule.

"Nah, it's okay. I'm used to her now. I really don't want to have to start over with someone new." Skylar dug through some notebooks and then bent toward the trash can.

"Is this it?" Nick asked as he held up an official-looking piece of paper.

Glancing over to see what Nick was holding, Skylar said, "Yes, that's it. Thank you."

"No problem. You were just using it as a coaster," laughed Nick.

Skylar shook his head in exasperation. "I really need to get organized." Walking over he took the paper from Nick, glanced over it, and laid it back down on the still unorganized table. "Okay, I can do it anytime after 2:30 p.m. if everything runs smooth for the day."

"I'll schedule it for four o'clock, which will give you a little breathing room." Nick started typing notes into his cell phone.

"Do you know if they're using the same supporting cast as they did in the first two films?" asked Skylar.

"I'm not sure about the entire cast, but I know you're screen-testing with Michelle Michaels."

"Okay, I've never worked with her, but I'm sure it'll be fine." Skylar thought about the brunette girl who had won an Oscar for her work in the first film of the franchise. *This should be interesting.*

Nick glanced up from his cell phone. "Oh, and one more thing! I spoke with your producer regarding the two fires here at the studios. Gray was concerned that you might be a target, but neither he nor the police could make that call based on the evidence they currently have. However, to be safe, he told me he was going to talk to you about tighter security."

"We did talk, and I don't think I need security. I haven't had any issues at home, other than the crazy fan-girl incident, but no other things that make me think someone is out to get me," said Skylar.

"What fan-girl incident?" This was the first Nick had heard about it, and he didn't like the sound of it.

"It was nothing—just an overzealous fan who found her way to my house." He held up his hand to stop the next question out of Nick's mouth. "Before you say anything, it was actually my fault. I was really drunk after the premiere party, and when she offered to drive me home,

I let her." Seeing Nick's frown, Skylar continued, "No need to worry. I have it straightened out now."

Nick wanted to ask more but decided against it. "Just think about it, and if anything else happens that involves you, I'll insist upon more security until they find out who is setting all these fires," said Nick.

"Fine," Skylar said quietly. He didn't like the idea of security. He wanted to be able to see Aiden whenever he chose without anyone leaking his personal life to the paparazzi. He could see Nick's face now at the news that he was involved with a man. *Wonder if I should give him a heads-up*, he thought. He looked over at Nick, who was already heading out the door. *Nah, I'll just wait and see.*

"All right, then, I'll see you later. If anything changes for Monday, let me know immediately. This is one role we really want. It'll put your career on an entirely different level. So let's not do anything to jeopardize it."

What the fuck? Can he read my mind? "You got it," promised Skylar as he looked away from Nick.

Nick walked out the door, leaving Skylar to think about his current situation. He knew Nick wanted him to maintain his current status as a single straight male who was tight with the gay community. So much so that he was willing to play the part when needed, without hesitation. That status gave him opportunities, and he appreciated them. Too many of his acting buddies had come out as gay, and from that point forward, they were only offered gay roles. There was the occasional exception, but Skylar knew for now, for his career, it was best to keep that part of his life private. Besides, he had never opened up to Nick about his sexual preferences. Why would he? He didn't answer to anyone about who he dated and slept with. *No, you big wimp, you just keep it all one big secret.*

CHAPTER 20

"WHERE HAVE you been?" Ben asked. He'd been waiting for Aiden when he strolled into the bay area of the firehouse.

"I was down at the fire investigator's office. I wanted to see if they had found out anything more on the fires at Monumental Studios," Aiden responded.

"And had they?" asked Ben.

"No, only what we already know. They were started by gasoline, and in each case, something was left behind with an initial on it. They do think it's an amateur because of the lack of sophistication in setting the fires. Their initial composite shows he's a young white male, most likely uneducated, or at least not sophisticated, and he may be doing it out of revenge for some reason. So, with that composite, we may be dealing with an ex-employee looking for revenge, or, in a long shot, someone wanting to hurt Skylar Murphy," explained Aiden.

He hated to even say that last part. Why would anyone want to hurt Skylar? Yes, he could be a slightly arrogant pain in the ass, but now that Aiden knew him better, he was positive Skylar was really a nice guy down underneath all that "celebrity crap."

"Any ideas on the letters being left behind at the scene?" Ben asked as he recalled their thoughts on the metal bars with the letters *L* and *A*.

"Not anything concrete. Obviously they are spelling out something, and believe me, the thought has crossed my mind that 'Skylar' has an *A* and an *L*. But I've spoken to him, and he truly believes there is no reason to think he's the target of the arsonist. However, I'm keeping my eye on him."

"I just bet you are," Ben said with a smile. He had heard about his young lieutenant going out with Mr. Hollywood.

Aiden blushed. "At any rate, I'm watching for signs of anything out of the ordinary, and meanwhile, the investigators are looking at other angles, such as the city of Los Angeles or the name 'Monumental.'"

There is an *L* and an *A* in that as well. At this point it could mean anything."

They were interrupted by the sound of the alarm going off. They grabbed their gear and headed to the truck. The case of the Monumental Studios arsonist would have to wait.

CHAPTER 21

EMMA DIDN'T know what to think. She was sitting in her little yellow VW Beetle outside of Monumental Studios, trying to decide what to do. Her thoughts were jumbled, and she was attempting to sort them out so she could understand what she had seen.

She had thought of little else since she'd seen Skylar and Aiden together. Skylar was gay. But how could he be gay? He had slept with her the night of the premiere. And he'd definitely known what he was doing, so sleeping with women had to be something he did often. Could he be bisexual? She had never known anyone bisexual, so the thought was foreign to her. Maybe he'd been drunk again and hadn't realized what he was doing? But thinking back at how he had gazed into Aiden's eyes, she knew down deep in her heart that there was something between the two men.

Sitting there fiddling with her dashboard flower, she felt betrayed and devastated. What should she do? What *could* she do? All of these thoughts were swirling around in her head. *Maybe it's a phase he is going through. If I wait it out, he will come back to me, and he will love me, I just know he will.*

"Hey, don't I know you?"

Emma jumped at the sound of someone talking to her. She looked out to see the red-haired girl who had been hanging around Skylar standing at her window.

"Who are you?" Emma asked. *And why are you bothering me?*

"I could ask you the same question." Sophie had been watching the girl just sitting in her car, not attempting to get out.

"I don't think you know me," Emma answered uneasily. She sensed animosity from the girl.

"Yes, I do. You were working the party at Gray Hudson's house a week or so ago!"

"Okay, so you know me. What do you want?" Emma asked as she glared at Sophie.

"Why are you just sitting out here? Do you need something? Or are you just looking for trouble?" Sophie asked accusingly. She remembered how Skylar had behaved at Gray's house and had demanded that she stay with him and not leave him alone with this chick. Sophie could tell that she was up to no good.

"I can sit here. It's public property," snapped Emma. "Besides, I'm waiting to talk to Skylar Murphy."

"This is *private* property, and no one is allowed on the studio grounds without an ID or a pass. You'll need to leave," Sophie demanded.

"I will not leave. I'm going to wait and talk to Skylar," Emma insisted.

"I can give him a message for you. But you must leave or I'll alert the security guard."

"Why are you being such a bitch? I just need to talk to Skylar. We're friends."

"Does Skylar know you're out here?" Sophie asked, although she already knew the answer.

"No, but I'm sure he'll want to talk to me once he knows I'm here."

Sophie rolled her eyes. "Somehow I doubt that. If you won't leave, I'll have security escort you off the property." To reinforce her threat, Sophie started to walk toward the security box at the main entrance.

"Wait!" Emma shouted. "Fine. I'll leave. But please give him a note for me." She reached down in her purse and pulled out a flower notepad. She wrote something on the notepad, pulled the piece of paper off the pad, folded it, and handed it Sophie. "Make sure you give it only to Skylar."

After handing the note to Sophie, Emma drove off, her little yellow bug squealing its tires.

Unable to help herself, Sophie opened it and read: *I saw you with Aiden the other night. We need to talk. I don't understand why you are angry at me and won't give me a chance to make things up to you. Please call me at 213-555-4795. Love you always, Emma.*

CHAPTER 22

SKYLAR WAS lounging in Kelly's dressing room trying to get her to run lines with him. Cary was milling around in his usual bad mood. Therefore, Skylar was anxious to leave.

"I'll be there in a sec," Kelly yelled from the bathroom.

"In Kelly-speak, that means about thirty minutes," Cary said sourly from his side of the room.

Skylar didn't know what Kelly saw in Cary. He'd had a run-in with Cary a while back, and he didn't want to spend any time alone with him. Cary had approached him late one night after a long day of filming and asked him out for drinks. Skylar was not interested. He was pretty hot and heavy with Kelly and the last thing he needed was her assistant hitting on him. Skylar had been a bit rude, but he was also tired and wanted to be left alone. He thought Cary had understood what a terrible idea that would be, but since then, Cary had kept silent around him unless it was to say something sarcastic in response to something Skylar said. *Oh well. No great loss.*

"Come on, I need to go soon," Skylar yelled in Kelly's direction. He was impatient and being stuck here in this room with Mr. Antisocial was not making it any more pleasant.

"I'm here! I told you that I was coming," Kelly remarked as she came into the room, holding her script. "Let's get started. Cary, would you mind leaving us for a bit?"

"Not a problem," Cary said as he immediately left the room.

"Wow, that is one sociable guy," Skylar remarked as he watched Cary leave.

"He's not so bad. He's excellent at his job. Therefore, he doesn't need to be a social butterfly. I like him as he is."

"That's your choice. Personally, I'd rather have someone who was a little more pleasant to spend time with."

"Like Sophie?"

"She's not so bad. Today, she actually went above the call of duty. She chased off a fan who's been following me around since the premiere. I was impressed," said Skylar.

This declaration of affection made Kelly jealous. She didn't particularly care for Sophie, and besides, now that she had Skylar in her dressing room, the last thing she wanted to talk about was the hired help.

Changing the subject, she asked, "Why haven't you come to the house lately?" She was referring to their usual meeting place, the pool house.

"I've been busy," replied Skylar. He wasn't ready to own up to her about his interest in Aiden.

"Well, I've missed you."

Shit. Here we go. "I'm sorry I haven't been around much. I've had a lot going on with the new movie prospect and all."

"How's that going?"

"I have an audition with Michelle Michaels on Monday. So I'm looking forward to that."

"I have no doubt you'll blow them away with that audition."

Kelly came over to sit by Skylar and started rubbing his leg with her fingertips.

"I hope you're right." Skylar was starting to feel a slightly uncomfortable because he knew the direction this meeting was going in. Strangely enough Skylar didn't want to go there. He was quite happy thinking about Aiden and didn't want anything to interfere with that.

Edging away from Kelly as tactfully as he could, he asked, "So, which scene should we start with?"

Not taking the hint, Kelly leaned over to nuzzle his cheek. "Do you want to run lines or would you prefer something else?"

Skylar moved farther away as he said, "I think we had better stick to running lines today. I'm a bit off on some of the scenes, and I need your help."

Visibly disappointed, Kelly sat up straighter. "If that's what you want." She might be disappointed but Kelly was always a lady. Grabbing her script, she started reading the first line.

CHAPTER 23

SKYLAR WAS running around the kitchen trying to get everything ready before Aiden showed up. He had sent him directions to the house earlier in the afternoon and asked that he join him for dinner. They had been dating for a few weeks now, but between the screen test for *Checkmate* and fourteen hours a day filming, this was the first time Aiden had been able to come to Skylar's house. Now it was almost time for Aiden to arrive, and Skylar still had to get the fire going in the living room. Tonight was going to be a special night, and he thought a glowing fire would set the night for romance. Earlier in the day, Skylar had found out that he, as well as Kelly, had been nominated for an Emmy, and he was on top of the world. Now, if he could only find out if he was going to be cast for the lead in *Checkmate*, his world would be complete.

He had worked all afternoon on his famous lasagna. When his mother would go into one of her self-imposed depressions and lock herself away in her room, it was either cook or survive off frozen pizzas; therefore, Skylar had learned to cook out of necessity. One of his specialties was lasagna, and he couldn't wait for Aiden to try it.

One last check on the lasagna and he was off to the living room. He reached down to turn on the pilot light on the fireplace and realized it was already on. *That's strange*, he thought. *I don't remember turning that on. Damn, I need to be more careful.* As Skylar watched the fire grow, he heard the doorbell.

He's here! Skylar could feel the excitement in his bones. He had waited so long for tonight to finally arrive, and now Aiden was here. He felt an unfamiliar tingling in his gut. If he didn't know better, he would think he was falling for this guy.

"Hey, there," Skylar said as he opened the door with a huge smile on his face, motioning for Aiden to come in.

"Hey there, yourself," replied a grinning Aiden as he stepped into the living room.

"Any problem finding the place?"

"Nah, I'm up here a lot with the fire department, so I knew the roads. So all I needed was your house number, and here I am."

"Yes, you are." Skylar couldn't stop smiling as he leaned forward and gave him a quick kiss on the lips.

Aiden followed Skylar in the living room. "Very nice!" Aiden was impressed as he noticed the beautiful soft glow from the fireplace.

Skylar looked at the fireplace, then at Aiden, and with slight shoulder shrug, he said, "I was going for cozy and charming."

"Then I would say you aced it." Aiden smiled at the knowledge that Skylar had gone to so much trouble for him.

"Would you like a glass of wine?" Skylar walked over to the counter where he had set up the wine and glasses.

"I would love one."

Skylar used the corkscrew to open the bottle of nice robust red wine and poured a glass for Aiden. "How was work this week? I'm sorry I didn't get a chance to talk to you for the past couple of days."

"No problem. I was at the firehouse anyway for my twenty-four-hour shift. But now I'm off for thirty-six, so I'm good to go."

Skylar handed Aiden his glass of wine, then turned around and poured himself a glass. Turning back to Aiden, he grinned and said, "I have some good news that I want to share with you."

"You got the part in *Checkmate*!" Aiden guessed.

Smiling, Skylar said, "Unfortunately, I still haven't heard anything about *Checkmate*, but I did get an Emmy nomination!" He was so proud of this, and sharing the news with Aiden made it feel more real.

"That is fantastic! I'm so happy for you!" Aiden was not surprised at all. Now that he had gone back and watched most of Skylar's work, he knew he was an amazing actor. Raising his glass, he toasted, "Here's to an Emmy win for you! No one deserves it more!"

They clinked glasses and stood there as they started to sip their wine.

"You know, I believe you'll win the lead in *Checkmate*," Aiden said as he grabbed a napkin beside the bottle of wine.

"I really hope so, Aiden. It would be such a fantastic move for my career."

Holding up his glass again, Aiden said, "Then I have another toast. Here's to getting the lead in *Checkmate* and to our wonderful evening together."

They clinked glasses again, then took a second sip of wine.

"I hope you like lasagna," Skylar said.

"Of course I do. Who doesn't like Italian?" Aiden replied as he smiled at Skylar and watched him taking another sip. The rippling of Skylar's throat caught his eye, and he was surprised how even such a small detail caused him to break out in goose bumps. Aiden was happy to be here. He'd had to practically shove Ryan out the door so he could leave on time, but he had made it with a few minutes to spare.

"Good. This is my special recipe." Skylar's words pulled Aiden out of his thoughts, and they walked over to the couch to sit down and enjoy their wine.

"I'm surprised you cook. I was expecting... well, I'm not sure what I was expecting." Aiden said, laughing.

Skylar glanced at Aiden's somewhat embarrassed expression and teased, "Oh, I know. You thought I'm a spoiled actor who employs a housekeeper, a cook, a driver...."

Aiden laughed again. "No, not a driver." Both of them leaned back against the couch laughing, knowing that Skylar probably did have those things.

"Okay, I admit it. I do have a housekeeper. But that's it. And *only* because I don't have a lot of time to clean this place properly." He continued, "And I'll have you know that I learned to cook a long time ago, as a kid."

"Now that's a cool mom. One who taught you how to cook early on. Smart woman," remarked Aiden as he took another sip of his wine.

Skylar pulled his leg up and stared at the almost empty glass now resting on his knee. "No, my mom didn't teach me to cook. I taught myself as she went in and out of periods of depression." Why *did I just tell him that?*

Aiden was taken aback, surprise visible on his face. "Oh, I'm sorry. I didn't mean to imply...."

"Hey, no big deal," Skylar said, waving off the implications as well as the memories. "It was either learn to cook or live on frozen meals. And I'm not your frozen-meal kind of guy. But I have to give her credit. Even if she would never win 'Mother of the Year,' at least she stayed. My old man hit the road," explained Skylar.

Aiden sipped his wine as he took in all this new information about Skylar. Feeling sorry that Skylar evidently went through a tough childhood, he said the only thing he could think of at the moment, "Well, I think you turned out pretty good, and look at you now, with an Emmy nomination and a chance at one of the top roles in Hollywood. She should be proud of you."

"I think she is," replied Skylar as he gulped down the rest of his wine.

Grabbing the bottle, he turned to Aiden. "Are you ready for a refill?"

Looking at his almost full glass, Aiden shook his head and said, "Not just yet. I'm still enjoying this one." Deciding to change the subject, Aiden stood up and wandered around the room. "Have you lived here long?"

"About six months."

Aiden looked around at the unpacked boxes and raised his eyebrows. Skylar noticed his slight gesture and got up off the couch himself, waving in the general direction of the boxes. "I know I still have some unpacking to do. I just don't have a lot of free time, and I don't want the housekeeper to do it. So the boxes are still here."

The timer went off in the kitchen.

"Lasagna's ready!" announced Skylar. "Follow me!" he instructed Aiden as he walked off into the kitchen to take care of dinner.

Aiden looked around and felt a pang of sadness as he followed him into the kitchen, where he found Skylar busy removing the lasagna from the oven. "That smells delicious," Aiden said as he sniffed the air.

"I hope you like it," Skylar said as he set the pan of lasagna down on the stove. "If you don't mind filling our glasses again, I'll serve the lasagna and salad."

"Certainly," replied Aiden as he gathered up both wine glasses and set them down on the table. He walked back into the living room to find the bottle of wine and paused for a moment to look at the fire roaring in the fireplace. He felt at ease here in Skylar's house. It was a comfortable feeling and one he hoped would continue.

As Aiden came back in and started pouring the wine, Skylar had already placed lasagna-filled plates down at each place setting. He had lit candles in the center of the table and was now bringing over the salads.

"Come sit with me," he said as he motioned to Aiden. "And in case you're wondering, I do have a dining room, but it's too formal for my taste." Glancing at Aiden from under his eyelids, he added with a wink, "Like I said, I was going for cozy and charming."

"And you aced it again." Smiling, Aiden put the bottle of wine down at the end of the table and joined Skylar at the place next to him.

"Another toast," Skylar said, raising his glass. "To many more moments like this." He clinked his glass with Aiden, and they proceeded to eat.

Aiden was immediately impressed with his date. The lasagna was really terrific. As he looked over at Skylar, who looked elegant in his black turtleneck, Aiden realized at that moment, it could have been the worst lasagna in the world and he wouldn't have cared. He was really falling for this guy.

"Now that I've shared a bit about my childhood—which, granted, wasn't stellar—tell me a little about yours," Skylar said.

"Not a lot to tell. I grew up here in Los Angeles. My mom and dad still live in the same house. They've been married for thirty years and are still as in love as the day they married. I hope to have that myself someday with the man I love." Aiden watched Skylar, who was now sipping on his wine, as he continued, "I knew I was gay fairly early. I never had any interest in girls, and when I developed a hopeless crush on the quarterback of our high school team, I knew."

"How did your parents react?" asked Skylar.

"They were understanding and never judged me. They told me that they wanted me to be happy and only I could decide what made me happy." As he looked at the man next to him, who was just staring at him with his sparkling eyes full of interest, he continued, "I realize every day that I'm one of the lucky ones."

"Sounds like you had amazing parents. No wonder you turned out so great," Skylar said as he reached out and touched Aiden on the cheek.

Aiden looked at Skylar with tenderness. "And when did you know you were gay?"

Skylar wasn't sure how to respond to that question but decided that in this case, honesty was the best way to go. "I don't know that I'm gay."

Aiden looked confused. "What do you mean?"

"I mean, I don't like to label myself. I find myself attracted to men and women. If it feels right and feels like something I want to do, then I do it. I don't let gender get in the way." As he noticed Aiden's surprise, he suddenly became nervous and took a big gulp of wine. "Okay, now that we have that out on the table, so to speak…."

Aiden wasn't quite sure how he felt about this. "So you're bisexual," he finally said. It was more a statement than a question.

"If you insist on labeling me, then yes, I guess I'm bisexual." Skylar slowly put down his glass, his hand shaking slightly, as he asked with a hint of hesitation in his voice, "Is that going to be a problem?" His heart skipped a beat because he realized he didn't want anything to cause a problem between himself and Aiden.

Aiden didn't know how to respond. He knew he really cared for Skylar and wanted to give them a chance, but was he ready for someone who might check out on him tomorrow for the hot young girl at the office? Or maybe the hot new male intern. To him bisexuality meant twice the opportunities—the best of both worlds.

"So…?" asked Skylar again.

As he looked into Skylar's intensely bright eyes and saw that they were full of hope, Aiden decided that instant that it was worth the chance. Shaking his head, he responded, "No, it isn't a problem. You just caught me off guard for a moment."

Relief immediately filled Skylar's heart, and he reached over to squeeze Aiden's hand. "Great! Now, if you're finished eating, let's take this conversation and our wine into the living room. I spent hours building that fire."

Both men laughed as they chose to put this part of their conversation behind them for the moment. After gathering up their wine glasses and grabbing the bottle of unfinished wine, they headed into the living room.

CHAPTER 24

EMMA HAD never felt so depressed. She had just joined her new friend, Chad, at the Red Oak bar on Sunset.

"I can't believe he didn't call," she moaned into her beer as she rocked back and forth on her barstool.

"Oh, I can. He's a self-centered asshole," said Chad as he chugged his beer.

Emma looked at him with questioning eyes before asking, "How do you know that? Has he done something to you?"

"A long time ago...." At her glance, he said, "And no, I'm not going to tell you. So just believe me, I know it."

After leaning in to take another gulp from her beer, Emma decided she didn't care what Skylar had done to Chad. She was in too much misery from her own problems with Skylar. Looking at Chad with hope, she said, "Maybe she didn't give him the note."

Shaking his head, he responded, "You said she was his assistant. It's her *job* to make sure he receives important correspondence."

Emma smiled at the thought that she might be considered important to Skylar. Then remembering he hadn't called her, she said, "Then what should I do? I really love him. I need him."

Chad gaped at her. *Oh wow... this is one pathetic girl. How disgusting can you be?* He had learned a long time ago that Skylar would never care for someone so pathetic.

"What? Don't you believe me?" she asked with fear in her voice.

I believe you're crazy... but still, maybe I can use this to my advantage. An idea popped into his head. Ever since he had started targeting Skylar with the fires, he had made it a point to always know where Skylar was and who he was with. Therefore, he knew that at this exact moment, Skylar was having a romantic dinner at his house with that firefighter. Chad leaned toward Emma and whispered, "Maybe you should go to his house and try to talk to him again."

"Oh no, I can't do that." She shook her head furiously. "He was so angry before. He might really hate me if I did that again," she said fearfully.

"Remember the day that I met you at the studios?"

"Yes…," Emma responded with hesitation.

"I told you then that I had known Skylar for years and was now working with him at the studio. So, I think it's safe to say that I know him pretty well."

Emma nodded in agreement.

"So, yes, he can be an asshole, but I bet if you go and knock on the door, rather than going in uninvited, he will react differently. And then you can make him understand how good you are for him, how special you are."

Rising to the bait, Emma's heart fluttered. "Do you really think so?"

"I really do think that. Go now. Go and give it a try," Chad said, taking her glass away from her. "I'll pay for this. You just make sure you get up there now before you change your mind."

"But what if he gets furious, like last time?" she asked, her eyes wide with fear.

Oh, believe me, he'll be so pissed off! The thought of ruining Skylar's night made Chad extremely giddy. All that he had been working for all these years would soon become a reality. But until that moment of truth, anything he could do to make Skylar's life miserable was added bonus points. He just had to be careful that Emma didn't find out his real name. Turning to Emma, he continued to reassure her. "I don't think he'll mind at all. You just caught him in a bad mood the last time you tried this."

"Okay, I'm going now." Emma hopped off the barstool, gave her friend a quick hug, and ran out the door.

Such a pity. I won't see his reaction. Emma was gone before she could hear his laughter.

CHAPTER 25

UNTIL NOW, Aiden had never understood the fascination of sitting in front of a fireplace, sipping wine with a hot date. Maybe it was the fact that fires were his job. Knowing how dangerous they could be took away some of the romance. But as he looked over at Skylar, who was staring into the fire, he couldn't help but think about how amazing this night had been. Sharing stories of their childhood made him feel closer to Skylar, and he knew he wanted to be with him.

As he watched Skylar, his eyes glistening from the glow of the fire, he noticed the veins on his forearm pulsing under his skin, and his hands, oh, his hands, were big and strong, and Aiden wanted nothing more than to have those hands all over him, touching, caressing. Aiden had never felt as happy as he did right at this moment. It was a strange sensation, this feeling of contentment with a man he had just gotten to know. But he liked it, and he would take it one day at a time.

Tentatively he reached out and touched Skylar's hair, running his fingers through the soft waves hitting his shoulder. Skylar turned to him and smiled, the warm glow of the fire dancing across his face. Neither man said anything as they just gazed into each other's eyes. The only sound was the soft music playing in the background.

Aiden placed his wine glass on the hearth and reached out to take Skylar's glass from his hand. Skylar handed it over without any hesitation, a mischievous glint in his eyes. Turning toward him, Aiden leaned over and gently placed his lips on Skylar's.

As their mouths touched, both men felt breathless. The electricity instantly sparked between them as they kept their mouths pressed against each other, both their heartbeats pounding in their chest.

Pulling each other closer, the kiss deepened, and Aiden kissed him hungrily as his tongue sought solace within Skylar's warmth. As he explored Skylar's mouth, Aiden could taste the earthy flavor of red wine and moved to capture Skylar's full lower lip and gently suck on it. Slowly moving his hands up Skylar's back, he could feel the muscles under his fingers and the sudden need to feel Skylar's warm skin stunned him.

Skylar, overwhelmed from the intimacy, reached out and started to unbutton Aiden's shirt.

Aiden pulled back and looked into Skylar's eyes.

"Are you okay?" Skylar asked, his voice raspy from lust.

Aiden looked at him for a moment before gasping out a whispered, "Yes."

Skylar leaned forward, capturing Aiden's mouth again in a deep intoxicating kiss. Then, slowly, he continued to unbutton Aiden's shirt. As the shirt fell open, Skylar ran his hands over the flatness of Aiden's tight stomach, feeling the muscles jump under his fingers. Just touching him was sending sensations through Skylar unlike any he had ever felt before.

Aiden's sudden intake of breath could be heard over the music playing in the background, causing Skylar to shiver. Somehow Skylar managed to remove his hands from Aiden's chest long enough to reach down and take off his own shirt. As he placed it on the floor, he looked up to see Aiden gazing at him with lust-filled eyes. Coming to action, Aiden leaned over and gently pushed Skylar backward until he was lying on his back, while over to the side, the fire was still glowing, leaving a toasty warm feeling in the room.

Skylar lay there as Aiden hovered over him and started planting openmouthed kisses down the side of his face, onto his neck, and down on his chest. As Aiden rolled his tongue around Skylar's nipple, he could feel it harden.

"Ah, baby....," Skylar barely managed to whisper as he dug his fingers into Aiden's soft blond strands, his breathing coming more rapidly now.

"You like that?" Aiden asked, his voice filled with hunger, right before he moved over to the other nipple, giving it the same mind-blowing treatment.

Skylar nodded his approval, and Aiden kept on kissing and licking as he let his hand travel down to find what he craved most. As Aiden tentatively rubbed his hand over Skylar's rock-hard cock, he heard Skylar moan out loud, the sound creating an undeniable pleasure within Aiden. He wanted to feel Skylar inside him, and he didn't want to wait any longer.

Just before Aiden moved to unbuckle Skylar's belt, his gaze roamed over the man lying beneath him. What was it about a bare-chested guy in jeans? To Aiden, it was a turn-on without fail, and he allowed his fingertips to follow the dark treasure trail that started just below his belly button and disappeared underneath Skylar's buckle. He quickly opened the buttons with trembling fingers and, grabbing hold on either side, started to slowly pull down his jeans. Skylar lifted his hips to speed things up, and Aiden couldn't help but smirk at his obvious eagerness. Noticing that Skylar had gone commando made his own cock twitch in the tight confines of his pants, and he carelessly threw the jeans on the floor behind him.

Skylar's cock was swollen and glistening with moisture. Aiden just gazed at him as he reached out and tentatively ran his finger across the engorged head, spreading the precum as if in a trance. Skylar's cock jumped at his touch, and his heaving chest began to shine with a sheen of sweat as their gazes met. No words were needed; both men knew what they wanted.

Looking back down, Aiden tenderly closed his fingers around Skylar's erection and began to rub him up and down while, with his other hand, he caressed the inside of Skylar's thighs as the fire sent warm rays over their bodies.

As Aiden brushed his fingertips along the outside of Skylar's balls, the sensation, between the warmth from the fire and the feel of Aiden's fingers, was too much. Skylar moaned as his hips jerked up, and he quickly grabbed Aiden's hand.

"Slow down, baby. I don't want to come yet." And then, with a less panicked tone, he continued, "I want this to last." Feeling completely overwhelmed with sensations, Skylar needed to have Aiden completely naked and under him. "Careful, baby." He gently put his arms around Aiden and rolled them over, allowing both men to lie on the soft rug decorating the hardwood floor. Both their bodies were flushed by both the warmth radiating from the fireplace, but also from the sheer adrenaline coursing through their bodies. Sliding up Aiden's body, Skylar leaned down to teasingly run his tongue across Aiden's warm lips and whispered, "I have never wanted someone so much."

Aiden hazily gazed up at him, his eyes an intoxicating blue, and said, "God, I want you too. More than you know."

As if to prove it, Aiden pushed up and kissed Skylar with a renewed passion.

Slowly pulling his lips from Aiden's, Skylar sat up to kneel between Aiden's legs and helped him to a sitting position. Reaching over, Skylar completely removed Aiden's shirt and then gently laid him back on the floor. He once again leaned down next to Aiden to capture his mouth with his. As he plundered Aiden's mouth with his tongue, Skylar used one hand to unbuckle Aiden's belt as he grabbed hold of the back of his neck with his other hand, digging his fingers into Aiden's skin.

After they both were completely naked, Skylar skimmed his fingers down Aiden's body, tracing his muscles, his flat stomach, as if to memorize it. As he finally reached Aiden's cock, he could see that it was completely hard, and he grabbed it in his hand to gently start pumping. Instantly a deep moan escaped Aiden, and he turned his head in search of Skylar's mouth. Skylar sensed his need and passionately started to kiss Aiden again. Aiden's mouth was wet and hot, and Skylar began to suck on Aiden's tongue at the same time he was pumping up and down on Aiden's cock.

Slowly Skylar lifted his mouth from Aiden's and began to move down his body, nipping and licking across his broad chest, savoring the taste of Aiden's skin on his tongue. Aiden's own fragrance was more than intoxicating, and within seconds, Skylar had replaced his hand with his mouth.

"Oh fuck!" Aiden's arms flew up, and, digging the heels of his hands into his eyes, he tried to keep himself from coming right there. Up and down, Skylar took him all the way into his throat while his moans reverberated throughout Aiden's entire being.

Skylar swirled his tongue around the head and down underneath, leaving a wet trail on the protruding vein.

Aiden was about to lose it. He moved his hands back to Skylar's head, grasping the long strands of hair as he pushed Skylar's head up and down, feeling himself getting closer and closer to orgasm. But he wanted Skylar inside him, and he had to have him now. After reaching down and pulling Skylar's face up to meet his, Aiden maneuvered himself so that Skylar was resting between his legs as their swollen cocks rubbed up against each other, making both men gasp.

Skylar grabbed a pillow from the couch and placed it under Aiden's hips for easier access, then lifted Aiden's leg up over his shoulder. Afterward, he reached underneath the sofa to retrieve a pack of condoms and a small bottle of lube. As Aiden watched the display, his eyebrows raised in mock amusement.

"You must have been pretty sure of yourself."

"Nope, not sure. But hope dies last, baby." With a playful smirk, Skylar handed him the condom, and Aiden eagerly tore the packet open with his teeth and started to slowly roll it down on Skylar's leaking cock with shaky fingers. Any playfulness was quickly forgotten, and Skylar temporarily squeezed his eyes shut and bit his lower lip in order not to attack Aiden right then and there. He was so excited he didn't know how he would manage to get inside him without coming instantaneously.

Once the condom was in place, Aiden opened the bottle of lube and huskily whispered, "Give me your hand." Skylar complied immediately, and Aiden squeezed a generous amount of lube on his fingers. After carelessly placing the bottle to the side, Aiden pulled Skylar down by his neck and started ravaging his mouth, hardly able to contain his eagerness for what was to come. Their mouths open, tongues tangling—it felt like the right moment.

Skylar reached down between Aiden's legs and gently began probing Aiden's tight entrance by carefully pushing one finger inside as he tried to prepare him. The sting caused Aiden to moan, but just as quickly, his muscles began to loosen up, and Skylar pushed in a second finger, scissoring them and listening to any sounds of discomfort due to the intrusion. Aiden opened his mouth and gasped into Skylar's mouth but soon began to move with Skylar, chasing his fingers like he never wanted to lose contact. The intensity between them was overwhelming.

"Now, babe... I need you inside me... please...," Aiden whispered to Skylar.

"Are you sure?" asked Skylar. "I don't think you're—"

"*Now*, Sky! Please...." The urgency in Aiden's voice wasn't lost on Skylar, and he quickly rolled into place. Aiden reached down and placed Skylar's swollen cock right at his entrance. He roughly grabbed Skylar's ass and pushed his hips so the tip of Skylar's cock slid inside him.

"Slow down, baby. I don't want to hurt you." Skylar's concerned tone forced Aiden to open his eyes, and the intense look in Skylar's eyes shot through him like a bolt of lightning.

"Can't…. Need you… now." Aiden was gasping for breath as he began to push up, as he couldn't wait another minute. The tightness was so intense; Skylar had to pause for a moment. Catching his breath, he leaned down and kissed Aiden with gentle passion as he very slowly pushed in until he was all the way inside. Aiden's breathing quickened, and Skylar stopped, watching his face intently.

"Are you okay?" he asked in concern, lifting his hand to Aiden's face to sweep some wayward strands of hair from his sweaty forehead.

"Just a second. Just give me a second," Aiden barely managed to get out.

Skylar was very large, and the pain was still there from the initial breach, and Aiden had to breathe through the pain, waiting for it to pass. "Okay, babe. Just take it slow at first." Aiden said.

Pulling all the way out and gently pushing back in made both men groan from deep within, and Skylar needed all his self-control not to ram into Aiden. He was close to coming apart, but hurting Aiden was the last thing on earth he wanted to do. The sensations of the newness of each other and the incredible intensity they shared were almost too much.

"Okay, babe. Go for it." Aiden emphasized his readiness by pushing down on Skylar's ass with the heel of his right foot.

Trying to be very careful, Skylar started to thrust in and out of Aiden with a gentleness that he seldom used. Suddenly he twisted just a little.

"Ahhh… *God*!" Aiden moaned with passion as he threw his head back and his back arched off the floor. "Jesus, don't stop, don't…. Yeah, keep it there, babe."

Knowing he was the one making Aiden feel like he was flying, completely overwhelmed Skylar with desire, his own need to orgasm almost undeniable. He made sure to angle his thrusts in just the right way, but gritting his teeth, he knew he wouldn't last much longer. Aiden was so tight, and Skylar was about to lose control.

Sweat began to run down Skylar's face, dripping onto Aiden's chest as his breathing became more erratic. As he reached down with one hand to start pumping Aiden's cock in rhythm of his thrusting, Aiden started grabbing at the thick carpet for leverage, their harsh breathing the only sounds in the room now. The music had long since stopped, but neither man noticed nor cared, concentrating solely on their mutual feeling of chasing their impending orgasms.

Skylar had started to feel his balls tighten when he noticed Aiden's neck muscles protruding, and the pressure in his groin became even stronger—he was ready to lose it. *Fucking sexy as hell*, he thought as he bent down to slide his tongue up Aiden's throat. His thrusts began to lose rhythm, just like his pumping motion on Aiden's engorged cock. A deep moan reverberated throughout the room when Skylar huskily demanded, "Look at me!"

When Aiden didn't comply immediately, lost in his own feelings of ecstasy, Skylar hoarsely insisted again, "Aiden, look at me. I... I need to see your eyes."

Aiden pried his eyes open, and as soon as he was met by Skylar's penetrating look, his pupils blown to kingdom come and his sweaty disheveled hair falling into his face, he lost it. "Oh Jesus, I'm gonna.... *Fuck!*" Stomach muscles clenching, Aiden jerked up and grabbed hold of Skylar's neck with both hands, forcing him toward him until their foreheads almost crashed together.

Skylar's jaw clenched as a deep, satisfying moan filled the air, and Skylar could feel Aiden coming in spurts all over his hand and down onto his stomach. That was all it took for Skylar, and he followed Aiden over the precipice with a husky roar, thrusting all the way inside one last time.

Their bodies spasmed for what seemed like minutes, and after Skylar milked Aiden dry, both men dropped back on the floor, Aiden's leg listlessly falling to the side. Skylar fell down onto Aiden's heaving chest, nuzzling into the crook of his neck as they both tried to catch their breaths. It had been so intense that they were shaking, and both could feel the other's racing heartbeat against their own overheated skin.

After a moment Skylar gathered up all his strength and reached down to grab the condom then carefully pulled out, in turn provoking an irritated groan from Aiden. As Skylar rolled off, he placed the condom to the side and then nestled up against Aiden, their gazes meeting once again. He could feel his lover's exhausted yet satisfied smile deep in his gut. Cleanup could wait. As they both continued to lie on the floor waiting for their breathing to get back to normal, the fire glowed brightly in the background, casting shadows on them.

Neither noticed the devastated girl watching them through the window.

CHAPTER 26

"I DID it," Emma confessed through her tears. She had called Chad, and they were back at the same place, beers in front of them. With her heart broken into a million pieces, Emma had every intention of getting smashed.

"I went to Skylar's house, but he was there with someone else," she said, tears falling as she remembered watching Skylar and Aiden make love. "Here. Look!" she said, throwing her cell phone at Chad. "See? I told you that he doesn't want me. He wants *him*!" And then she started to cry harder. Why had she ever agreed to go to Skylar's house?

Oh my God, this couldn't be more perfect. Chad was almost giddy glancing at the photos on Emma's cell phone. Lady Luck was definitely on his side. Now to think of something toxic to do with this delightful information.

Remembering Emma was watching, Chad turned his charm back to her. Putting an arm around Emma, he cooed, "Oh, sweetie, I'm so very sorry." Squeezing her closer to him, Chad patted Emma's hair, trying to calm her. "You know, I'm not going to let him get away with this. He has to pay for hurting you in this way."

"What do you mean? What are you going to do?" she said, her voice choking with emotion.

"Not me, darling. You," he said while lightly stroking her hair. "I want you to mail these lovely photos to Skylar's manager." As she started to protest, she felt Chad place a finger over her mouth. "No... listen to me. I have the address. You send these photos to his manager, and I promise you that Skylar will no longer be able to see this guy."

"How do you know?" Emma asked.

"Because, darling, not only do I know your beloved Skylar, I also know his manager. He is a money-hungry, no-talent piece of crap. He will not want anything out there that might damage the scheme he has going with Skylar."

"I still don't understand."

Losing his patience Chad continued to stroke her hair and whisper promises. "Just trust me. Send those pictures anonymously, and soon you'll see that these two boys are finished."

Emma could only nod in agreement.

CHAPTER 27

"WHERE THE hell did you get these?" Skylar was pacing back and forth in front of Nick's desk. He really needed his antianxiety medicine because this was sending him over the edge. Things were going really well between him and Aiden, and while it shocked Skylar that he liked Aiden so much, it was a fantastic feeling and Skylar was reveling in it. Now that amazing feeling was being threatened, and he was about to go ballistic.

Lying in front of them on the desk was a stack of photos someone had taken of Skylar and Aiden in front of the fireplace at Skylar's house. Judging from various things, Skylar believed it had to have been the night they had full-on sex for the first time.

Skylar picked up the stack and glanced through it. There were photos of them drinking wine, sitting in front of the fireplace, and kissing. There was only one in which Skylar had his shirt off, but that was enough to send him further into panic mode. With his heart in his throat, Skylar nervously looked for more intimate, thus damaging, photos. But he didn't find any.

Skylar repeated his question. "I'll ask again. Where did you get these?" he said, his voice barely above a whisper.

"Someone sent them to me anonymously through the mail," Nick responded as he pointed to the brown envelope tossed over to the side of the desk.

Skylar picked up the envelope and began to turn it over and over, searching for anything that might give away who had taken the photos and who could possibly be stalking them.

"You won't find anything. Believe me, I've looked all over that envelope. And the address is typed, so we don't have a handwritten sample either," Nick explained as he took the envelope from Skylar. "Just in case you're not aware, this isn't good."

"Okay, so what do you want me to do about it?" Skylar was already in defense mode because he knew where Nick was going with this.

"I want you to stop seeing him."

"I can't do that. I *won't* do that," he said with conviction. The anxiety that held Skylar hostage was now moving into anger. He could feel the resentment building up inside him.

Nick walked around to stand in front of Skylar. Looking at him with an intense look, he said, "Skylar, you know that normally I don't give a rat's ass about whomever you might be screwing, but right now we have an important deal about to happen, and if you want to *keep* that deal, you have to stay on the straight and narrow, and yes, I did intend my pun."

Blood near boiling point, Skylar exploded. "That's fucked up! Why does it matter who I'm sleeping with?" *Damn*, he hated nothing more than being told what to do, especially where his love life was concerned.

Nick, not missing a beat, responded, "Because you know damn well that the fact that you'll take on controversial roles is a huge selling point that I use to get you work."

Skylar couldn't help but roll his eyes at this statement.

"Stop rolling your eyes. We make damn good money at those roles that other actors won't touch. But if you *are* gay and take on gay roles, where's the controversy in that?"

"It was never my intention to be projected in that way," Skylar protested.

"I understand that, but it worked out that way, and we have a good thing going, so why would we jeopardize it now, *especially* when you're so close to booking the most important gig of your career?" Nick was getting angry. He was not going to let Skylar mess this up for them. He had to convince him to stop seeing that boy.

Skylar walked over and picked up the photos again, so angry his hand was shaking. Attempting to find a positive thought, he suggested, "Maybe this person has no intention of doing anything with the photos."

"I think the fact that they mailed them to your manager says otherwise," Nick bit out, waving his hands toward the incriminating photos.

Anger taking over his thoughts, Skylar growled, "For fuck's sake!" Sweat was threatening to break out as he neared panic mode for the second time. Running his hand through his thick wavy hair, Skylar walked over to the window of the office and looked out. After taking a deep breath, he said, "Okay, let's think for a moment." There was silence in the room as both men tried to think of an answer. Turning toward Nick, he asked, "Why would my being perceived as gay hurt my chances at *Checkmate*? It's not a gay character."

"Skylar, you know the answer to that. This is an action-hero role. They want a hot, powerful, intense leading man. And you *are* that man. You rocked their world when you auditioned with Michelle a few weeks ago."

"But I still don't see how my being perceived as gay would change that," protested Skylar.

Nick was becoming very frustrated. He walked over to Skylar and put his hands on his shoulders. "Listen. Right now, you have the reputation of being an actor who steps into controversial roles, unafraid of the consequences. You can bring in all audiences, whether it's gay, straight, or bi, because you're seen as brave and unconcerned with typecasting. Everyone loves you! However, if the studio thinks for a minute that you haven't been doing anything controversial, you have just been playing yourself, lying about your sexuality, I think they won't see the specialness in you any longer. Besides, you know as well as I do that once you are labeled gay, those are the only roles you'll be offered."

Skylar looked directly at Nick. "Frankly, Nick, I think that's a bunch of bullshit."

"Maybe, but do you really want to take that chance?"

Skylar walked over to a chair and sat down. Putting his head in his hands, he thought, *This was fucking insane. Who is trying to ruin my damn life?* "I don't know what I want, but I do know that I don't want to stop seeing Aiden." *Especially when someone is telling me that I have to.*

Nick was tired of this. He didn't understand Skylar, and his blood pressure had to be peaking at a dangerous level. What was a piece of ass when you might lose your shot at the big time? Shaking his head he paced the office as he tried to think of a solution.

Stopping for a second, he turned to Skylar, "At the very least, we have to do some sort of damage control. If these photos get leaked to the press, then we need to be in front of it with another angle."

"What sort of angle?" Skylar asked as he looked up at Nick. He wasn't sure what Nick had in mind, but he did have the distinct feeling he wasn't going to like it.

"Let me think. I haven't gotten that far," Nick said as he restarted his pacing. After about a minute of silence, Nick turned back to Skylar. "Okay, I may have an idea that will allow you to still see your boy toy *and* fix this situation. At least until casting is announced by the studio."

"Don't fucking call him my boy toy!" Those words automatically pissed Skylar off. Sometimes he wondered why he had ever hired Nick.

"Fine. Whatever." If Nick didn't calm down, he would explode. Skylar was his biggest client, and he was being unreasonable. "Okay, how about this? What if we rig it to where you are seen all over LA with a hot girl? She can be your new girlfriend. A few well-placed paparazzi and photo ops, and we'll have everyone convinced that you're straight and in love."

"Are you fucking kidding me?" Skylar asked incredulously, standing up to look Nick square in the eyes. "Where am I supposed to find this girl? And what will I tell Aiden?"

"You tell Aiden that you have to do this for your career. If he wants to be with you, he'll agree and get over it. As for the girl, how about that assistant of yours? She's pretty hot."

"I haven't dated Aiden very long, but I can assure you that he will *not* get over it."

"Then you need to decide what you want most—your boyfriend or the most anticipated role in Hollywood." Nick was tired of fighting with Skylar. He was trying to protect the boy and help him have a great career, but this was bullshit. Skylar should be listening and not fighting him.

As angry and pissed off as Skylar was, he knew Nick had a point. Although it was getting better, Hollywood was still hung up on actors being gay and the preconceived ideas that came along with that. He had no choice if he wanted this role but to do as Nick suggested.

"Okay, fine, I'll do it. But let me talk to Aiden first, before any photos are out of Sophie and me."

Nick knew better than to disagree with Skylar. "Just make it fast. We need to get in front of this immediately. I don't know what this person has in mind for these photos."

Skylar was already walking out the door. He had to talk to Sophie and get her to agree, and then he had to talk to Aiden and convince him this was the only choice they had. Somehow he knew neither conversation was going to be a piece of cake.

CHAPTER 28

SOPHIE COULDN'T believe what she was hearing. "You want me to pretend to be your girlfriend?"

"Just until the *Checkmate* role is cast, and then we will casually 'break up,' and that will be the end of it." Even as the words came out of his mouth, Skylar knew the entire scenario was crap.

At his request Sophie had hurried over to Skylar's trailer. All the way there, she had worried about what she had done wrong, how had she made him angry. Now, hearing this story, she couldn't believe what he wanted her to do. She couldn't decide whether she was insulted or flattered. Besides, she was not an actress, so how on earth would she pull this off?

"What would I have to do?" She sat down on the sofa, her head spinning at the thought of all this might entail.

After sitting down beside her on the sofa, Skylar looked at her solemnly and tried to explain. "Just hang out with me. We'll go to a few places in Hollywood where the paparazzi hang out, and we'll make a scene so they'll take the bait. After that, it'll be easy. Once they have us in their mind as a couple, they'll follow us."

"But we have to act like we are in love?" Then it hit her. Whipping her head around, fear in her voice, she asked, "Will we have to… you know… sleep together?"

She said the latter part with such hesitation that Skylar almost laughed. "Sophie, they don't follow you into the bedroom. We may have to go to my house or your house and pretend we are staying there, but no, we don't have to actually sleep together. However, we may have to kiss. Will that be a problem for you?"

Kiss him? Now Sophie was nervous. She looked into Skylar's big blue eyes and thought that normally, no, it wouldn't be a problem. But this was her boss! How could she do this convincingly?

"I don't think so," she weakly responded.

"Good. I'll try to avoid that as much as possible." Skylar grinned to himself. *This might actually be fun.* He could practically see Sophie sweating.

"When do we start?" Sophie asked.

"As soon as I talk to Aiden. Oh, and I guess I should explain it to Kelly." Damn, who else did he have to explain his faux love affair to? Skylar stood up, turned to Sophie, and held out his hand to her. "But for now, let's practice. Walk with me to the car. We'll hold hands and smile, you know, just in case there's someone out there."

Sophie stood up, straightened her clothes, and took Skylar's hand. He was much taller than her, so it felt kind of nice and safe to be that close to him. Skylar led her out the door and toward the parking lot. They walked over to Skylar's car, and Sophie gasped in surprise as Skylar pulled her to him and kissed her right on the mouth!

Good... got that out of the way, thought Skylar, smiling to himself. He glanced at Sophie long enough to see that she was standing there with her mouth hanging open. He blew her a kiss and hopped into his car to head over to Aiden's. *Now for the tough one.*

CHAPTER 29

"HEY, BABY!" Aiden said as he opened the front door. He leaned in and hugged Skylar tight. Aiden loved the way Skylar smelled. Nuzzling his neck, he wanted nothing more than to pull Skylar inside and ravage him again in the doorway.

Smiling, he said, "What brings you by? I wasn't expecting you until tonight."

"I have something I need to talk to you about. Is now a good time?" Skylar asked as he peered around Aiden into the hallway. The last thing he needed was Ryan around to put in his two cents.

"Sure, come on in." Aiden stepped aside so Skylar could come inside. "Sorry the place is a mess, but I just got home from my shift at the fire station."

Skylar walked past him into the living room. "Hey, you've seen my place. So it's not a problem," Skylar said with a shaky laugh. He walked over and sat down on the sofa.

"Would you like a beer?" Aiden asked as he came over to rub Skylar's shoulders. Judging from the strain on his face, a good massage might relieve some of the tension he seemed to have. And besides, Aiden enjoyed helping him relax.

"No, thank you. Just need a few minutes to talk to you," Skylar responded in a nervous voice as he reached up and pulled Aiden down on the sofa next to him.

Sitting down beside Skylar, Aiden sensed something wasn't quite right. The uncertainty caused butterflies to start fluttering around in his stomach. Nervously, he asked, "What is it?"

On the drive over, Skylar had decided that he should just say it all at once, get the emotional reaction out of the way and then figure out a way to make Aiden understand. Taking a deep breath, he said, "Listen, baby, this isn't easy for me to say, so please hear me out before saying anything."

"I'm listening." Aiden could feel his own shoulders beginning to tense up. He didn't like how this conversation was starting. So far, it didn't sound very promising.

"I'll just cut to the chase and tell you straight out." Aiden sat there in silence, as Skylar blurted out, "Unbeknownst to me, someone was at my house one night, and they took photos of us."

Processing this information, Aiden looked at him with wide eyes and slowly asked, "Which night?"

"The night we had sex in front of the fireplace," Skylar responded as gently as he could, looking down at the floor. Somehow he knew this was all his fault, and he hated having to tell Aiden.

The silence was almost deafening except for the ticking of the clock over the mantel. Aiden sucked in his breath as he remembered that night—the wine, the fireplace and yes, the lovemaking. The sinking feeling he'd previously had was now turning to sheer fear. He could feel himself on the verge of freaking out. "Who the *hell* would do that?" he asked once he was able to find his voice.

"We have no idea."

Feeling the tension in his shoulders intensifying, Aiden asked, "Who is 'we'?"

"Don't worry. It was only my manager and I. Someone sent the photos to Nick's office," Skylar explained as he tried to remain calm and focused.

"Photos? As in photos of us having sex?" Aiden asked, his voice rising.

"I don't know." Seeing the panicked look from Aiden, he clarified as fast as he could, "I mean, there were photos of us kissing, and one of me without my shirt, but so far they haven't sent any of us actually having sex."

"But they must have them!" Aiden was now in full panic mode.

"I won't lie to you. I'm sure they do, but right now, I don't know if they plan to share them." Skylar sounded very calm on the outside, but inside he was a bundle of nerves. He didn't like having to tell Aiden something like this and even more, he didn't like all this drama.

"Okay… so what does all this mean?" Aiden asked hesitantly.

Skylar took a deep breath and continued, "You know that I'm up for the lead in the movie *Checkmate*, right?"

"Right," responded Aiden slowly as he started to realize where this was going.

"Well, Nick seems to think, and I somewhat agree with him, that if word gets out that I'm involved with a man... bisexual... it might end my chances of getting the part."

Aiden felt like he had been hit in the chest, the air knocked out of his body. With his heart in his throat, he looked down at his hands in his lap. Choosing his words carefully, he looked up into Skylar's eyes. "Okay, so I assume he told you to stay away from me, and you've come to tell me good-bye."

Skylar could see the pain all over Aiden's face. His eyes were so full of sadness that it made Skylar ache inside. He wanted nothing more than to reassure Aiden that it would all be okay. Reaching up to touch Aiden's cheek, he gently answered, "He did, but I told him that I won't agree to that." *And I never will.* Skylar surprised himself with this last thought that went through his head.

Skylar could almost see the relief on Aiden's face as he gave him a half smile and said, "You don't know how happy I am to hear you say that. I felt for sure you would cave."

He didn't want to hurt Aiden again, but Skylar knew he was giving him the wrong impression. Reaching out to hold Aiden's hand, he continued. "But wait. I'm not finished."

Aiden drew back his hand. "What?"

Skylar began to stumble over his words as he tried to explain. "Aiden, you have to understand how it works in this town. Hollywood is run by gay men, but when it comes to hiring gay men for their films, if you're not already an established actor, you can forget it. You'll be pigeonholed from the time you come out."

"So what, exactly, are you saying?" Aiden felt like he was on an emotional roller coaster. One second, his heart felt like it would break, the next second, he felt happiness, and now he was back to heartbreak.

Damn! I knew this wasn't going to be easy, thought Skylar as he ran his hands through his hair.

"I have to let the paparazzi see me with a woman." At Aiden's puzzled look, he continued, "Okay, not just any woman, but with my assistant, Sophie. She knows the deal, and we've already worked it out. The plan is for Sophie and me to pretend we're dating and falling in love."

Again, Aiden felt like he had been kicked. Skylar recognized the look and pointed out quickly, "But this won't affect you and me. We'll still continue to see each other privately. Nothing will change between us other than having to stay under the radar for a little while."

As he watched Aiden take a deep breath and lean back on the couch, Skylar was losing his nerve. He didn't blame Aiden at all for feeling like this, but couldn't he just "try" for his sake? Slowly Skylar began to speak again, his voice full of tenderness. "Baby, I'll still be with you. This thing between Sophie and me will be nothing more than an illusion for the press."

Aiden just kept sitting there, not saying anything.

"Say something," Skylar pleaded.

Looking over at Skylar and seeing the pleading look in his eyes, Aiden said, "There's nothing to say. It seems you have it all figured out, and all I need to do is go along with your little plan."

"Don't say it like that. It's not forever. It's only until they officially cast the movie."

"So you are telling me that as soon as it's announced you're the lead, we can be ourselves and go out in public as a couple?" Aiden looked at Skylar with hope in his eyes.

Why does this have to be so complicated? Skylar thought as he tried to explain how they could handle this situation. "Well, maybe not at first. I'll have to stage a breakup with Sophie, and then slowly we can become a little more public."

"Slowly?" Aiden said sarcastically. His eyes shone with disappointment.

"Aiden, you know that I don't allow my personal life to be out in the news." Skylar was beginning to feel the need to defend himself, and he didn't like it at all.

"But you *will* allow it when that so-called 'personal life' consists of you and Sophie—a woman."

This is really not going as planned. Frustrated, Skylar pleaded, "I just explained that to you. Can you just try this for me, just for a little while?"

"Sky, I'm not going in the closet for anyone. Not even for you," Aiden responded with conviction. This was killing him. His heart was on the verge of breaking as he said the words.

Skylar felt a deep ache inside as he listened to Aiden. But he was not going to back down. He couldn't. He really wanted this part, no matter what it took. "Who said anything about going in the closet? We just need to hide the fact that we're dating for a while, and after that, we can go back to normal."

"That's the same thing," yelled Aiden. "I would have to hide my relationship with someone I care for a lot."

Equally frustrated, Skylar pointed out the obvious. "It's not like we broadcast it now." On that note, Skylar reached out to hold Aiden's hand.

Aiden let him take his hand, but he was very confused at how he felt about all of this. "We don't broadcast it, but we don't hide it either." Then Aiden had a different realization as he remembered the dark restaurant. "Or do we?"

"*No*! It's just that I've never spoken to the press about my personal life." Skylar squeezed Aiden's hand as he looked directly into his eyes. "I don't want to be labeled and suddenly have work disappear. I've worked a long time to reach a point in my career where they actually *ask* me to audition for a role. I don't want to lose that." Skylar was running out of things to say to try to convince Aiden. The thought crossed his mind for the first time tonight, what if Aiden would not go along with this. What would he do if that happened?

Aiden tried to take all this in. He didn't pretend to understand show business or the life of an actor. Ryan had told him stories regarding how previously closeted gay actors would come out and suddenly disappear except to occasionally appear in gay roles. He wasn't ashamed of himself, and he certainly wasn't ashamed of his love—*was this love* for Skylar?—but he didn't want to cause him unnecessary problems either.

Resigned, he asked Skylar, "How long are we talking about?"

Skylar looked at him with renewed hope in his eyes, "I'm not sure, but I think no longer than a month or so. Believe me, Aiden, I can't think of any other way."

"What about the photos?" Aiden asked as he remembered the primary reason for this huge scam they were getting ready to undertake.

"I have no idea who is doing this or *why* they are doing it, but Nick thinks that if we put it out there that Sophie and I are a couple, even if they were to put the photos of us online, we can downplay the effect with this 'new' love."

"But what if they put *sex* photos out there?" Aiden was getting a headache from all this fake Hollywood bullshit.

"If they do that, I won't have any choice but to come out that I am bisexual and hope that wouldn't cost me the part," Skylar reasoned to himself more than to Aiden.

"Because being gay would be so much worse," Aiden said, shaking his head.

Skylar rubbed Aiden's hand. "I honestly don't know what kind of response that would bring, but I hope we'll never have to deal with it."

"Okay, I'll agree to try this for you…. only for you. And just in case you're not aware, I'm *not* happy about this." Aiden didn't see how this could work, but he felt he had to give it a try, for Skylar.

Relief washed over Skylar, surprising even himself. "And *that*, baby, is why you mean so much to me," Skylar said as he squeezed Aiden's hand. "I won't let it get in the way of our being together. I promise," he whispered as he leaned down to kiss Aiden.

CHAPTER 30

"HAVE YOU seen this spectacle?" Cary asked Kelly as he pointed to the television.

The evening entertainment giant was broadcasting their weekend highlights, and Kelly always tuned in to see if they discussed her or *The Executives*. Kelly glanced up from her needlepoint in time to see a photo of Skylar and the girl, Sophie, arm in arm, leaving a famous LA nightclub the previous night. Underneath the photo was the caption, "Does Hollywood have a new super couple?"

Frowning, she ordered, "Turn off that nonsense. Sky has already told me all about his 'new' relationship with his assistant. Of *all* people," she muttered.

Cary could have taken that remark regarding "the assistant" as an insult but decided to not rock the boat. Kelly had been hell on wheels since Skylar explained to her that he was now seeing Sophie and that his and Kelly's "relationship"—for lack of a better word—would have to end.

"I think it's kind of strange, the two of them falling in love. Hell, I didn't think Skylar was capable of loving anyone but himself," remarked Cary as he continued writing in Kelly's appointment book. Kelly looked up at Cary in disbelief. *Does he really believe that farce?*

"Oh *please*! You don't believe that ridiculous instant love story, do you? Really, Cary, I thought you were smarter than that."

"What? Are you saying it's not true?" Cary couldn't believe he had fallen for that.

"No, it's not true. Skylar told me that his manager wanted him to get additional press in order to push the final decision on *Checkmate*. He has the Emmy nod, but his manager thought a beautiful love story all over the news would be the perfect accent to that."

"Why not leak the news about you and Skylar?" Cary knew that would piss her off, so he waited for the inevitable burst of anger.

"Have you lost your mind, Cary? He *can't* speak about our affair because our producers would have our heads. It has to be someone else!" Kelly couldn't believe Cary would even suggest such a thing. But his question now caused her to worry that others might think there was something wrong with *her* and that was why Skylar had chosen the younger woman.

"Well, it's definitely giving him headlines. The new 'Super Couple of Hollywood' is taking precedence over his Emmy nod," Cary informed her, while backing away.

Kelly was completely riled now but, wanting to appear nonchalant, she bit out, "Frankly I couldn't care less who Skylar Murphy is sleeping with. I have more important things on my mind, such as the Emmys."

Kelly put down her needlepoint and walked over to Cary. "Since Skylar is up for best actor and I'm up for best actress, I need to focus on making that a double win for us and for *The Executives*. Even if we don't bring home the statues, we should make sure to take advantage of all the press available to us. And Skylar is already ahead of the game."

"Why do you care if Skylar wins for best actor? If I were you, I would only be concerned about myself." Cary handed her the schedule he had just completed. "As I see it, you're the leader in your category because you have the advantage of having fans from years ago who still remember you and will want to see you out in front again. So the members voting will surely get that right."

Noticing that this was the second negative thing Cary had to say about Skylar, looking him up and down with a puzzled expression, Kelly asked, "What do you have against Skylar? Has he done something to you that I should be aware of?"

Cary looked at her, his face full of annoyance and irritation. "I just don't like the guy. I think he uses and abuses people for his own purpose, and I think you're better than that."

That shocked Kelly, as she'd had no idea Cary didn't care for Skylar. "He's not as bad as all that. Yes, he can be selfish and a bit egotistical, but I've seen a different side to him that not many people see. You should give him a chance before dismissing him that way."

That will be the day, thought Cary. "Maybe I will," he responded as he walked away from Kelly to finish working in the other room.

CHAPTER 31

SOPHIE AND Skylar had just left the restaurant. Sophie felt giddy with excitement. Teasing the paparazzi had been so much fun. Much more fun than she had imagined when she had agreed to help Skylar. They had found the most popular restaurant in Hollywood and put on a display that would have won her an award had she been a real actress.

Skylar started it off by squeezing in beside her in the booth. Taking every opportunity to nuzzle her neck, kiss her cheek, and squeeze her hand, Skylar had worked it to perfection. And she had to admit, it had felt good. He was so handsome, and she didn't mind the kissing nearly as much as she had initially thought she would.

"No wonder you are up for the Best Actor Emmy," Sophie whispered as she leaned against Skylar as they waited on their car to be pulled around.

The valet showed up with Skylar's BMW, and as they walked over to it they passed several paparazzi along the way, who had been more than happy to take their photo. As Skylar opened the car door for Sophie, she giggled as she slipped into the passenger seat.

Skylar got into the driver's seat, leaned over, and brought her face around to his. After making sure a camera was right outside the window, he started kissing her passionately, until she was breathless. Finally he pulled away and whispered to her, "Yes, I'm one damn fine actor, if I do say so myself." Laughing, they drove away while the paparazzi continued to snap photos as quickly as they could.

CHAPTER 32

RYAN FINISHED serving up his famous chicken parmesan and set it down in front of Aiden. He was concerned because Aiden had been acting miserable all night long.

Tapping the table in front of Aiden's face, Ryan said, "Come on, honey, eat up. I made your favorite meal, and you know I don't do leftovers."

Aiden looked at him, "I'm not really that hungry." However, to not upset Ryan, who was only there to cheer him up, he took his fork and slowly began to pick at his dinner.

"Are you still upset over the beautiful Skylar creating paparazzi heaven all over Hollywood?"

Aiden just glared at him. "Well, I'm not exactly shouting for joy at seeing my boyfriend posing all over town, kissing some beautiful girl. How the hell do I know he won't fall for her?" Now it was out. One of the main reasons that Aiden was so hurt that he kept seeing the photos of "Hollywood's Latest Super Couple" was the fact that Skylar was bisexual. Nothing was keeping him from falling for Sophie. She was beautiful, sweet, and worshipped Sky. No, nothing was keeping that from happening.

"Sweetie, just because Skylar finds himself attracted to men and women doesn't mean he can't control his lust. And from what I've seen, his lust is only for you! That man is crazy about you!" Ryan reached out and rubbed Aiden's arm. "Now eat!" he ordered.

"You must have not noticed the gossip rags today. It was a miserable thing to see, and damn if they weren't in every magazine rack at the grocery store. I couldn't miss them!" Aiden felt like his stomach was in knots as he continued, "And not only in the magazines. Tonight, TMZ was showing photos of the two of them at the premiere of that new musical." Just the thought had his heart pounding like a jackhammer.

"Aiden... come on. He always comes back to you." Hoping to remind Aiden of this, Ryan asked, "Tell me, when was the last time you saw him?"

"I think it was Wednesday, when I was off shift. I went to his house around midnight so I could make sure no one saw me. Ryan, do you have any idea how much I hate this?" Aiden was frustrated and confused, and his insides were clenched tight.

Ryan felt bad for him. Aiden had fallen hard for the Greek god of television, not that Ryan could blame him. Skylar was so damn hot, and judging from what he had witnessed, Skylar was crazy about Aiden as well.

"I told you how this crazy Hollywood life works," Ryan reminded him. "It's all an illusion in this town. Nothing is real. Nothing is for sure. You just grab what you can while you can and hope for the best."

"Yeah, well, maybe my relationship with him isn't real either." Aiden's voice was barely above a whisper. The ache in his chest was almost unbearable. "Why did I ever start this? Why didn't I listen to myself that first day when I told him that dating him would be a bad idea?" His voice cracked as he finished his thoughts.

"Because you looked into those beautiful blue eyes and all your brains turned to mush. I know that's what happened to me when I saw him on that episode of *Royal Family* without his shirt. My brain turned to mush so fa—"

"You're not helping!" Aiden said, interrupting him.

At the same time, they heard a knock on the back door. "What the hell time is it?" Aiden asked as he got up to see who was at the door. As he opened the door, he froze.

Ryan, who was still at the kitchen table, could see Skylar standing at the door holding a bouquet of flowers as Aiden took a step back. *Oh my God*, Ryan thought, putting his hand over his heart as if to keep it inside his chest. *This is just like the movies!*

"Can I come in?" Skylar asked from the back steps, a shy smile on his face.

Aiden, who was still frozen at the sight of Skylar standing there, came to his senses and stepped aside. "Oh... sure, I'm sorry. I didn't expect to see you tonight."

Skylar walked into the kitchen, shutting the door behind him. "These are for you," he said as he handed the bouquet of pink and white camellias to Aiden.

Aiden didn't know what to think about all this, but the second he'd seen Skylar standing there, the tension in his shoulders had immediately eased.

"Thank you," Aiden said as he took the flowers and walked over to the kitchen sink to look for a vase in one of the cupboards.

"Hey, Skylar!" Ryan yelled from the kitchen table.

Skylar, who had not seen Ryan up to that point, looked over at him with a surprised glance. "Oh, hey, Ryan! How are you?"

"I'm good. Just hangin' with my boy," he said as he blew a kiss to Aiden. Sensing that the two of them needed to talk, Ryan decided he had better do the noble thing. "But actually, I'm on my way out. Just please do me a favor and make sure he eats," he said, motioning toward Aiden.

Skylar, confused, glanced at Aiden, who was placing the flowers in a vase of water. "Sure... yeah, sure, I'll take care of him."

Ryan walked over to the sink, gave Aiden a kiss on the cheek, and hugged him from behind. "Okay, honey, I'll check on you tomorrow?"

Aiden didn't turn around as he said, "That's fine... and thank you, Ryan."

"No need to thank me. That's what best friends are for." He walked over to Skylar and gave him a bear hug. "Now, *that* was for me," he said, smiling as he left out the back door.

Now that they were alone, Skylar walked up behind Aiden and started nuzzling on the back of his neck. "Baby, I've missed you so much."

Aiden, still feeling hurt and confused, pushed himself away from Skylar and walked out of the room.

What the hell? Skylar followed Aiden into the living room, where he was standing in front of the television, playing with the remote. "What's going on, Aiden?" Skylar asked as he walked up behind him. Deep inside he knew exactly what was going on, but he thought they had worked through all of this.

"How was your date?" Aiden asked as jealousy filled his heart.

"Ahhh... I had a feeling that was the problem." Skylar said. "Aiden...." Turning Aiden around to face him, he gently said, "Look at me. You know it's not real. It's all an act for the press." He cupped Aiden's face in his hands. Leaning close to softly kiss him on the lips, he could feel Aiden's lips quivering beneath his. "Oh, baby, please tell me you're not really believing any of this 'thing' with Sophie?"

"It looks pretty real to me. And do you *really* have to kiss her the way you've been kissing her?" Aiden mumbled. He hated this feeling of jealousy, but it didn't stop him from removing Skylar's hands from his face.

"I have to make it look real. You know that," pleaded Skylar.

"It definitely looks real. If I didn't know better, I would believe you were in love with her."

"Well, I'm not. You don't ever have to worry about that. Believe me." *Because I don't believe in falling in love.* "Now come here, I've missed you so much," he said as his voice cracked with desire. Reaching out for Aiden and pulling him into his arms, Skylar leaned over and took his lips with a hunger that begged to be satisfied. Pushing open Aiden's mouth, Skylar searched for his tongue while holding the back of his head as tight as he could. He plowed his fingers through Aiden's fine blond hair, his mouth completely covering Aiden's.

They both felt the intensity of their passion at once.

Aiden gave in to the feelings enveloping him and kissed Skylar back with equal enthusiasm. Reaching up to unbutton Skylar's jacket, he quickly removed it and dropped it on the floor.

Skylar let go of Aiden's mouth long enough to plant wet, hot kisses down the side of his neck, licking and nipping as he went. Their hearts pounding, sweat beginning to glisten on both their foreheads, they knew they had to get out of their clothes. Both wanted to be totally naked and touching each other. Stepping back they removed their shirts and pants. Before long both were completely nude, standing in front of each other. As they gazed at each other with a longing that neither had felt for any other person, Aiden reached out and took Skylar's hand. "I think it's time we made it to the bed."

Aiden guided Skylar into the bedroom and shut the door behind them. Skylar was slightly taller than Aiden, so when Aiden leaned up to capture Skylar's full glistening lips with his, he felt light-headed with love. *I love him. I really do love him*, he thought as he kissed Skylar deeply. With these thoughts in his head, he ran his fingers down

Skylar's chest, breathing in his scent that was creating an intoxicating effect on him.

"Aiden... babe...." Skylar was groaning with passion in between sucking on Aiden's tongue. He was kissing him with a fervor that was close to devouring him. What was going on with him? Whatever it was, he didn't care. He just wanted to be close to Aiden in every way.

After walking Aiden backward to the bed, Skylar gently helped him lie back. Leaning down Skylar continued kissing Aiden passionately. Their lips were red and swollen, and their cocks were already rock hard as they rubbed against each other, creating a fever pitch inside them both.

Not wanting to wait a moment longer, Aiden pulled his mouth away from Skylar's long enough to open the bedside table drawer and pull out lube and a condom. He was shaking as he ripped open the package and threw the paper down beside the bed. Reaching out to the top of Skylar's cock, he ran his fingers lightly over the head. It was glistening with precum, and he could tell that Skylar was about to burst. Gently, he rolled the condom down on Skylar and looked up at him with pure love in his eyes.

Skylar had been watching Aiden's every move and saw the affection radiating from his beautiful blue eyes. Normally, seeing such affection would send Skylar packing but right now he wanted nothing more than to kiss Aiden and sink deep inside him. Wanting to be as close as he could get was all Skylar had on his mind.

Suddenly Aiden reached up and flipped them over so that he was now on top.

With an amused expression, Skylar laughed and said, "So, baby... you want it this way?"

"You bet. Unless, of course, you want me inside you," Aiden whispered in his ear right before nipping him in the earlobe.

"Uh... not yet, baby. I've never bottomed for anyone before," Skylar said as he pulled Aiden's ass closer to his cock.

"There's always a first time," whispered Aiden as he sucked on Skylar's bottom lip.

"I say there's too much talking. I need you," Skylar said, trying to change the subject as he moved Aiden into position.

Aiden laughed as he said, "No worries, baby... I'll take you any way I can have you."

Aiden knelt over Skylar and reached for the lube, then put some on his fingers to prepare himself. Skylar just watched him, growing more excited by the second as Aiden's head fell back, causing his neck muscles to protrude. Skylar couldn't help but slide his knuckles down Aiden's warm chest, making Aiden's skin break out in goose bumps.

Once he had prepared himself, Aiden lifted his head and leaned down to kiss Skylar as deeply as he could. He reached behind him and positioned Skylar's cock right where he needed it to be. Then he started to sink down onto him, slowly at first as he became accustomed to his size. With every inch, Skylar fought his own instincts to thrust upward, his fingers biting into Aiden's strong thighs, until he was buried inside, as deep as he could.

When Aiden started moving, Skylar felt his breath being taken away. Moaning in between his gasps, he pleaded, "Slow down... baby... oh my God... so tight, so deep." Skylar was simply in sensory overload and didn't know where to touch first. Aiden placed both hands on his chest for better balance and started an up-and-down rhythm, his eyes squeezed shut as blond wisps of hair began falling into his face. After beginning with careful thrusts, Skylar was no longer able to hold back. "Gotta move, babe... I can't...." Panting between kisses, he moved one hand to Aiden's right hip, digging his fingers in so deep he was sure to leave small bruises, but neither man cared.

"God, yes, move... move! I need—" Aiden's words were cut off by a deep moan as Skylar thrust deep and hard, leaving Aiden breathless. Aiden sat upright and grabbed hold of Skylar's thighs behind him, changing the angle of Skylar's thrusts and hitting his magic spot.

"Oh *God*...." His head fell back as Skylar's cock continued to stroke his sweet spot, causing small electrical currents to course through his body while he tried to keep in rhythm with Skylar's strokes.

The scent of sex, clean sweat, and the remnants of cologne permeated the air while the only sounds to be heard in the room were their mutual panting breaths. Skylar was about to lose his mind. "A... Aiden, I...."

Aiden knew instinctively what Skylar needed and leaned forward to wrap his hands around the wooden headboard while lifting his ass a bit. "Go for it, babe!" With those words Aiden bit his lower lip and let the newfound feelings he had for the man beneath him completely overwhelm him. He let himself go, allowing Skylar to completely take over.

Skylar planted his feet flat on the mattress and grabbed Aiden's neck with one hand while he moved the other to Aiden's rock-hard erection. They were lost in each other's gaze as Skylar began pounding into Aiden, leaving both men breathless. Skylar was too close to be gentle, but he would be damned if he allowed himself to come before Aiden. He wanted—no, *needed*—for them to come together.

Aiden's body began to shake uncontrollably, his orgasm only seconds away as he held on to the headboard for dear life. Never in any of his previous relationships had he felt this connected, this out of control.

"I'm gonna come, babe! I can't... ohhh fuu-uuck!" His body trembled as he leaned forward to ravage Skylar's mouth with his while an orgasm of epic proportions ripped through him. The same instant, Skylar froze underneath him, his fingers leaving bruises on Aiden's smooth skin as he filled the condom deep inside his lover. Long muffled moans wafted through the room as their lovemaking came to a climactic end.

Several minutes passed, during which neither man spoke nor moved. How was it possible to be so in sync with another person? Skylar began to run his hands up Aiden's sweaty back, mapping the muscles across his shoulder blades. Right now, he couldn't think of anyone more perfect than Aiden, and he reveled in these new feelings. He would enjoy them as much as possible for as long as this, whatever they had, lasted.

CHAPTER 33

EMMA THREW the magazine at Chad, who was staring at her with amusement.

"What's your problem?" he said as he caught the flying magazine. On the front was a photo of Sophie and Skylar kissing in a car, with the headline, "Hollywood loves their new 'It' couple."

Emma looked at her so-called friend and angrily said, "*You* are my problem! I didn't follow your advice so that Skylar would simply drop Aiden and find *another* girl! He was supposed to come back to me!"

"Seriously? Did you really think he was going to come back to you?" Chad was through with all this drama and this stupid little girl.

"Yes! And I thought you believed that too." Tears were beginning to spill over as Emma sat down in defeat.

Chad did not try to hide his disgust as he said in a nasty voice, "Listen up, little girl. When are you going to realize that Skylar is out for himself, for numero uno? He's selfish, arrogant, and never… and I repeat *never* going to fall in love with a fan who throws herself at him, begs for his affection, and continues to do stupid stunts to get his attention."

Emma gasped, and realizing that Chad was not what he said he was, she started to cry. "I thought you were my friend."

"And why on earth would you think that? You were simply a means for me to get back at Skylar, and it seems to be working."

"But why? Why would you want to hurt him? He's really a good person. I'm the messed-up one." Emma continued to cry as she finally realized that the things she had done were the actions of a very mixed-up person. "I never wanted to hurt him."

"Well, I do, and I'm not finished yet. But I am finished with you!" With that, Chad got up to leave.

"But, Chad…."

Turning, he looked at Emma one final time. "By the way, my name is not Chad."

Emma sat there sobbing quietly, her dreams shattered, as he walked out of the room.

CHAPTER 34

THE ATMOSPHERE on the set of *The Executives* was high energy. The news about the Emmy nominations had created so much buzz for the show that the ratings had soared, prompting the network to order a second season. Also, today was a stellar day because the executive producer for the new movie *Illusions* was on set to check out the action. Skylar had heard the rumors that he was there to look at him for a role in the movie, but Skylar didn't want to buy into that. He felt like that movie was way out of his reach. He wanted *Checkmate* and knew he had a good shot at it, but *Illusions*—that was really big-time. It had Oscar buzz and hadn't even been shot yet.

Kelly and Skylar were over on set preparing for a scene in which Kelly's character, Martha, finds Skylar's character, Toby, in his apartment, drugged out from cocaine. The scene would be very dramatic, dealing with lots of emotion. Therefore, they needed to bring their A game.

The director was giving out directions to everyone, and the scene was ready for its first take. The AD showed Skylar his mark on the ground. Skylar took his place, his makeup perfected to show a drug addict. Kelly was out of sight, off set, waiting on her cue to come into the apartment. This was a crucial scene as it laid the groundwork for the next part of the series as the mother/son dynamic took a turn for the worse. The director yelled, "Marker," and the assistant snapped the clapboard, and then the director followed up with, "*Action.*"

Kelly knocked on the door, and upon receiving no answer, she used the key to open the door. She came rushing in and saw her son lying over on the floor in a drug-induced haze.

"Toby! Darling! Answer me!" Kelly said in character. Skylar began to moan and flail around as Kelly tried to lift him up off the floor. "Mom... stop. I'm fine... just leave me alone." Skylar loved playing these scenes. He loved playing the damaged, broken character as it gave him so much range to act with.

That was when Kelly began to shine. She and Skylar finished the scene, a roller coaster of emotion and dramatics. The two actors battled with all they had, and when the director yelled "Cut," everyone on set applauded.

Later, in the community dressing room, which had been repaired from the fire a few weeks before, Kelly and Skylar were excited beyond measure.

"Did you see the guy from *Illusions*?" Kelly asked.

"I think he left before we finished." Skylar mulled that over for a second. "Maybe he wasn't impressed."

"Oh, don't you think that! You rocked that scene, my little A-lister," Kelly said to Skylar as she hugged him.

Skylar laughed as he grabbed her face and gave her a kiss on the mouth. "No, lady, *you* rocked it!" Judging from the look on her face, Skylar immediately realized what he'd done, and in response he dropped his hands.

Immediately noticing the hand drop, Kelly raised her eyebrows and asked, "Is this thing with you and Sophie for real?"

Judging from the way Kelly was looking at him, her eyes full of lust, Skylar knew he had to tread carefully. Not for Sophie, not for Kelly, but for Aiden. Skylar had always slept with whomever he wanted, whenever he wanted. However, since he had met Aiden, he hadn't felt a desire for anyone but him.

"No, it's not, but I don't want to do anything that might jeopardize that image." After deciding that he needed to come clean, he continued, "Besides, Kelly, I have to be honest with you. I don't think we should continue sleeping together. I think it's best if we just cool it for now and see what happens down the road."

Disappointed and, judging from her facial expression, hurt, Kelly reached up and gave him a quick hug. "That's probably best for both of us. I need to get to my trailer, but I'll see you on set later."

Shit! I hurt her, he thought as he watched her walk out the door. *I seem to be hurting everyone these days. All for what? A role in a movie.* For the first time since all the pretending had started, Skylar was beginning to regret his choices.

CHAPTER 35

"DON'T WORRY. You don't have to hide it from me," Aiden said as he walked up on Paul trying to hide that he had been reading the latest *People* magazine, with Skylar and Sophie on the cover.

"Sorry, man. I was just trying to find out what they were saying about it. Since you told Ben and me about your deal with Skylar, I've wanted to follow this dog and pony show, like the sick fuck that I am."

"Come on, let's get some coffee," Aiden said, turning to walk out of the room.

Paul followed Aiden back into the kitchen, where Ben had just finished brewing a pot of coffee.

Since they were the only three there, Paul kept talking. "How long does this charade have to continue?" He reached into the cabinet and took out three coffee cups.

Aiden kept walking until he was on the other side of the table, then grabbed a chair and sat down. "Who knows? But if it doesn't end soon, I may lose my mind. For example, tonight I'm meeting him for dinner, and we have to act as if we are business partners or something."

"Is it hard for you? Having to act as if you are not involved with him in any way other than buddies?" Paul asked as he handed Aiden a cup for his coffee. Paul knew he shouldn't be asking, but he had known Aiden a long time and had never known him to behave this way.

Taking the cup, Aiden scooted his chair up under the table. "Yeah, to be honest, it really is. I mean, I've spent my entire life being myself, being upfront about who I am, and trying to stay true to myself. And along comes Skylar, and suddenly I'm hiding who I am, hiding who I'm dating, and lying to everyone I know. I hate it!"

"Then why do it?"

"I ask myself that every day. I guess I love the guy. I mean, I'm sure I love him, but sometimes I wish I had listened to myself in the beginning and stayed far away from him and his Hollywood scene."

Aiden looked so miserable as he sat there rubbing his thumb over his coffee mug that Paul felt sorry for him. "Well, just so you know, if you want to talk, I'm here to listen. Or better yet, we can go to the local bar and get shit-faced drunk. Just say the word."

"Thanks, Paul. I may take you up on that offer. And I apologize to both you and Ben. One of the things I hate the most is lying to the other guys, and because you both know the truth, it puts you in a bad position. But it's best if they just think the scam is true and that Skylar is with Sophie."

"Hey, don't you worry about us or the other guys," Ben said as he brought the pot of coffee over and started pouring it into their cups. "They don't need to know everything, and once it is over and you and your guy can date properly, then they can just think it's a new relationship."

"If it ever ends." Aiden sighed as he thought about this mess. Wondering how he had allowed himself to become involved in it, he sat back to try and enjoy his coffee.

CHAPTER 36

SKYLAR WAS waiting for Aiden at their favorite Italian restaurant at the Santa Monica Pier. It was the place they had gone on their first official date. They loved it because of its quaint old-world atmosphere. The only light was candlelight in the center of each table, accented with small lights every few feet on the wall. It was the perfect place to hide, yet feel safe and secure.

Skylar had arrived before Aiden so that it would not appear that they had come together. Upon arriving, he had ordered two glasses of wine and asked the waitress to keep the glasses filled. He didn't want the bottle on the table for fear it would look like a date. The more he had to make these types of arrangements, the more Skylar was beginning to hate this situation. He wondered if he would be able to continue it for much longer.

He waved Aiden over when he saw him come through the front door. Aiden was wearing a leather jacket that accented his broad shoulders. *He looks so fucking hot*, thought Skylar. All he wanted to do was wrap him in his arms and kiss that tempting mouth of his. He could feel his jeans getting tighter at the thought.

"Hey, babe… er… I mean Sky," Aiden said as he sat down across from Skylar. Catching himself saying an endearment was the least of his worries. He had to make it through dinner and not show the world how he really felt about this man.

Skylar smiled at the almost slipup. "Hey, Aiden." Then, lowering his voice to almost a whisper, he said, "Hey, baby." Immediately, Aiden's face lit up.

Smiling back at the beautiful man in front of him, Aiden asked, "How did your day go? Wasn't today the day you filmed that scene with Kelly? The one you were so concerned about?"

"Yes, and it went better than I expected. At least the scene did. I was hoping the producer for that movie *Illusions* would stay around, but he left. Guess it wasn't meant to be."

"What producer? What movie? *Illusions*?" Aiden was confused. He really needed to brush up on all that was Hollywood.

"It's a huge blockbuster film that all the studios wanted because the screenplay is said to be phenomenal. But, really, Aiden... it's way out of my league. However, it was nice that he came by to check out our scenes today."

"I can't imagine that anything is out of your league," Aiden teased.

"Yeah, you and Kelly... my two biggest fans," Skylar said as he toasted the air with his wine glass. At Aiden's mock "shocked" face, Skylar continued. "Seriously, Kelly even calls me her little 'A-lister.'"

"At the risk of sounding stupid, what's an 'A-lister'?"

"It's a name given to celebrities who are the top of the food chain. The moneymakers, the ones that sell movies on their name alone, like Brad Pitt or Tom Cruise."

"Ah... okay, got ya."

"Anyway, long story short, I was worried that we would have to stay late into the night, but as you see, we finished in two takes, and here I am."

No one was happier than Aiden that Skylar had finished his big scene in time. Aiden himself had just left the firehouse. He had been counting down the time until shift change, hoping no call would come in and make him miss this date with his man. His man. Aiden loved the sound of that. Realizing that he was sitting there with a goofy grin on his face, he coughed and made a straight face.

As the waiter came up and took their dinner order, it was all they could do not to touch hands, whisper to each other—anything that would put them in a more intimate setting.

Skylar, with a mischievous look on his face, took out his notepad and a pen. Smiling as he wrote, he slipped the note to Aiden.

Aiden picked up the paper and read it. *You look incredibly hot tonight. I want you.* This both surprised and turned Aiden on. Taking out his own pen, Aiden thought, *Two can play at that game.* After writing, *Meet me in the men's room. Two minutes,* he slipped the note over to Skylar.

As Skylar read the note, grinned, and placed it in his pocket, Aiden excused himself to the men's room. Skylar was beyond excited.

He didn't understand this deep affection he felt for Aiden, but he hoped it would last for a long time. Trying to relax he counted down the seconds until he could excuse himself as well.

As he sipped his wine, anxiously anticipating meeting his lover in the restroom, he jumped when he heard the screams from the kitchen. He looked up to see the hostess and several workers from the kitchen running out into the dining room. "Everyone, please get to the exit—there's a fire in the kitchen." The hostess was going table to table, trying to maintain control, while at the same time trying to get everyone out of the restaurant.

Skylar's only concern was Aiden. The fire was in the same direction that he had seen Aiden walking. He jumped out of his seat and started walking back toward the men's room. The hostess grabbed him and said, "Please, sir, you're going in the wrong direction. You have to leave the building."

"My friend has gone to the men's room. I won't leave without him." He pushed by her and ran back in the direction of the men's room. "Aiden!" he yelled as he opened door after door. The smoke was so intense he couldn't see very clearly. "Aiden! Where are you?" he yelled in panic.

"Sky." Skylar heard Aiden's voice as he walked by one door. "Sky... I'm in here."

Skylar pushed open the door and saw Aiden lying on the floor in front of the sink. He was holding his head, and Skylar could see that it was bleeding. Skylar ran over to him as Aiden tried to sit up. He started to fall backward, and Skylar grabbed him before he hit the ground again.

"Someone walked in behind me and hit me over the head with something," Aiden tried to explain.

"Shushhh... shushhh, baby... I have to get you out of here. There's a fire in the kitchen, and the whole place could go up in flames." Skylar put his arm around Aiden, supporting him, and led him out of the men's room and back in the direction that he'd come. The smoke was intensifying, and when they reached the dining room, Skylar could barely see which direction to go.

"Get down on the floor, Sky. We can crawl toward the exit sign," Aiden ordered as he pointed toward the bright red exit sign. His senses were coming back to him, and his firefighting skills were instinctively coming out. They could hear the sirens outside as the firefighters arrived. Slowly they crawled together toward the exit sign until they hit a door. After shoving it open, they could see that they were outside. Both men got up, and with Skylar helping Aiden, they ran out into the parking lot.

They sat on the ground, far away from the fire, and watched as the firefighters began to fight the fire.

"Are you guys okay?" an EMS worker asked as she came over to them.

"He's not," Skylar said, pointing to Aiden. "Someone hit him over the head while he was in the men's room. We think it happened just before the fire broke out."

The EMS worker crouched down beside Aiden. "Sir, can you look at me?"

Aiden looked up at her, and she used her light to look into his eyes.

"Sir, I need you to follow the light for me."

Aiden followed the light with his eyes. The dizziness was slowly going away, and he didn't feel nauseated, which he knew were signs of a concussion.

"I think I'm fine. I'm a firefighter, so I know the symptoms to look for."

The EMS worker looked up at him in surprise but had to agree with him from her initial assessment. "Do you want to be transported to the hospital?"

"No, really, I'm fine. Please go and make sure the other people are okay," Aiden suggested as he waved her off in the general direction of the others patrons who were still outside sitting or lying on the ground.

"You, sir," she, said talking to Skylar. "Are you with him?" Skylar nodded, and she continued, "Please see that he gets home safely. And someone needs to stay with him tonight. If he doesn't want to go to the ER, then make sure someone wakes him every two hours. We don't want to overlook a concussion." Looking at Aiden's head wound, she said, "I think this is a superficial cut, but it will need a bandage. I can fix you up if you will walk over to the truck with me."

"Ma'am, really, I'm fine. I do this for a living. I can talk my friend through whatever is needed as soon as I get home. I just want to leave. Unless you need my help with the other people here who may be hurt."

Skylar just listened with admiration as Aiden again put others before himself. But Skylar's concern was not the others; they had the EMS and the fire department here. Aiden was his concern and he wanted to get him out of this place. "Aiden, come on. I'll take you home."

"I think that's a good idea," said the EMS worker.

Aiden had to agree. Skylar stood up, then leaned down and grabbed Aiden's hand to help him off the ground. Slowly they walked to Skylar's car.

"What about my car?" Aiden asked as he looked around to where his car was parked.

"I'll have Sophie take care of it tomorrow," Skylar responded as he opened the door for Aiden. "Let me take you home and take care of you."

Aiden wanted nothing more, and the two men got into Skylar's car and drove toward Aiden's house.

When they arrived, Skylar parked and started to get out of the car. Aiden grabbed his arm to stop him. "Are you sure you should be seen bringing me into my house? We've already risked people seeing us together enough tonight."

"I don't give a damn about that right now. You're hurt, and I'm going to make sure you're going to be okay." He went around to Aiden's side of the car and helped him out and up the steps into his house.

"Maybe you can call Ryan to come over and stay with me tonight."

"I will not call Ryan, at least not to stay with you. I'm going to be here with you tonight. I'll leave early in the morning, because I do have an early call, and I need to study my lines. That is, *if* you are okay," Skylar said with conviction. He wasn't about to go anywhere until he knew Aiden was okay.

Aiden just smiled as Skylar helped him back to the bedroom.

After helping him lie down on the bed, Skylar went into the bathroom to look for bandages and ointment.

"They're in the closet over to the side. Top shelf," yelled Aiden from the other room.

Skylar found the supplies and came back into the bedroom. "Here, let's clean that head wound." After placing a warm wet washcloth on the wound, Skylar took special care to clean it and take a good look at it. "It's just a small cut, but I'm still going to stay here with you tonight. I don't want to leave you here alone and find out later you had a concussion."

Once Skylar finished taking care of Aiden's wound, he leaned over and gave him a quick kiss on the forehead. "Okay, baby, time to get you out of these clothes and let you rest."

"Please stop treating me like I'm going to break," protested Aiden. "I'm fine, I keep telling you that." He wasn't used to this type of pampering, but deep down he had to admit he kind of liked it.

Skylar looked at him, cupped his face, and leaned in to kiss him lightly. "Can you just bear with me a few minutes more? I'm enjoying myself. Who knows when I might have to play a paramedic," he said, trying to add some comedy to the stressful situation.

"Okay, Mr. Actor... have at it."

Removing Aiden's clothes was always fun, but not nearly as fun as the last time. Skylar remembered kissing and stroking as he removed all Aiden's clothes and threw them in the hamper. After finding a clean T-shirt in his drawer, Skylar helped Aiden put it on. Aiden raised his arms so that Skylar could easily slide his shirt down. Once Aiden was ready, Skylar helped him under the covers before going over to remove his own clothes.

From the bed, Aiden watched as Skylar stripped down to his underwear.

Skylar climbed into bed and snuggled up to Aiden, kissing his shoulder. "What a night. I can't believe that happened again. What is it with me and fires?"

"I don't know, but there is definitely something going on, and I'm going to figure out what it is," Aiden promised.

"Not tonight, you're not," Skylar said as he leaned over and kissed Aiden, then wrapped him in his arms.

CHAPTER 37

"YOU NEED to make this quick—I have an appointment at three." Nick was frustrated that his afternoon was being interrupted by the young girl sitting in his office. He had a million things to do and this was not on his list. She had only been given access because she had insisted on seeing him, telling his secretary that it was an urgent matter relating to Skylar. *Well, it damn well better be urgent.*

"What did you say your name was again?" he asked the young girl.

"Emma Langley," she responded timidly as she sat clutching the brown envelope. After Chad had left her in tears at the bar, she thought a lot about what she had done, and she didn't want Chad to be able to use her photos to hurt Skylar any longer. Therefore, Emma had decided she needed to come clean. Since she was terrified to face Skylar, she thought the next best thing would be to bring the photos to his manager's office.

"What can I do for you, Emma Langley?" Nick asked as he looked at her from his side of the desk. He was curious to know what she had in the envelope that she seemed to be holding in a death grip.

After taking a deep breath, her heart in her throat, Emma confessed, "I'm the person who sent you photos of Skylar Murphy and his friend Aiden... the ones at Skylar's house."

Nick was surprised. He'd never expected the person stalking Skylar would be this seemingly innocent girl. He looked at her with a menacing glare. "You do realize that by telling me this, you just opened yourself to a lawsuit?"

Emma started trembling. Apparently she hadn't thought of that possibility. Shakily, she continued with her story. "To be honest, it wasn't my idea to send them. I had someone, who I thought was a friend, giving me advice. He told me that I should send the photos to you so that Skylar would have to break up with Aiden."

"Just who was this friend? And why did he care who Skylar is seeing?"

"He said his name was Chad, but that wasn't really his name."

"What did this Chad look like?"

"He's a little taller than me, dark hair, glasses. He said he knew Skylar."

That could be anyone, thought Nick. "Okay, that's a pretty vague description. However, the fact remains that you're the one who mailed the photos. What did you intend to accomplish by doing that?"

"Because, like I said, I thought it would make Skylar stop seeing Aiden and he would come back to me. What I didn't realize is that Chad just wanted to hurt Skylar."

She now had Nick's full attention. "Hurt Skylar how?"

"He didn't say. He just said that Skylar was spoiled, arrogant, and always got what he wanted, and he wanted to hurt him."

"Can you get in touch with Chad now?"

"No, I tried last night. His number was disconnected." Emma looked down at her feet. "It was probably a temporary number anyway."

Sensing that this could have something to do with the fires, Nick carefully watched Emma's face as he asked, "Do you know anything about the fires that have been happening?"

Emma looked totally confused. "What fires?"

Judging from the blank look on her face, she didn't know anything about the fires. However, he couldn't shake the idea that there was a connection between the fires, the photos, and this Chad guy. Not wanting to discuss this any longer with Emma, he decided to let it go for the moment. "For now, why don't you give me *all* the photos and delete them from your cell phone, and I won't say any more about this."

"Really? You would do that for me?" Emma couldn't believe he wasn't calling the police.

"Not for you, but for Skylar. I don't want this to go any further. Give me the photos, and let me handle it."

"Okay," she said as she handed him the envelope full of photos. "There are no more on my cell phone. I deleted them last night."

"What about this Chad? Does he have access to any of these photos?"

"No. I just showed him the photos on my phone. He didn't get any copies."

"Good." He got up and walked over to Emma, then took her arm. "Thank you for bringing these by to me. I'll make sure they're destroyed. But again, please don't mention any of this to Skylar. I'll tell him that everything has been taken care of." He led her to the door. "How can I get in touch with you if I need to talk to you?"

Emma hesitated. She just wanted to go away and forget all about this and Skylar. She had been hurt enough and wanted it gone. "Why do you need my number?"

"I may need to call you to identify this Chad person, if we can find him. I think he has something to do with the fires that have been happening around Skylar."

"Oh my God! I didn't know he was capable of something like that. Please don't let him hurt Skylar." Strangely enough, even though Skylar had hurt her, she still loved him and wanted to protect him.

"I'll take care of it. Here, write your number down," Nick said as he went back to his desk and grabbed a pen and paper.

Quickly, Emma wrote down her cell number and handed it back to Nick. "I'm so sorry for my part in this. Please believe me when I say that I would never hurt Skylar."

"I do believe that or else I wouldn't be letting you walk out of here. Now, Emma, I have to get to my appointment. Thank you for bringing those by," Nick said, pointing to the photos on his desk.

"Okay, and… thank you," Emma said as she left the office.

Nick walked over and picked up the envelope. He opened it and began to glance through the photos. Seeing there were indeed sex photos, he decided he would keep quiet for now. The minute Skylar knew Nick held all the photos, he would feel safe and want to stop the charade with Sophie. Nick couldn't let that happen. He knew that this love affair—real or not—was helping with Skylar's image. *He can keep dating his assistant until I decide it's okay to stop it.* With that thought he placed the photos back into the envelope and then walked over and locked them in his safe.

CHAPTER 38

IT HAD been a week since the fire at Giovanni's, the Italian restaurant, and Aiden still had not heard any word on the cause of the fire. Paul had told him that another metal piece had been left at the scene, this one with the letter *I* on it. This confused Aiden because he had been so sure that it had to do with Skylar. But there was no *I* in Skylar. Regardless, he had to figure out who this arsonist was and what game they were playing. Most of all, he wanted to rule out that the fires were related to Skylar.

He was driving down Hollywood Boulevard, heading to work the premiere after-party for the new blockbuster scheduled to come out this weekend.

Looking at his cell phone, lying on the seat beside him, Aiden realized he had not spoken to Skylar all day. Now that he thought about it, he hadn't spoken to Skylar since yesterday afternoon. Granted, he had been at the firehouse until this morning, but normally Skylar called at least once a day. *Maybe he's just busy.*

After pulling into the venue parking lot, Aiden wheeled into a parking space near the back and headed inside. Once inside, he found Jamie, and she gave him instructions for the night. As the party attendees started filing into the ballroom, Aiden loaded his tray with glasses of champagne and started making his rounds.

He was passing a group of young actors, whom he recognized as the main stars of the movie being premiered, when he heard the familiar voice to his right. He glanced over and saw Skylar and Sophie standing in a small group. They were speaking to an older gentleman Aiden didn't recognize. Aiden stopped dead in his tracks and quickly turned away. He was struggling to not freak out. *Damn, damn, damn! What the hell do I do now?* He looked around for a quick exit. He'd had no idea that Skylar was going to be here, and he wasn't sure how to handle the situation. They hadn't discussed how they would behave if they were to run into each other at an event. Aiden's heart was pounding as he grew more anxious. *The least he could have done is warn me!* Aiden was torn—should he speak to him or dart behind the tall guy standing over to his left and work the other side of the room?

His dilemma was solved when the older gentleman standing with Skylar motioned for him to bring over the tray.

"Here, sir, could we please have some champagne? I want to toast this beautiful young couple."

Those words felt like a punch in the gut. Struggling to keep a smile on his face, Aiden had no choice but to walk over to the group. Just as he reached them, Skylar turned around. Skylar's startled look at seeing Aiden standing there almost gave him away.

Quickly catching himself, Skylar took two glasses off Aiden's tray and handed one to Sophie and then one to the older gentleman. Turning completely around to face Aiden, so his face was out of sight of the gentleman, Skylar gave Aiden a look that said "I'm sorry" as he took his glass.

Not knowing what to do, Aiden bowed his head in dismissal and started to walk away. As he was leaving, he heard the older gentleman toasting, "Here's to the brightest couple to hit Hollywood. May your days together be full of joy and happiness." Then he added, "And to Skylar. I look forward to working with you on *Checkmate*." Aiden heard the clinking of glasses as he walked as quickly as he could in the other direction.

The rest of the night went by in a blur. Every so often he would look over the crowded room in search of Skylar. Each time, he would feel a jab in his heart as he watched Skylar play his role as a man in love with a beautiful girl. He knew this particular producer was the one Skylar had to keep up this pretense for, but that didn't ease his pain or soften the blow at watching Skylar with Sophie. He wanted to throw his tray when he saw Skylar stroke Sophie's hair and lightly touch Sophie's waist as he led her from one group to the next. Aiden continued to work the room in a daze. He felt as if his life was a fucking television movie of the week. No, you couldn't make this crap up.

The night seemed endless. The more he watched Skylar with Sophie, the more Aiden began to feel like a fool. He kept thinking the same thing over and over. *Look at me, hiding behind my tray of champagne while my boyfriend pretends to be in love with his assistant.*

How the hell did I allow this to happen? He needed to grow a pair and stop letting Skylar do this to him.

About that time he saw Skylar walking toward him, motioning toward the back entrance of the venue. Aiden took his tray back to the kitchen and told Jamie that he was taking a quick break.

As Aiden walked out the back entrance, he found himself in a dark, deserted alley. After his eyes became accustomed to the dark, he saw Skylar over to the side, standing alone. Walking over, he heard Skylar say, "Follow me." They both walked down the alley until they were a safe distance away from the party. It was a cold night, and there was no one around. The light from the streetlamp across the road created just enough light that they could walk without tripping over the small rocks that lined the alley.

When he reached a particularly dark spot, Skylar stopped and turned around. The second Aiden was within range, Skylar grabbed him and kissed him, his lips warm and searching. "Hey, baby," he whispered in Aiden's ear as he kissed his earlobe.

Aiden, who had seen enough acting tonight, just pulled away. "Really, Sky, I'm in no mood for this."

Skylar let go of him and stepped back. As he looked at Aiden, he saw the look of betrayal. Realizing Aiden truly was in no mood for games, he said, "I know you're upset at seeing me with Sophie, but how was I supposed to know you would be here tonight?"

"I'm working! Besides, if you had bothered to call today, I could have told you. The better question is, why are *you* here?" Aiden hated this intense feeling of jealousy. This was not like him and it had to stop! Why was he allowing this to happen? *Because you love the idiot, that's why.*

"The producers for this movie will also be producing *Checkmate*. They invited me."

"And you just had to come and bring her," Aiden said, motioning toward the building where Sophie waited for Skylar.

"I figured it would be a great place for Sophie and me to be seen together." Pulling Aiden over to him, he whispered, "Babe, you know how this works."

As Aiden jerked away from him for the second time, Skylar found himself becoming very frustrated. He was really tired of all the dramatics. How many times did he have to explain to Aiden why he was doing this? It was times like these that Skylar remembered why he liked to keep his sex life simple.

"Unfortunately, I do. And Skylar, I'm over it." As Aiden said the words, the thought hit him that he truly was over all of this. With an ache in his chest, Aiden continued, "I'm so tired of seeing you with her on magazines, on television, every fucking place I look. Damn! I can't even go to work without having to watch the two of you parade around like some fucking super couple of the year!"

"Aiden...."

"Don't! I'm done with all of this. Either you drop this charade, or we need to end this... this... whatever it is we have." Turning around so Skylar wouldn't see the tears forming in his eyes, Aiden realized how upset he was. He hadn't spent his entire life being his own person to have it yanked away by Skylar.

"You don't mean that." Skylar was upset. *Why is he being like this?* Running his fingers through his hair, Skylar was trying to think of what to say or do when he heard the pain in Aiden's voice.

"I do mean it. I don't want to mean it, but I do." Aiden could hear his voice cracking as he fought the impulse to take back everything he said.

Skylar grabbed Aiden by the shoulders and turned him around to face him.

"Please think about what you are doing. Why do you want to ruin what we have? It's almost over. Just give it a few more weeks." Skylar didn't know what to do. Part of him was pissed off and tired of fighting over this, but another part of him really didn't want to let Aiden go.

"What am I ruining, Skylar? We have to hide our relationship from the world, if you can even call it a relationship. I'm lying to all of my friends every day, and now I get to watch you mingle and cozy up with a hot girl all night. The *only* thing I'm ruining is my self-respect."

"Come on, don't you think you're overreacting a little?" Skylar asked as he tried to reason with Aiden. "Let's just talk about this tomorrow."

But at this point, Aiden had made his decision. He wasn't going back to hiding from everyone, keeping their relationship a secret. He had to make a stand, and he was making it now. Tears filled his eyes as he looked at Skylar. He fought the desire to reach up and push back the hair falling so gently on Skylar's face. "No, I don't want to talk about it tomorrow. If you care about me, you'll stop this charade of yours, and tell me that you want to be with me, and accept that I love you."

Love? *Who said anything about* love? Suddenly the frustration was gone, and the only thing Skylar could feel was fear. It gripped his heart and sent tingles down his arms and legs. *Love?* Dropping his hands away from Aiden's shoulders, Skylar said with a slight warning, "Aiden… I think we really need to stop this conversation before we both say something we can't take back."

"What, Sky? Did the word 'love' freak you out?" He took Skylar's face in his hand. "Look at me," he said forcefully. Then, dropping his voice to a whisper, he continued, "I love you. Plain and simple. I love you."

Skylar slowly removed Aiden's hand as the fear gripped his heart even more. He could swear he was seeing darkness closing over his eyes. He had never felt fear like he was feeling it right now. *Why did he have to mention love and ruin everything? How am I going to salvage this?* Speaking in a voice barely above a whisper, Skylar looked at Aiden and said, "Baby, we have fun. I like you a lot… a *lot*. But I don't know if I'm capable of loving someone. I've never been in love. Shit, I've never told someone I love them, and honestly, I'm not even sure I could say the words."

Aiden could feel his heart breaking. From the minute he had met Skylar, he had feared the day this would come. His eyes brimmed with tears, and he felt like there was a hole in his chest as he told Skylar, "If that's how you truly feel, then we really do need to go our separate ways. Because I'm in love with you, and if this… this thing we have is going to end, then it needs to end now."

Skylar, still freaked out by the declaration of love from Aiden, reached out and ran his hand down Aiden's face. "I'm so sorry, baby… so sorry." As he looked into Aiden's blue eyes, he could see the tears causing his beautiful eyes to glisten. Skylar felt tightness in his chest, a feeling he was not familiar with. Maybe he had gotten too close to Aiden? He hadn't intended to. The last thing he wanted was to be attached to someone. That never worked out. So maybe it was better if he just bowed out now and moved on.

With that realization Skylar leaned down and gently kissed Aiden on the lips. Then he straightened up, took a deep breath, and walked back toward the building.

Aiden, devastated, stood there with his heart completely shattered.

CHAPTER 39

"YOU NEED to snap out of this," Nick said as he sat on the edge of the counter and watched a depressed Skylar moping around his trailer. "You have everything to be excited about. The Emmys are in a couple of weeks, and you're favored to win. That win alone will boost your asking price up a few hundred grand. What's not to be happy about?"

"I would never expect you to understand. Hell, I don't understand it myself," Skylar responded with a shrug as he walked over and flopped down on the sofa. All he really wanted to do was go home and be alone in his thoughts. He had felt lower than dirt ever since the night he and Aiden broke up. He didn't understand why this breakup was troubling him so much. In the past, he had always felt bad for a day or so and then moved on. But that was not happening. He struggled to get a grip on himself. Running his hands through his hair, he sighed loudly. Nick was right; he needed to snap out of this self-imposed depression he was dealing with. He had a lot of things going for him, and he needed to recognize that.

They were both startled when there was a knock at the trailer door. Skylar slowly got off the sofa and walked over to open the door. "Oh, hey, Sophie," he said, leaving her standing outside. As he immediately lay back down on the sofa, feeling lost, he thought, *Okay, so not off to a great start.*

Sophie stepped inside. Feeling the presence of someone else, she glanced over and saw Nick. Not recognizing him, and feeling as if she was intruding on something, she quickly said, "Oh, I'm sorry. I didn't know you had company."

"I'm not company, darling," Nick said as he walked up to her. "I'm his manager, Nick." Smiling broadly, he reached out and took Sophie's hand. "It's about time I met the love of Skylar's life."

Sophie was immediately confused, and Skylar couldn't hide the disapproving look on his face. Looking back and forth at Skylar and Nick, she stammered to Nick, "Uh… you do know it's not real, right?"

"Of course I do, honey. I was just teasing you." Nick smirked under his smile.

Still confused and not sure how to respond, Sophie chose to ignore the situation and turned to Skylar. "You're wanted on set in five."

"Fine, I'll be there." Skylar didn't want to go anywhere. Not if it meant moving from his sofa. His body felt weighted down, as if he had worked out at the gym for hours. He didn't want to close his eyes because all he saw was the look on Aiden's face when he'd kissed him and then walked away. *Why did I do that? Why can't Aiden understand? Why did he say he loved me?*

Sophie, noticing that Skylar seemed lost in his thoughts, asked him, "Are you okay?" As he looked at her with such sadness in his eyes, Sophie became concerned. She knew something had happened between him and Aiden. He had been behaving very strangely since the night of the movie party. He had gone outside, and upon coming back in, he immediately wanted to leave. He had grabbed her hand and said, "We have to go." After picking up their coats, they'd just run out the door, without a good-bye to anyone. He had been so upset she hadn't asked any questions that night, but now he seemed even worse. He just moped around, not talking to anyone, and even on their "outings," he didn't seem himself. He barely smiled for the cameras and didn't seem to care if they were there or not.

"He's fine. Aren't you, Sky?" Nick stepped up and responded before Skylar could answer. Skylar glared at him. Nick was really beginning to tick him off. First of all, *no one* called him Sky but Aiden, and if Nick made one more comment, his ass was going out the door. Besides, it was his fault he and Aiden had broken up. Well, Nick and all his scheming.

"If you would do your job and find out who sent those photos so that Sophie and I could stop this charade, I *would* be fine!" Skylar growled at Nick.

Nick bristled. "I'm trying, okay? Do I look like the flippin' FBI?" *If you would be more careful who you screwed, we wouldn't even have an issue.* Oh, that was on the tip of Nick's tongue, but he knew better than to say it out loud. Besides, he still had an ace up his sleeve. He was still keeping it to himself about Emma, the photos, and this Chad guy. He wanted to get *Checkmate* in the bag, and then he would deal with Skylar.

Therefore, he steered the conversation in a different direction. "They haven't sent any more photos, so I think my idea is working quite nicely. Just don't go fucking it up because your feelings are hurt. Besides, you always get over it. Why are you so touchy about this one?"

I wish I knew. Skylar looked at Nick with ice in his eyes. He didn't like Aiden being referred to as "this one." "Listen, you need to remember you work for me." Both men stood staring at each other, as if in a standoff.

Nick, realizing he had pushed Skylar a little too far, tried to rein back in his money tree. "You're right. I'm sorry. But listen, we only have a few more days. I have it on good authority that the producers of *Checkmate* are going to offer you the part. I think they're waiting to see how you do at the Emmys."

"Honestly, Nick, I'm really over *Checkmate* and their rules and their expectations. I'd better get this fucking role after all I've given up for it." *Given up? Did I just say that?* Then, feeling a pain in his chest, he thought, *Damn, I miss Aiden.*

"Like I said, just a few more days. I don't think we need to worry about the photos anymore, but let's keep up the affair until casting is announced. Then, slowly, we'll stage a breakup, and then you'll be free to go back to your fireman, and Sophie can get back to her job."

Skylar looked at Nick and hoped like hell that Nick knew what he was talking about. Then, sadly, he remembered. *My fireman is gone.*

CHAPTER 40

RYAN FELT like his sole purpose in life these days was to cheer up Aiden. He had spent the past week trying to find anything to put a smile on that boy's face. Nothing was working.

"You can hit me if you want," Ryan said as he plopped down on the bed beside Aiden, who was laid out in the middle of bed, staring at the ceiling.

"You're not the one I want to hit," Aiden responded with a slight edge to his tone.

Shaking his head Ryan continued, "I *am* the one who convinced you to go out with the boy wonder. If I hadn't gone on and on about those rock-hard abs, those crystal blue eyes, those plump, moist lips...."

Seriously, Ryan, shut up. Without moving his eyes from the ceiling, he said, "Ryan, please. I don't want to think about any of those things right now." As he rolled over on his side, Ryan cuddled up behind him and hugged him.

Aiden realized it had been his choice to break up with Skylar. He had been the one who pushed Skylar to walk away, but now that he was really gone, Aiden felt as if his heart had shattered, and his life was over. "Maybe I was wrong to break it off with him. Maybe I shouldn't have given him that ultimatum," he whispered for the tenth time today.

Snuggling up closer to Aiden, Ryan tried to comfort him. "No, sweetie, you did exactly the right thing. If he wasn't going to let you any closer and it was going to end eventually, it's better you cut your losses now."

"I know you're right, but it doesn't feel like it."

"It'll take a while. You know the drill," Ryan reassured him.

"Yeah... I know."

Suddenly Aiden pushed away from Ryan and jumped up off the bed. He walked over to the dresser and pulled out a manila folder. There were newspaper clippings and official-looking documents inside.

"What's that?" asked Ryan.

"This is all the information on the three fires that have occurred around Skylar and me."

Ryan couldn't believe it. Aiden couldn't stop thinking about Skylar for half a second. This was going to be one *long* road. "Uh, can I ask why on earth you are looking at that mess now?"

"I can't think about loving Skylar but I *can* think about helping him. I *know* there's a connection between him and those fires. I just have to find it." He sat back down on the bed and emptied the folder on the bed between them.

"Okay, so let's start digging," said Ryan as he gave in to Aiden's newest way of handling the breakup. They shuffled through newspaper clippings, looking for anything that might stand out.

Aiden reached around to the nightstand for a pen and paper. After finding both, he turned back to Ryan. "I still think it has something to do with those letters that the arsonist leaves at the scene. I just can't figure out what it is."

"Okay, so let's start with that," suggested Ryan. "What are the letters?"

"Let's see." Aiden started scanning each newspaper article. "Here, you write them down as I call out the letters," he said, handing Ryan the pen and paper.

Ryan took the pen and paper and waited patiently while Aiden scoured the articles.

Aiden said, "Here is the first one; it's an *A* as in apple."

"Or *A* as in ass…. Oh look, we are talking about Skylar," Ryan teased.

Aiden looked at Ryan with an amused expression. "Are you going to help or are you going to throw out insults all night?"

"Is that a half grin I see there?" Ryan was excited now. He had made Aiden smile. Wanting to keep things moving in a positive direction, he said, "Okay, I'm here to help, so let's go." Ryan jotted something down on his paper. "*A*… got it."

Aiden kept scanning articles. They all stated the same thing: gas and rags were used to start the fire, with the exception of the one in the community dressing room. In that case, the arsonist had decided to just use the curtains that were already there.

"Here's an *I*," exclaimed Aiden as he found the letter from the Italian Restaurant.

"So, we have an *A* and an *I*. Those are two vowels. It could say anything in the world," grumbled Ryan.

"Just hold on. I know there was one more," said Aiden as he went through the pile of articles again.

"Why do I feel like I am playing the arsonist version of *Wheel of Fortune*? Except instead of winning the big prize, we'll be saving Skylar's pretty ass." Ryan liked helping Aiden, but this was a bit far-fetched to him. Besides, he would rather be helping Aiden get over his heartbreak by watching hot pretty gay boys on television. And *not* that certain blue-eyed sex god.

"Because you *are* quite possibly saving his ass. So pretend I'm Pat Sajak and get to work," ordered Aiden.

Retrieving the last article regarding the community dressing room, Aiden said, "Okay, write down an *L*."

"Finally we have a consonant. Let the games begin." If Ryan had to play this silly game, he might as well enjoy it.

Aiden looked at the letters and started guessing. "*A, I, L*…. All in LA? *L, I, A*? What the fuck? This makes no sense at all. It spells nothing." This was so frustrating, but Aiden knew it had something to do with Skylar. It had to.

"Try this," suggested Ryan. "*I, L, A*." Both men thought for a second. Ryan continued, "Is that some kind of terrorist agency that sets fires to kill off hot actors?"

"Not that I've ever heard of." Aiden took out another pen from the nightstand and proceeded to write his own arrangement of the letters. Mumbling to himself, he tried to make heads or tails of the three initials.

Ryan took his pen and wrote slowly. "How about we put them in order of the fires? *A*… what was the second fire? The dressing room?"

"Yes."

"So we have *A, L, I*. Is there an Allison in the picture?" Ryan asked as he continued to play with the letters.

"There is a Sophie, but no Allison… well, not that I know of," replied Aiden.

"Maybe *A* is a word and the *L* and *I* are another word? *A* can stand alone, you know." Ryan was grasping at straws, but somehow something had to make sense.

Aiden sat on the bed, twirling around his pen, and he thought out loud. "*A. L. I.*… wait! Oh my *God*! I know what it spells!" shouted Aiden.

CHAPTER 41

SKYLAR THREW himself onto his sofa the minute he was in his house. This had to have been the longest day of his life. He'd had to deal with Nick all afternoon and then film the show until late in the evening. However, the day had really hit bottom when he and Sophie had to attend a jewelry store opening on Rodeo Drive. Inwardly he groaned at the thought. When would he ever be able to say no to those types of events?

However he and Sophie had shown up, arm in arm. They'd given their usual show of PDA until the manager of the store created chaos by suggesting that Skylar buy Sophie a ring. It would not have been such a big deal except for the fact that a few dozen photographers were standing there waiting for his response.

Thankfully Sophie had been on her A game and saved the day. She politely informed the reporters that when the love of her life finally decided to buy her a ring, it certainly would not be in front of all of them. That moment had to be saved for a special night, with flowers and candles. The photographers loved it. They got their romantic story, and Skylar was off the hook.

And now, he was officially off for a few days. It was the weekend, and he had no plans to do anything except lie on the couch and drown in his misery. And miserable was exactly how he felt.

He couldn't remember a time when he had felt so lonely. As he looked over at the fireplace, he could almost see Aiden lying there with no clothes on. Skylar could still taste the sweat on Aiden's abs as he had licked down his taut, rippling stomach. Damn! Just thinking of Aiden that way gave him a warm feeling in his gut. Or maybe that was his groin. Whatever it was touching, it worked for him. Skylar sighed. His heart hurt as he realized how much he really missed him.

Skylar heard the noise at the same time he saw the shadow. He jumped off the couch in time to feel something hit him in the top of his shoulder, glancing off the back of his head. The force was enough to knock him to his knees. A hot pain shot through the back of his head as he reached around to grab the back of his neck. He felt a sticky wetness, and his vision went in and out of focus. Groaning, he fell to the ground.

"Finally, you son of a bitch, I'm going to finish you off." Skylar immediately recognized the voice as he looked up to see a bat coming toward his head.

The bat came down again, but Skylar rolled out of the way. The bat hit the ground, barely missing where Skylar had been lying.

Holding his head Skylar managed to crawl behind a chair. "What the *fuck* are you doing?" he screamed as he struggled to put the chair between the two of them.

Looking over at his assailant, his vision continued to go in and out of focus. He was in shock seeing Cary standing there, ready to swing the bat again.

"You couldn't just die in one of the fires, could you? So now I have to take care of this one on one," said Cary with pure hate in his voice.

Skylar couldn't believe what was happening. Why would Cary be trying to kill him? Had he lost his mind?

Trying to reason with him, Skylar tried to stay calm as he said, "Cary, listen to me. What's going on? Why are you doing this?" Never letting Cary out of his sight, Skylar tried to stand up. The throbbing in his neck and down the back of his head was now so painful he could barely open his eyes.

Cary calmly walked over toward Skylar. As he got closer, he squinted at Skylar and said, "You really don't remember me, do you?"

"Of course I remember you. I just saw you today!" Skylar spat.

"*No*! You idiot! From New York!"

"What are you talking about?" Not only was Skylar confused, he was now pissed off. "I have *no idea* what you're talking about!"

Thinking back to his senior year in New York City, at the private school that he attended with Skylar, Cary remembered very distinctly everything that had happened that year.

"Remember senior year at Camden Academy?" Cary was now so close he was almost upon Skylar. Leaning down so Skylar could clearly see his face, he snarled, "Remember that young skinny kid who idolized you? Worshipped you? *Loved you!*"

Skylar struggled to remember what Cary was talking about. "There was *never* a kid who idolized me at the academy."

"Oh, there was… you were just too popular and self-absorbed to notice me." Cary grew angrier at the thought.

"*You*? You were never at the academy," Skylar said as he looked at Cary in total confusion.

"I was. I looked different then. The fire changed my face, but my mind stayed the same, and I remember how much I loved you, how I followed you around and begged for your attention." Cary rolled the bat around in his hand. "To no avail, I might add. You never glanced at me for more than a second before you were off chasing one of your pretty young girlfriends." Cary's heart still ached at the memory of watching Skylar walk away from him time after time, never giving him a second glance.

"Cary, honestly, I don't know what you're talking about," Skylar said as he looked around, searching for anything to use to protect himself.

The fact that Skylar didn't remember him, his attention, or his love infuriated Cary to an entirely different level.

"*You fucker! You're the reason I was in that car that caught on fire!*" Cary screamed at Skylar as he swung the bat again.

Skylar quickly grabbed a lamp and attempted to ward off the blow. The bat hit the lamp with such force it shattered the lamp into pieces, knocking the bat out of Cary's hand.

Taking his chance Skylar lunged at Cary. The two men hit the ground as they fell beside the sofa. Skylar punched Cary in the face as they rolled around on the floor, and Cary pounded Skylar over and over on his ribs and on his head, each man trying to win the struggle.

Skylar was at a steep disadvantage due to the injury to his head and his vision continuing to go in and out of focus.

Using Skylar's injury to his advantage, with one final lunge, Cary threw himself over Skylar, landing on top of him. Using one hand to block blows to his face from Skylar, Cary reached over with his other hand to grab the bat that was now lying very near.

Skylar could see that Cary almost had the bat, so with a sudden burst of energy and strength that seemed to come out of nowhere, Skylar flung his body upward, causing Cary to fall over to the side. Skylar jumped up and tried to run toward the kitchen, where he had a gun hidden in a drawer. Skylar felt the bat hit him in the side. He felt himself falling toward the fireplace, an intense pain in his head, and then everything went black.

CHAPTER 42

AS AIDEN ran out the front door, with Ryan right on his heels, Aiden tried in vain to call Skylar.

"It's going to voice mail! Why is it going to *voice mail*?"

"Slow down, Aiden, just slow down. Where are we going? What are you doing?" Ryan was completely confused. One minute, they're playing "*Wheel of Fortune—The Arsonist Edition*," and the next thing he knew, Aiden was jumping off the bed, yelling, "I know who it is!" Now they were racing out the door to the car, and Ryan didn't have a clue what was happening.

"I have to warn Skylar. If he won't answer his cell phone, then we have to go to his house!"

"Warn him about what? Who?"

"The *arsonist*! I know who it is! It's Kelly Bane!" As he said the words out loud, even Aiden had a hard time believing it.

Ryan stopped midstep. "Are you serious? Kelly Bane is *not* an arsonist." As he could see Aiden starting to protest, Ryan held up his hand to stop him. "Pleeeasseee, before you go accusing a '70s It girl who just left her 'has been' status behind her to find fame again, I would think long and hard about accusing her of attempted murder. You won't make enough money in your lifetime to pay off that defamation-of-character lawsuit that she will slap on your happy ass!"

"It *has* to be her!" Seeing Ryan roll his eyes, Aiden continued. "Listen, Ryan. Skylar once told me that when they were alone, Kelly referred to him as her 'little A-lister.' Get it? *A L, I*, Lister... get it now?"

Ryan contemplated this new information for a moment. "I understand what you're saying, but believe me, there's no way in *hell* that woman would risk her comeback with something like this. And besides, what would her motive be?"

"Maybe because he stopped sleeping with her?"

With mock calmness, Ryan reached out to pat Aiden on the arm. "Okay, sweetie, I'm sure he's the sex god to end all sex gods, but I believe you're giving the man way too much credit. Besides, didn't the fires start *before* Skylar and Kelly stopped sleeping together?"

Sighing, Aiden had to admit Ryan was right. Leaning on the car in frustration, he rubbed his eyes and thought about the scenario again. "Yeah, you're right. It's most likely not her." As Aiden thought about it for a few minutes, another idea began to form. Standing straight up he said, "But it could be someone close to her. Maybe it's that slimy assistant of Kelly's. He seems to really dislike Skylar."

To Ryan, this made more sense. That Cary dude seemed more the criminal type. "You may be on to something there," he admitted. He reached for the car door, climbed inside, and locked his seatbelt. Looking over at Aiden, who was still standing there, lost in thought, Ryan called out, "Coming?"

Not having to be prompted a second time, Aiden ran around to the driver's side of the car and climbed in. Throwing the phone at Ryan, he said, "Here! You keep trying to call him. We need to get up there and tell him what we think before whoever it is strikes again." After throwing the gear into drive, he tore off down the highway, barreling toward Skylar's house in the hills.

CHAPTER 43

WHEN SKYLAR came to, he could see his fireplace moving in and out of focus. The soft glow of the fire appeared to be dancing in a beautiful array of orange and gold. Attempting to reach out for something to grasp, it shocked him to find that he couldn't move his hands. He slowly started to realize that he was lying on the floor with his hands tied behind his back. His head was throbbing with a pain unlike any he had ever felt. *I wonder if this is how I'm supposed to die*, he thought. *And worse is the fact that Aiden will never know how much I missed him or… loved him.* Loved? *How hard had he hit his head?*

"Well, Sleeping Beauty did finally wake up."

Skylar instantly recognized the voice, and the events of the evening came rushing back. Groaning, Skylar just laid his head back on the ground. With his hands and feet tied, it wasn't like he was going anywhere.

"Hey. *Hey!*"

Skylar felt a kick in his back.

"Don't you dare go back to sleep. Before I finish you off, I want you to know why this is happening."

"Cary, I don't know what in the hell you're talking about. I've never done anything to you!" Skylar was frustrated, hurt, angry, and so sleepy. All he wanted to do was sleep. Maybe he had hit his head on the hearth.

"Well, let me refresh your memory," Cary said in an intimidating voice. "Take yourself back to our senior year. Remember the night of Judy Carver's party? Her parents were out of town, and we were partying at her house. You had your usual harem of girls hanging all over you." Cary remembered this with distaste. Shaking his head he continued, "You never could make up your mind. Girls, boys, boys, girls… you could screw anyone you wanted, anytime you wanted. They *all* wanted you." After pausing for a second, Cary leaned down to Skylar and whispered in his ear, "Even me."

Wearily, Skylar said, "Cary, I don't even remember you."

"You didn't let me finish!" Cary yelled as he glared at Skylar with hate and contempt. Then, after taking a deep breath, Cary lowered his voice and said, "Yes, you slept with them all, except me." With his voice barely above a whisper, Cary finished with, "You didn't want me."

Skylar tried to sit up but fell back onto the floor. Moaning, he said, "Dammit, Cary, listen to me. I'm sorry if I hurt you. But how could I have rejected you *or* wanted you if I didn't know who you were? I'm being honest when I say I don't remember you."

"Don't you *ever* listen? I told you earlier, you don't know this face!" Cary snapped at Skylar. "Let me finish my story, you ungrateful brat." Cary was determined that Skylar would know exactly why he had spent all this time trying to get revenge. He continued with his story. "No, when your highness was too busy screwing his latest conquest up in Judy's *parents'* bedroom, I was chosen to make a beer run. And let me just add that I was chosen by *your* buddies, who said they would make sure you knew it was me who got the beer. I guess my following you around like a damn puppy was obvious to everyone except *you*." Leaning down closer to Skylar, he continued, "Yeah, great friends you had there. Even though I was also only seventeen, they convinced me to go downtown to a guy they knew who sold beer under the table to underage kids. And me, being stupid crazy over you, agreed so you might finally see that I existed."

Now Skylar was beginning to remember where this story ended. It was not a happy ending, and while he had felt bad about the accident, he had never known it was directly related to him.

HE HAD been upstairs, fooling around with Mandy, when he heard a lot of commotion downstairs. Afraid that Judy's parents had come home early, Skylar and Mandy had quickly gotten dressed and run downstairs.

As they came down the steps, Skylar could see that something was wrong. Everyone was running around in a panic, saying they had to leave. He found his best friend, Stephen, and asked what was going on.

"There's been a wreck!" Stephen was nearly hysterical. "That guy Cary.... Chad, something like that... you know, the one who always

follows you around...." Noting the blank look on Skylar's face, Stephen continued, "You know the guy! Tall, skinny, gawky! He is everywhere you are. Man, the dude has a massive crush on you."

Skylar ignored all that. He only wanted to know about the wreck. "Tell me about the wreck. Was this Cary guy in a wreck?"

"Yes! About a mile down the road. Tommy was on his way here for the party when he saw Cary's car skid off the road. It went down the embankment, and the front part of his car is on fire! Tommy called 911, and the paramedics and firemen are down there now." At this point, Stephen was tired of talking; he wanted to get the hell out of there before the policemen learned of the party and showed up asking questions.

Now Skylar was beginning to freak out. "Is he okay? Did he get out of the car?"

"Man, I don't know. The emergency crews are there now. I'm sure he's fine, so I'm getting the hell out of here before the cops get wind of this party and start nosing around. The last thing we need is to get busted for underage drinking."

Feeling overwhelmed and also not wanting to face any authorities, Skylar said, "Okay, I'll come with you." Turning to Mandy, who had been standing behind him silent all this time, Skylar said, "Mandy, do you need us to take you home?"

"Yes, please take me with you." Mandy ran over to the coat rack and grabbed the only coat remaining. Everyone else had already left.

"Let's go," Skylar said, and the three of them left the party as quickly as they could. Later, driving by the wreck, they could see someone lying on a stretcher as paramedics gathered around him.

JUDGING FROM Skylar's silence, Cary knew he was either remembering what happened that night or he'd passed out again.

Standing up Cary said, "So you see, asshole, you're the reason I had to endure three surgeries on my face. Part of it had to be reconstructed. If I hadn't been trying to impress *you*, I wouldn't have left the party to go on that beer run."

Skylar tried once more to reach Cary. "Cary, listen to me. I didn't know about the beer run. How can you blame me when I didn't know until this minute that you'd left to go on the beer run for me?"

"See, comments like that are why I hate you," Cary snapped out. "Did you bother to find out if I was all right? *No!* You have to be the most egotistical, ungrateful, uncaring person in the world!"

Skylar realized he was getting nowhere with Cary. "So, what's this big plan, Cary? Why am I tied up like this?"

Cary had almost a delighted look on his face as he looked down at Skylar. "I'm going to leave you tied up, set this place on fire, and call your little boyfriend to come and save you. But he'll be too late, and if I'm lucky, he too will get caught up in the blaze."

The thought of Aiden getting hurt made Skylar desperate. *"No!* Leave him out of this!" Skylar demanded in anguish.

"Ahhhh… so I've touched a nerve there. Is it possible that the uncaring, noncommittal Skylar Murphy has actually fallen for someone?" Cary was beside himself with glee. This was perfect. Now he definitely had to make sure Aiden went down with his man.

"He's nothing to you, Cary! This is between you and me and no one else." *Please don't hurt Aiden,* he thought as he tried to keep his sanity. His head felt like it was going to detach itself, and he was terrified at the thought of Aiden getting hurt, especially because of something he had inadvertently done in his past. "Please just leave Aiden out of this," pleaded Skylar. As he said those words, Skylar knew that for the first time he actually cared about someone more than he cared about himself. Was that what love felt like? Skylar wasn't sure, but he instinctively knew he had to do anything he could to protect Aiden, even if it meant giving up his own life. These feelings were so new to Skylar they almost knocked the breath out of him.

"Oh, stop with your pathetic whining! Do you honestly think I give a rat's ass who you want hurt and who you don't want hurt? *You* are finally going to feel what I felt all those years ago. You're going to understand the feeling of pain, hurt, and helplessness." Cary was finished with this entire conversation. It angered him more to learn that Skylar did love someone enough to want to protect him. He had come here for a reason, and now it was time to stop talking and get on with the action.

As Skylar struggled to think of a way to stop Cary, he watched him walk around the living room with a gas can. He was pouring gas all along the walls of the living room and dousing the curtains that hung near the fireplace. Skylar used this time to concentrate on trying to untie his hands.

"Don't bother. You won't be able to untie them in time," commanded Cary from across the room.

"Cary, think about what you are doing. You'll go to jail for the rest of your life! Stop now, and I won't press charges." Skylar had every intention of putting this nutcase away forever, but he had to think of something to change Cary's mind.

"Not happening," said Cary as he continued to throw the remaining gas in the can around the living room. Slowly, Cary bent down and set the curtains on fire, and then he slowly walked out of the room as Skylar screamed for him to stop.

CHAPTER 44

"*FUCK*! THERE'S a fire at Skylar's house! Oh my God, are we too late?" Aiden roared into the driveway and raced up to the house, while yelling to Ryan, "Call 911 *now*! Give them Skylar's address, and tell them to get up here." Aiden said the last part as he was jumping out of the car and running toward the house.

Ryan grabbed the phone and with shaking hands dialed 911. He couldn't believe this was happening. Just like in the movies! He and Aiden had figured out the puzzle, and now they had arrived to save Skylar's life! Just like the superheroes! After giving the 911 operator all the information, Ryan felt a burst of energy that could only be described as a combination of fear and courage as he took off toward the house to help.

Running past Skylar's car, Aiden felt sheer terror in his heart as he yelled, "*Sky*! *Skylar*!" He ran up the steps to the back door but found the door locked. Since he couldn't get inside that way, he did what he had been trained to do. He felt the door, and it was still cool. There was no fire on the other side! He stepped back and ran at the door, hitting it with his shoulder and all the strength he could muster. He almost fell as the door swung open, and he barreled through at full force.

"*Aiden*! Be careful!" warned Ryan from outside.

"Skylar... where are you?" Aiden yelled as he went from room to room, trying not to breathe in too much smoke. He quickly realized that the main fire was in the living room. He could hear the wood crackling under the heat of the fire. After covering his nose and mouth with his shirt, he lowered himself to the floor, and he started to inch his way into the room. He could barely make out someone on the ground. He instantly knew it was Skylar. His eyes stinging, Aiden crawled over to Skylar, as his mind refused to believe that he was dead. Skylar had to be all right. He just had to be!

Reaching Skylar, Aiden immediately saw that he was tied up. After a quick feel for his pulse, Aiden knew Skylar was still alive, just unconscious. He didn't appear to be badly burned, but Aiden knew he had to get him out of there quickly. Slowly he put his arms under Skylar's and started to pull him out of the living room. As the smoke began to overwhelm him, Aiden pressed his mouth and nose up against Skylar's back as he continued to pull him along the floor toward the kitchen. The fire was fully blazing over on the other side of the room, and the heat was rising. Aiden feared that there would be a flashover, igniting everything in the room at once. Therefore, he *had* to get them both out of there and now!

Ryan was standing at the back door not knowing what to do. In the movies this part always looked so easy. But in real life, he was in near panic. He hadn't seen Aiden since he took off inside the house. Should he go after him? Should he stand here and yell so they know the way out? He was terrified at not knowing what to do next.

Something flashed in the corner of his eye. He glanced over and saw someone running toward the woods. Suddenly a feeling of pure adrenaline flowed through Ryan. That *fucker*! Ryan knew that it had to be that Cary dude, and he had to stop him. So he did the only thing he could think to do: he started chasing after him.

Ryan, a former high school track star, quickly caught up to Cary, and at the last second, he jumped, landing right on Cary's back. Ryan wrestled him to the ground. As they rolled over and over, all of Ryan's frustration of having to deal with his friend's heartbreak and his beautiful actor boy being terrorized came out. He found strength he never knew he had as he threw Cary down with one final fling while pulling Cary's arms behind him, nearly breaking one. He sat on him, holding him down firmly on the ground as Cary struggled to get away. But he wasn't going anywhere—Ryan had his man!

Back in the house, Aiden had managed to pull Skylar out of the living room. They were now in the kitchen, and the door was just ahead of them. The smoke was thicker now, and the heat was continuing to build. The combination of the two had Aiden on the verge of passing out. However, his love for Skylar gave him renewed strength and courage as he kept struggling to pull the both of them out of the house. He pulled and pulled until he felt the opening of the back door. Aiden gave one last pull, and both he and Skylar fell backward out the door onto the concrete steps.

Shit! That hurt, Aiden thought as he took the brunt of the hit. But they were outside, and now he had to get Skylar far away from the house. *Where is Ryan?* he thought as he continued to struggle to get them both to safety. He could hear the fire trucks in the distance and knew it was only a matter of seconds before they arrived.

As the sirens got closer, Aiden used the last of his strength to get them away from the house and on the ground near the cars. Once he felt that they were at a safe distance, Aiden gently laid Skylar on the ground and leaned down to see if Skylar was breathing. He couldn't hear anything, so, panicking, he grabbed his wrist again. It took him a second, but he found Skylar's pulse. He was alive! Then Skylar began to cough. "Shush... baby, it's okay. You're okay. Just breathe." Skylar was still barely conscious, but at least he was breathing on his own.

The smoke had Aiden's eyes tearing, but through his tears, he could see the firemen arrive and run toward the house. Aiden recognized Paul and called him over. "Paul! We're over here."

Surprised to see someone he recognized, Paul exclaimed, "Aiden!" Upon seeing Skylar in Aiden's arms, Paul put two and two together. "What the hell? Did you pull him out alone?" Knowing the answer to his own question, he continued, "Are you okay?"

"Just a lot of smoke in my eyes, but I'll be okay." Looking down at the man he loved, Aiden said to Paul, "Please get a paramedic as fast as you can. Skylar is still semiconscious, and I'm not sure of the extent of his injuries."

Paul didn't have time to react. A paramedic was already running up to them with her medic bag.

"Okay, sir, if you can, just move to the side so that I can get a good look at him."

Another paramedic brought around a stretcher as Aiden reluctantly let go and moved back so they could reach Skylar. The female paramedic cut off Skylar's bindings and checked him over as Aiden looked toward the house, which was now completely engulfed in flames. The firemen were trying their best to extinguish it.

Ryan? Where in God's name is Ryan? The last time Aiden had seen him, Ryan was calling 911. But that felt like ages ago.

"*Ryan!* Where are you?" Aiden yelled out over all the noise. Looking down at the paramedic, his heart was back in his throat. "Will he be okay?" he asked as he looked at Skylar, who still appeared to be out of it.

"We don't know for sure," the paramedic said. "We need to get him to the hospital." They started loading Skylar on the stretcher, and Aiden looked around for Ryan. He was torn between worrying about Skylar and his need to find Ryan.

Suddenly he heard Ryan yell out, "I'm over here!"

Aiden glanced at the paramedic and said, "I'm riding with him to the hospital."

The paramedic looked up and said, "That's fine." She continued to help move Skylar onto the stretcher.

"I'll meet you at the ambulance. I have to find my friend who was with me."

"We're leaving in one minute," she warned.

"One minute is all I need," replied Aiden.

Touching Skylar's arm and feeling an overwhelming sensation of love for him, Aiden forced himself to walk toward Ryan's voice. "Ryan, where are you?"

"Here, with this nice policeman."

Aiden looked over to his right to see a policeman taking notes from Ryan, who had a huge grin on his face. As Aiden's eyes fell to the police car, he saw another policeman putting Cary into the backseat. Aiden gave Ryan a questioning look.

"I caught that fucker. Nobody messes with my boys," Ryan said proudly.

Aiden smiled for the first time that night.

CHAPTER 45

SKYLAR WOKE up to the bright lights of the hospital room. As he tried to focus on his surroundings, the throbbing inside his head intensified. Reaching up he felt a thick bandage that circled the top of his head. All the events of the previous night came rushing back.

Skylar still couldn't believe that Cary had tried to kill him. Had he really been that careless as a teenager? So caught up in his own world that he didn't notice someone following him around? Someone who obviously had a crush on him? And worse yet, had he really been so indifferent that he never bothered to find out who was in the wreck and if they had survived? Shit! A part of him could almost understand Cary's anger, but still, trying to kill him was fucking crazy. He wasn't sure who he had overheard, but he was positive that during one of his fading in and out moments, he'd heard someone say that Cary had been caught and was now in police custody. He certainly hoped that was the case. He glanced to his left to see Aiden asleep in the armchair next to his bed. He remembered at some point during the ambulance ride waking up long enough to see Aiden sitting beside him, all covered in soot. Without a doubt, he knew that Aiden had saved his life. Now watching him sleep quietly, Skylar's heart warmed as he fought the urge to reach out and wake him. This notion caused him to shiver. Sometimes when it came to Aiden, he felt overwhelming emotions that he didn't understand. But he knew he didn't like it. Emotions such as those could cause him to lose control, and he needed to be in control at all times.

He thought back to the previous night, when Cary had threatened to hurt Aiden, and how desperately he had reacted to that. He had been totally out of control at that moment. He had been so frantic to keep Aiden safe that it occurred to him that he might actually love him. However, now that he thought about it again, he knew—deep down— that wasn't true. Love was just a bunch of bullshit, and he wasn't going to buy into that nonsense. His entire life, he'd always left when the other person got too close, and Aiden was not going to be an exception. Therefore, as he looked over at Aiden sleeping so peacefully, he decided his intense feelings had to be due to some sort of overwhelming gratitude for Aiden having saved his life.

A tap at the door interrupted the calmness in the room. Aiden sat straight up out of his sleep and turned to see who was coming through the door. It was Sophie, who was holding a vase of beautiful blue and yellow flowers in her hand.

"I'm so sorry. I didn't realize you were sleeping," she said as she saw Aiden start to rub his eyes.

"I didn't mean to fall asleep. I guess everything finally caught up with me."

Skylar coughed to get their attention. Both of them turned to see him awake.

Aiden felt happiness wash over him but resisted the urge to run over to Skylar and kiss him until he screamed for mercy. He had missed Skylar so much, and seeing him sitting there with his head wrapped in a bandage, having barely escaped death, Aiden wanted nothing more than to go to him and wrap his arms around him forever.

Skylar looked at Aiden, who still looked amazing, even with his unkempt hair and disheveled clothes. *Does it really matter if I don't love him? Surely he'll want to continue to hang out and have fun*, he thought as he motioned for Aiden to come over. When Aiden didn't move, Skylar knew his answer. They might have been through a major ordeal together, but nothing had changed, at least not between them. *Maybe it's for the best*, Skylar thought.

"There you are, sleepyhead!" Sophie said, breaking the silence. After she brought the flowers over and set them on the bedside table near Skylar, she reached out and grabbed his hand. "You had us all scared to death!"

"I was pretty scared myself," Skylar replied as he continued to stare holes through Aiden.

Noticing the tension between the two men, Sophie decided to say her hellos and then get out of the way. They obviously needed to talk. "I bet you were. I'm still in shock that it was Cary who set all the fires."

"Me too. Apparently he had wanted revenge for many years." Shaking his head in disbelief, Skylar continued, "All the time that he worked for Kelly, I never had any idea that I had known him years ago at Camden Academy. Strange story, but one that I'm very glad is over."

Sophie squeezed Skylar's hand. "Well, it's not completely over."

Skylar looked up at her. "What do you mean?"

Sophie continued to hold Skylar's hand as she explained. "I hate to be the bearer of bad news, but you need to know. The media has had a field day with this, and it's all over the news. So you and I have to prepare our response before you can leave." Seeing Skylar frown at this news, Sophie continued. "I know, I hate telling you all of this now, but Nick already called this morning with instructions that we're to keep up the pretense, especially now that there were a few rumors out there."

"What rumors?" Skylar looked over at Aiden, who had been silent the entire time.

"Don't look at me. I've been in this hospital room since you arrived," replied Aiden.

"Apparently, there were a few journalists asking questions about how Aiden knew to find you." And then turning to Aiden, yet continuing to speak to Skylar, she quietly added, "And there is a photo of Aiden sitting here by your bedside."

"Who in the hell took that photo?" Skylar tensed up. Couldn't the press leave them alone for a second?

"I don't know, but they were asking questions about why Aiden was here and not me."

"Shit! Can't they just leave me alone?"

Aiden looked over at Skylar, surprised that he sounded so tired of it all.

Skylar continued speaking. "Sophie, can you give me a few minutes? I need to speak to Aiden first before I do anything else." He glanced over at Aiden, and the two men looked at each other, both feeling awkward.

"Sure, I can do that," Sophie replied quietly. "Why don't I leave now and come back later?" She leaned down and kissed Skylar on the cheek, she noticed that Skylar was looking at Aiden with a strange expression. *He acts like he really loves him*, she thought. Making her way to the door, she turned to shut the blinds. Then she quietly let herself out.

As the door clicked behind her, Aiden was the first to break the gaze. Walking over to Skylar's bed, he said, "So how do you feel?"

"My head hurts like a bitch, but other than that, I think I'll live."

"Yeah, you had a slight concussion. Cary hit you with something because we can see the deep tissue bruising, and from the sharp angular gash on the side of your head, we think you must have fallen at some point against the corner of the fireplace. Thankfully, it was not a severe concussion, and you should be out of here by tomorrow."

Skylar reached out for Aiden's hand. After hesitating for a moment, Aiden gave his hand to Skylar.

"I know you saved my life," Skylar whispered in an emotion-filled voice that surprised even him. "I remember you being there and helping me when the paramedics arrived, and I came to for a moment in the ambulance, and I saw you there with me." Just saying those words, Skylar felt his insides turn to mush.

"Thank *God* we arrived in time," Aiden said. With a shaky voice, he continued, "It was the clues that Cary left at each fire. Ryan and I sat down and sorted through all of the crime scenes. We figured out that the letters he had been leaving spelled out 'A-lister,' and I remembered you telling me that Kelly often called you that."

Skylar was surprised. "Unbelievable. I would have never guessed Cary had anything to do with the fires or that the fires were directed at me. I still can't get over that," Skylar said as he held on to Aiden's hand tightly.

"Well, you definitely have a way of impacting people's lives. Some good, some not so good," teased Aiden, trying to lighten the conversation.

"I'm just glad that it's over."

Realizing what he was doing, Aiden slowly removed his hand from Skylar's grip. "Yes, he confessed everything to the police, and I think he'll be put away where he belongs, and, hopefully, get some help as well."

Skylar didn't like that Aiden had taken his hand away. "Why are you pulling away from me? Please come here."

The pleading sound in his voice and the painful look in Skylar's eyes were too much for Aiden to take. His heart was aching with an intensity that he didn't understand, and he wasn't sure what to do.

"Last time it was you who pulled away from me," Aiden responded with a raspy voice. The hurt was still there.

Suddenly a loud booming voice said, "Hello, fellas! And how is my favorite client today?"

Both men were startled, causing them to jump.

Nick was standing in the doorway with a huge bouquet of flowers.

Aiden quickly walked back over behind the chair, giving Nick space next to Skylar's bedside.

"Hope I wasn't interrupting anything," Nick said.

Just my life, thought Skylar. "What are you doing here so early?" he asked, frustrated.

"Skylar, it's not early. It's four in the afternoon." After looking around for an empty spot to place his flowers, Nick moved Sophie's flowers out of the way and put his bouquet smack down in front of it. "I wanted to run by to check on you *and* to give you some fantastic news."

Skylar, who was not interested in this conversation, said, "And what might that news be?"

"Prepare yourself, handsome! You got the part!" Nick could barely contain his excitement.

Hearing those words shook Skylar back to reality, and his mood changed 180 degrees. "What?" With a huge smile, he asked, "Are you serious? They offered me the part in *Checkmate*?"

"Yes, sir! This morning they sent over a tentative offer for the part. We're now talking money, and let me just say, with all the press you're receiving from this fire, your hospitalization, *and* the 'love story' that you and Sophie have been spinning, it'll be a big payday for both of us!"

Upon hearing Sophie and Sky's names together as the "love story," Aiden's heart sank. He knew exactly where this was leading, and he didn't particularly want to be around for all the details.

"About that…," Skylar began. "I was actually hoping that we could put the 'Sophie and Skylar' story behind us."

"Don't even go there, Skylar," Nick warned. "You are *this close* to having the best role of your career."

Seeing Skylar hesitate, Nick continued, "Listen, you only need to keep up this pretense until we have signed the final contract. Obviously, the movie studio won't admit they are looking at that, but believe me, they are!"

Skylar's head was reeling between the conflicting emotions he was feeling for Aiden and his desire to have this role. He was going to try to talk to Aiden and see if they might work things out, hang out together again; however, deep down, he knew Nick was right. He really wanted this part, and since he had carried on the charade this long, he couldn't stop now. Aiden would have to understand. If not, then things would just have to stay the same between him and Aiden. *Why do I have to be such a bastard?* Skylar asked himself.

Lying back down on the bed, he sighed and said, "I guess you're right."

Aiden looked over at Skylar with disbelief in his eyes. "I think I'm going to go now," he said as he grabbed his coat.

"Aiden, wait. Can't we talk?" Skylar sat up so fast his head started spinning. The second he saw Aiden standing up to leave, it hit him that maybe he didn't want things to stay the same. But maybe... just maybe, he could convince Aiden to wait it out for just a little while longer.

"I think there's been enough talking, so I'll be going now. See you around." Aiden felt like a knife was plunging into his heart as he headed toward the door.

"Aiden, wait!" Skylar pleaded. Turning to Nick, he said, "Nick, *please*, can you give us a few minutes alone?"

"Okay, I'll go for now, but call me within the hour, Skylar," Nick demanded as he turned to leave. As he walked by Aiden, he leaned in close to Aiden's ear and quietly said, "Remember, this movie could make his career. Think about that before you sabotage it."

Aiden was not a violent person, but at that moment, he wanted to deck Nick. But all he could do was glare as he watched Nick walked out the door.

As the door closed, Skylar looked at Aiden, reached out his hand, and whispered, "Baby, please come over here."

Aiden, still ticked off at Nick's closing comment, walked over to Skylar's bedside. Not taking Skylar's hand, Aiden calmly said, "Sky, we've been through this before. I can't live like this. I can't be with someone who can't—no, *won't*—acknowledge our relationship. And more importantly, I can't be with someone who doesn't love me in the same way that I love him." Aiden looked away as he remembered telling Skylar that he loved him and watching Skylar panic at the words and walk away from him.

"Aiden, why can't I make you understand that those words scare the hell out of me? Why can't we just go back to the way we were? Just having fun being together, talking, hanging out?"

"Because I'm past that point, Sky. I know that I'm in love with you, and now I have to protect myself. If you are incapable of loving me back, then I have no choice other than to walk away while I still can and try to move on with my life."

Falling back onto his pillow, Skylar sighed and said, "I don't know how to respond to that." He knew deep in his heart that the damage was done, and they were over. And he was too tired and too overwhelmed to continue the conversation. Sadly, he looked up at Aiden and said, "Okay, if you have no other choice, then I guess this is good-bye… again." Damn, why was his heart hurting so fucking much?

Aiden was a quivering mess of heartache. Slowly he inched his way to the door. Turning back to look at Skylar one last time, he struggled to hold back tears as he said, "I'm happy you are okay. I'm happy Cary is behind bars, and most of all, I'm happy for you that you got your part in the movie. I hope it will be everything you think it will be."

Skylar, not knowing what else to say, could only lie there and watch his lover walk out the door.

CHAPTER 46

THE EXCITEMENT could be felt all though Hollywood as the Emmys approached. It was all over television, newspapers, and the Internet. The weekend was shaping up to be an exciting one, and anticipation was filling the air. Skylar had been told he was in the lead to win for "Best Actor in a Drama Series," yet instead of feeling excited, he felt nothing but emptiness.

Since the day Aiden had walked out of his hospital room, Skylar had thought of nothing else. He would often find himself touching his lips as he remembered the feel of Aiden's lips on his during the kisses they had shared. He was lonely and miserable. And to make matters worse, he knew it was his own fault.

Nick had told him that the tentative offer for *Checkmate*, along with Skylar's salary request, had been approved by the production company. It was going to be a huge payday! And to top that off, Nick was certain that *Illusions*, the biggest movie of the decade, would come after Skylar next. So why wasn't he happier? This was everything that he had worked for, and now he had it in the palm of his hand. But all Skylar felt was miserable.

He really missed Aiden. He was having a hard time working; he didn't want to eat. What was wrong with him? He had never had this problem. When he was finished with something, it was finished. But no one had ever affected him the way that Aiden had. Shit, even sleeping at night was becoming a problem.

He had tried to call Aiden many times, but there was never an answer. Skylar just couldn't understand why Aiden had to go and mess up a perfectly good arrangement by saying that he loved him. But as he sat alone in his dressing room, he had a feeling that it was him who had messed up. He was one miserable son of a bitch.

A knock at the door brought him back to reality. Kelly opened the door and peeped in.

"May I come in?" she asked.

"Sure, come on in. I'm just sitting here wallowing in my own self misery." A self-pitying remark if there ever was one.

Kelly sat down beside him on the sofa. Taking his hand she tilted his chin up so that he was looking at her. Staring into his big blue eyes, Kelly could see why so many became obsessed with him. Reaching up to move a soft strand of hair out of his eyes, she said, "Darling, I haven't had the chance to talk to you alone, but I really want to say again how very sorry I am about Cary and all that he put you through."

Skylar squeezed her hand as he said, "It wasn't your fault, Kelly. How could you know that he was crazy?"

"You're right, and while I didn't know the extent of his craziness, I did know that he never liked you very much."

"Kel, we all knew that, yet none of us ever thought he would go this far." Skylar really didn't want to talk about Cary ever again. The trial would be here soon enough, and until then, he wanted to forget it all. "Let's change the subject, okay? I'm feeling really lousy."

"Is there anything I can do to help? You look so miserable." Kelly was truly worried about Skylar. He had forgotten his lines twice this morning, and it wasn't like him to let things get in the way of his work.

"Kel, I never told you the truth about something." Skylar was in such a state of misery that he thought if he told someone, maybe he would feel better.

"Tell me what, darling?"

"Do you remember when we were still sleeping together and I told you that I had a lot going on and I ended it, without ever really giving you an explanation?" Now that he had started this conversation, Skylar was already regretting his choice. After all, how do you tell a woman that you were sleeping with on a regular basis that you met someone else? And to top it off, that someone else was a man?

"Are you going to tell me that you fell in love with that handsome firefighter I saw you with on several occasions?" Kelly already knew the answer but wanted to hear Skylar admit it.

Skylar looked at her with shock. "*You knew?*" Stumbling over his words, he clarified, "I mean, I didn't fall 'in love' with him, but I did start seeing him."

"Of course I knew, darling. I may have a few years on you, but I'm *not* stupid."

"I'm really sorry, Kelly. I should have been upfront with you and told you the truth from the beginning. It just happened, and then the movie role came up, and Sophie and I had to go out—"

Kelly interrupted Skylar as he took a breath. "Darling, you're rambling. Slow down. Tell me… what is really going on here?"

"Hell if I know. Aiden—that's his name—and I started going out, and I was crazy about him. It was the strangest thing, Kel. It was as if he was connected to me in some way. I thought about him all the time, wanted to be with him all the time. Then… boom… someone took photographs of us together, and Nick insisted that I stop seeing him."

"And why would Nick want you to stop seeing him? Because of the movie?"

"Yes! Nick thought that the *Checkmate* producers would not want me in the role if they found out I was dating a man."

"Well, I would love to say that is the stupidest thing I've ever heard, but in all fairness, Nick was probably right."

"I know… but now I'm not sure it was worth it."

"What do you mean?" Kelly was genuinely interested.

"I'm not sure what I mean. One minute we're fine, I mean, there were fights about Sophie and all that shit, but I thought we were okay. Then one night at a party, Aiden decides he can't handle it anymore because he loves me. Can you believe that shit?" Skylar stood up and walked across the room. There was silence for a moment, and then Kelly spoke.

"Can I believe what, Skylar? That he loves you?"

"Yes! He knows I don't believe in love and all that crap, yet here he goes telling me that he loves me. How else did he expect me to react?"

"How did you react?"

"The only way I could. I walked away." As Skylar said the words, they felt all wrong. Turning to Kelly, he asked, "Do you think I did the right thing?"

Kelly looked at Skylar and watched how desperate and anxious he was becoming. She knew without a doubt that Skylar was in love with Aiden as well, but he couldn't see it for himself.

"Darling, can I ask you something?"

Skylar turned to Kelly and walked back over. "Sure. Anything."

"How would you feel if you could never see Aiden again? I mean, gone forever and there was no way for you to see him again."

Skylar thought about it for a minute. The thought of never seeing Aiden again was devastating to him. A sinking, hopeless feeling overtook him. Slowly, he whispered, "I think I would be miserable for the rest of my life."

"Okay, let me ask you something else." Kelly carefully worded her next question. "Have you considered the possibility that you could also be in love with Aiden?"

"I don't even believe that could be a possibility."

"Skylar, listen to me. Love is not a bad thing. It can be wonderful if it's with the right person. If you truly believe that you would be miserable for the rest of your life without Aiden, then I think you must consider the possibility that you're in love with him."

Skylar thought back to the night of the fire and how desperately he'd wanted to keep Aiden safe. "Well, I do know that when Cary threatened to hurt him, I would've done anything to stop that, even if it meant dying."

Kelly just sat there and slowly nodded. Skylar thought some more about the strange feelings he had, the feeling of emptiness without Aiden. Could it be true? Was he really capable of loving someone? Being in love with someone?

Looking at Kelly, he asked with all sincerity, "Do you honestly think I could actually be in love with him?"

"I believe you are." Kelly adored Skylar and loved having sex with him, but she had enough class to step aside when he was so obviously hurting over someone else.

Sitting down beside her, Skylar put his face in his hands. What a miserable fucking feeling. He had always known that love was nothing but misery. And here he was, miserable as hell. So what now?

"Okay, let's say that I am in love with him. I don't have a clue what to do about it. Besides, I think it may be too late." He groaned and put his head down again in his hands.

Kelly drew Skylar over to her and laid his head on her shoulder. Stroking his hair, trying to comfort him, she said, "It's never too late to tell someone that you love them."

Groaning, he said, "Kel, I wouldn't begin to know how to tell Aiden that I love him. I have never said those words out loud to anyone. Besides, at this point, I don't think he would believe me."

Kelly was silent for a moment as she thought about what to say next. "Seems to me that you need to convince him."

"But how?"

"That, my darling, is the million-dollar question."

CHAPTER 47

AIDEN AND the others were on the fire truck headed back to the fire station. They had just left a fundraiser in downtown LA and were trying to get back to the 101 so they could return to Hollywood. It was Emmy night at the Nokia Theatre, and it was already becoming a madhouse between the fans, paparazzi, and the celebrities.

Paul was driving and having a hard time maneuvering the huge fire truck through the maze of cars and people.

"I guess it's Emmy night," Ben murmured as they pushed their way past the limousines and Hummers. He and Paul were the only two in the firehouse who knew about Aiden and Skylar, and neither was going to mention his name. Nor were they going to mention Skylar's nomination for Best Actor at the awards show. It was just another day, and they were firemen, not actors or show business people.

Thirty minutes later they turned into the firehouse, and Aiden jumped off the truck and went inside.

"Damn! I really hate to see him like this," said Paul as he pulled his equipment off the truck. "He should have known better than to get involved with a self-absorbed actor. They're all alike."

"Well, if I were you, I wouldn't be mentioning the so-called self-absorbed actor," warned Ben.

"No need for the warning. However, I was going to catch the show, if I can. I'll just turn it on in another room, away from Aiden," Paul responded. At the sideways glance from Ben, he continued, "Hey, I like the award shows… so sue me."

The men finished unloading their gear and walked inside the firehouse. Aiden was already in the kitchen starting their dinner. No one said a word as they went about their everyday business.

CHAPTER 48

APPLAUSE WAS radiating off the walls of the Nokia Theatre. *The Executives* had won for Best Drama, and the entire cast had just walked offstage after accepting the award. They were now backstage in the winner's area, taking group photographs. As they finished up, one of the Emmy producers walked up and asked them to please go back to their seats, as they were getting ready to announce the category for Best Male Actor and Best Female Actor.

The Emmys award show was being televised live; therefore, when the commercial break began, the cast and crew all started going back to their seats. Skylar sat down next to Sophie. Still under the impression that they were a couple, the producers of the Emmys had assigned them seats together. Skylar had not said a word, nor had he shown any affection toward Sophie. No kisses, no hand-holding. As far as Skylar was concerned, that story was finished.

"Are you okay, Skylar? Your show just won Best Drama, and you didn't smile the entire time on stage," Sophie complained.

"I'm fine," replied Skylar as he stared straight at the stage.

Sophie didn't understand what was going on. She didn't care about the "love story," but she did want to keep her job. Therefore, she didn't ask any more questions and just listened as other categories were named and the winners announced.

Skylar felt his phone buzz and glanced at the text message. It was from Nick: *That's two crowd shots centered on your group and nothing from you and Sophie. What's up with you?*

Skylar ignored the text and kept staring straight at the stage. His heart still felt shattered and had been that way for over a week. His talk with Kelly had answered a lot of questions for him, and if given a chance, he knew what he had to do. And he also knew that what he was about to do could end his Hollywood career in a heartbeat.

The music started, and the commercial ended. The host was back on stage introducing two new Disney musical stars to announce the winner of Best Actor in a Drama Series. Sophie glanced over at Skylar, who was still staring straight at the stage.

After a bit of ad-libbing and reading from the teleprompter, the teenagers finally announced the nominees, and as they giggled, the younger one said, "And the winner is... *Skylar Murphy!*"

Skylar felt his heart drop to his knees as he stood up. The applause was thunderous as he walked up to the stage to accept his award. This was the moment he had worked for his entire career, and now it was his moment to shine. And he intended to make it memorable.

CHAPTER 49

"HOLY CRAP!" exclaimed Paul. Skylar had won! He wanted to tell Aiden so badly but knew it would be a bad idea. Therefore, he did the next best thing. He yelled, "Ben. Ben! Come here! Quick!" Little did he know Aiden would also come to see what was going on, along with the rest of the fire station.

As all the guys gathered around the television, Skylar was walking up to the stage.

"You brought us in here for this? Dammit, Paul! You sure are slow on the uptake. What part of 'We don't talk about Skylar Murphy' do you not understand?" complained Ben.

The rest of the guys looked on in amazement. They had no idea what was going on, but judging from the tone of Ben's voice, it definitely had something to do with that actor on stage.

"It's okay," Aiden said as he walked up from the back of the room. His heart was in his throat. He hadn't seen Skylar in well over a week, and just seeing him on the television screen was heartbreaking and shattering. He felt like his insides were gutted.

"We can turn it off," offered Paul. "I'm sorry, dude. I was just excited because we've met him and stuff."

"No, don't turn it off. He deserves this win, and I want to watch him accept it," replied Aiden as he watched his ex-lover walk up to the microphone.

CHAPTER 50

THE APPLAUSE died down as Skylar stepped up to the microphone. His voice was shaking as he addressed the audience.

"First of all, I want to thank everyone who voted for me. This award is something I have strived for many years. Thank you." The audience erupted in applause again.

Skylar waited for the applause to die down. After taking a deep breath, he said. "I want to take this opportunity to say something to the fans and to everyone watching." At this point his heart was pounding so hard Skylar could only hope that the words would come out as he continued. "Some of you might not think this an appropriate time for me to do this, but I feel it's the absolute perfect time. For several months I've done many things that I'm not proud of. I have betrayed my fans and friends by pretending that I was having a love affair with my assistant, Sophie." The camera immediately panned to Sophie, who sat there in shock, her mouth dropped open. There was silence across the venue as the audience waited to hear more.

"I was pretending to date and fall in love with Sophie so that I wouldn't jeopardize my chances at a role in a new movie. The truth is, I am totally and completely in love with someone else." Skylar could hear the buzzing in the auditorium as the audience started to whisper.

"I was pretending because the person I'm in love with is a man. His name is Aiden, and, Aiden, if you're watching tonight, I love you. I've never known what it was like to love someone, but I know now that I love you. This past week without you has taught me many things. But mostly it has taught me that I don't care anymore if my love for you will cost me the role of a lifetime, because the truth is, without you, I'm no one." Skylar lowered his voice as he whispered just loud enough for the microphone to pick it up, "I have no life, unless you're part of it."

Judging from the relative silence in the audience, Skylar didn't know if he should continue or not. Glancing over to the host of the show, who motioned for him to continue, Skylar finished up his speech.

"Therefore, I want to apologize to all my fans, friends, and colleagues for all the lies and betrayal. However, most of all I want to apologize to Aiden. He's the reason that I won this award. He was the one behind my strength to finish scenes that were difficult for me. He was the one who never betrayed me. He was everything to me, and I didn't realize it until it was too late. I'll never forgive myself for that. Thank you."

After those final words, Skylar, with tears streaming down his face, lowered his head and walked off the stage. At first the silence continued. Then there was one clap, followed by more clapping, and then the audience started cheering and gave him a standing ovation.

CHAPTER 51

THE FIRE station was roaring! The firemen had just listened to Skylar's speech, and they were overjoyed!

"Shit! Aiden! He just fucking told the entire world he loves you! What an acceptance speech," Paul said, laughing.

Aiden was shell-shocked. Tears were falling down his face, and his heart was pounding as he tried to grasp what had just happened. His cell phone started ringing, and without looking, he knew it was Ryan. He answered the phone. "Hey."

"Oh my *God*! Did you see, did you see? *I knew he loved you*!" Ryan was yelling so loud the entire room of men could hear him.

"I know. I can't believe it," responded Aiden. His heart was bursting with love for Skylar, and yet he didn't know quite what to do.

"What are you waiting on? Get your ass to the Nokia Theatre! *Now*!" Ryan was beyond excited.

"I can't just go to the Nokia Theatre… can I?" asked Aiden.

"You sure as hell can. Now hang up, and go get your man!"

As Aiden hung up the cell phone, Ben was already handing him his jacket. "Go, Lieutenant. You are officially off duty for the night. Go get that boy," Ben said as he gave Aiden a half hug and pushed him out the door.

CHAPTER 52

SKYLAR FOLLOWED the presenters around to the backstage area. He was greeted by several people as he made his way to the winner's area for photographs. Gray Hudson walked up to him and patted him on the back.

"Skylar... son... that was a touching speech. I'm sorry you felt like you had to go through that alone. I wish you had talked to me. I might have been able to help you."

Skylar smiled for the first time that evening and said, "Thank you, Gray. That means a lot to me." He shook Gray's hand and then walked on to the photographer's circle.

Holding up his Emmy for the camera, his emotions were all over the place. He was glad he'd admitted to loving Aiden, but where would that leave him? Would he be accepted as he was? Or would he be forced to give up his acting career? As he smiled at the photographer, he knew none of that would matter if only he had Aiden with him. But he didn't have Aiden, and that was his greatest regret.

Slowly he walked back to his seat, aware of the stares from some and the smiles from others. Shaking it off, he sat down next to Sophie, who leaned over and hugged him tight. "I'm *sooo* proud of you," she said with tears streaming down her face. Laughing, she wiped away her tears and hugged him again. "After this is over, you have to go and find him... you have to."

Without looking up, he said, "It's over, Sophie. I just had to tell the world so I could make things right. I've done that, and now I have to accept that Aiden is gone."

As he sat there, waiting for the show to continue, he thought about everything. He had thought he might feel better if he tried to make things right, but it didn't work. He was still miserable.

He felt a buzz in his pocket. Pulling the phone out, he looked down and saw that it was Nick: *Great job, Skylar. Just got a text from* Checkmate. *They withdrew their tentative offer. It's off the table.*

Skylar couldn't muster enough feeling to care, so he didn't respond. He wanted nothing more than to leave the Nokia and go home and stay in bed for a month. His cell phone buzzed again.

What the fuck were you thinking? You just blew the biggest payday of your career. And for what? A nobody who doesn't give a fuck about you. I should have let that bitch Emma print those photos. Saved us all a lot of fucking time.

That last text made Skylar sit up and take notice. Shaking, he texted back, *What the fuck did you just say? You* knew *it was* Emma *who took the photos? Are you telling me that you let Sophie and me go through this hell for nothing?*

Nick knew he had gone too far but he didn't care. He was finished with Skylar and all of his crap. *Yes, I knew. I was only trying to help you, but in the end, you fucked it up all by yourself.*

Skylar had one more text for Nick before turning off his cell: *You are fucking* fired*!*

CHAPTER 53

AIDEN DROVE up to the entrance of the Nokia Theatre, jumped out of the car, and practically threw his keys to the waiting valet. As the valet yelled that he needed a ticket, Aiden ran into the lobby. The theater was beautiful. Surrounded in glass, it resembled the lobby of a small coliseum. Aiden looked in both directions but there wasn't a soul to be seen. He kept walking until he saw a lady at what appeared to be a ticket window. He ran up to the window just as she was getting ready to pull her shade down.

"Please, is there any way I can get inside the auditorium where the Emmys are being held?" Aiden asked as he ran up to the window.

"Not unless you have a ticket," she responded without hesitation.

"May I purchase a ticket here?"

"No, sir. The event is almost over, and we're closed for the night."

Defeated, Aiden thanked her and started to walk around to look for another entrance. Not finding one, he made his way back outside and walked around to the back of the theatre. From all the catering work he had done, he knew there had to be a back entrance for employees.

"Sir, can I ask what you are doing here?" a voice said out of the darkness.

Jumping at the sound of the voice, Aiden quickly turned to find himself face to face with a stocky, crew-cut-wearing police officer.

"I'm sorry, sir. I was looking for a back entrance. I'm Lieutenant Moore from the Los Angeles Fire Department. Station 11." Aiden, quick on his feet, realized those credentials might help him out in this situation. He took out his ID and presented it to the officer.

Immediately concerned, the policeman asked as he looked at the ID, "Is there a fire inside? Do I need to evacuate?"

"No... no need for that. I just need to get inside to check out some damaged wires."

Suspicious, the officer narrowed his eyes as he asked, "Shouldn't you be going through the front door rather than lurking around back here?"

Aiden, realizing that his lies were working against him, decided to come clean. "Okay, Officer, I'll tell you the truth. My boyfriend is Skylar Murphy, and he just won the Emmy for Best Actor. During his acceptance speech, he told the entire world that he loves me." Aiden couldn't help beaming with love at the memory of Skylar's speech. Continuing, he said, "And as sketchy as that sounds, it's the truth, and I just want to get inside to tell him that I love him too."

The officer broke out into a huge smile. "So you're the one. My wife just called to tell me that story and read me the riot act for never professing my love for her in such a grand way. Tell that boyfriend of yours he just made it hard on the rest of us guys. It's going to be next to impossible to beat that!"

Aiden smiled and said, "I'll be sure to tell him that." Looking back at the locked door, he asked the policeman, "Can you help me get inside to him?"

"I think I can manage that. Better yet, I'll get you inside the awards ceremony."

Aiden couldn't believe his luck. He had never felt so insanely happy.

The police officer took out his keys and opened the door for Aiden and himself. Turning to his colleague who was walking up, he said, "Hey, we need to go inside for a minute. Cover my area until I get back, okay?"

"Sure thing," replied the other officer.

Aiden and the officer walked through the door and into the kitchen area. "Just follow me," instructed the officer.

Together, they maneuvered their way through the sinks, dishwashers, and waiters until they were out on the other side. Inside the dining area, Aiden looked around. The place was huge and filled with beautifully decorated tables, obviously set up for an after-party.

"This way," the officer said to Aiden. They walked along the walls, avoiding tables and decorations until they reached the front doors. The officer opened another huge door and then they were inside the main part of the venue. Off to his right, Aiden could hear loud applause and voices magnified by a microphone. He knew that was where he would find Skylar.

The officer walked with him up to one of the main doors, which were guarded by even more of LA's finest. When he reached the main policeman standing guard, Aiden's new friend said, "This guy is okay. He needs to get into the main room."

Looking at Aiden with a little suspicion, the guard asked, "Are you sure?"

"Sure, I'm sure," replied the officer. "Show him your ID," he ordered Aiden.

For the second time that night, Aiden pulled out his LAFD ID, and the guard standing between him and finding Skylar moved aside and opened the door.

Once the door opened, the brightness of the lights on the stage took some getting used to. The officer who had arranged Aiden's way through the center said, "I'll just stand back here and wait for you."

Turning to him and shaking his hand, Aiden said, "I don't how I can ever thank you."

"That's enough," said the officer, laughing. "Now go and find your man."

Aiden didn't have to be told twice. He started walking down the aisle, looking for Skylar. He had no idea where Skylar was sitting, but he knew he had to find him.

CHAPTER 54

SOPHIE HADN'T said a word since she saw Skylar slam down his cell phone. She knew it had something to do with his acceptance speech but wasn't sure if it was Nick or Aiden that he was angry with.

The show was almost finished; they were on their last category. Hopefully, after that, she and Skylar could just quietly leave without bringing any more attention to themselves.

Over to her left, she heard some commotion among the guests. She glanced over and nearly fell out of her seat. Aiden was walking down the outside aisle, looking for someone. She hit Skylar in the side with her elbow. He turned and said, "What?" She motioned toward her left, and as he looked, his gaze caught Aiden's.

Aiden stopped walking, and Skylar stood up. As if in a trance, Skylar made his way down the row. The other guests had seen what was happening and were more than happy to let him through. He couldn't believe Aiden was there. How had he gotten in? Had he heard his acceptance speech? So many questions were flying around in his head.

Aiden's heart was practically bursting. Skylar looked absolutely gorgeous in his tuxedo. As they walked toward each other, they were oblivious to everyone else in the auditorium or what was happening down on the stage. They only saw each other.

They kept walking, gazes interlocked, until they were standing in front of each other.

"Did you mean it?" asked Aiden.

"Every damn word!" replied Skylar.

They met in a kiss that would be remembered for years by anyone watching the display in front of them. Skylar found Aiden's lips and clung to them as if they contained the very life of him. Aiden opened his mouth and allowed Skylar's tongue to find its way inside. After passionately kissing for what seemed like an eternity, Aiden broke away. "Do you have to stay until the end?"

"Not a chance, baby. Come on, let's go home."

CHAPTER 55

THEY REACHED Aiden's apartment in less than ten minutes. There was no talking during the ride home, just rubbing each other's hands and kissing at stoplights. It was as if they didn't want to spoil anything by talking. They just wanted to be with each other.

As they walked into the apartment, Skylar grabbed Aiden, turned him around, and captured his lips. Gently sucking on his bottom lip, Skylar teased Aiden with his tongue. Aiden, full of love for the man, wanted to devour him.

Slowly Skylar walked Aiden backward as he kissed him. They made their way to Aiden's bedroom and fell down onto the bed.

"I thought I had lost you forever," Skylar whispered, pushing his hands through the soft strands of Aiden's hair and nuzzling his lips as if he never wanted to stop kissing him.

"I thought the same thing," said Aiden in a lust-filled voice as he ran his tongue along Skylar's lips in an attempt to taste every part of him.

Groaning, Skylar sat up to try to get out of the tux. In his rush, he was struggling.

Aiden laughed and said, "Here, let me help." Quickly, he removed Skylar's jacket, then reached for the bow tie. After tossing the bow tie off to the side, Aiden started working on Skylar's shirt. As he unbuttoned each button, he looked up to see Skylar was looking at him with pure lust in his eyes. This only intensified Aiden's hunger for Skylar. Shoving apart Skylar's shirt, Aiden moved his hands up and down Skylar's taut muscles. Just feeling the rippling stomach muscles made Aiden hard as a rock.

Skylar, feeling the same intensity, leaned down to take possession of Aiden's mouth. He shoved his tongue inside and instantly tangled his tongue with Aiden's. Sucking, nipping, they kissed as if to erase the time they had been apart.

Moaning in between each erotic kiss, Aiden finished unbuttoning Skylar's shirt and helped him take it off. Leaning forward, Aiden started to plant soft kisses on Skylar's stomach and chest. Skylar was coming unglued. He wanted Aiden with everything he had inside him. He leaned down and pulled Aiden's shirt over his head. They were half naked and neither could wait for the other clothes to be gone. Skylar stepped off the bed and removed the remainder of his clothes. Aiden watched him and then started to take off his own clothes. Soon both men were naked and back on the bed.

Aiden took over. He gently kissed and nipped at Skylar's neck as he made his way down to his chest. Skylar felt like he could die any minute, and he would die happy. He had never felt like this. The love that he felt for Aiden overtook him in a way he had never expected. His entire being was content in Aiden's arms.

Slowly Aiden made his way down to Skylar's stomach. He licked and tongued the rock hardness of his stomach. After kissing each abdominal muscle, he made his way down and gently took Skylar's cock into his mouth.

Skylar almost came right then. "Holy fuck," exclaimed Skylar. He was shaking down to his toes in preorgasmic feelings. "Stop… stop… stop, baby." Pulling Aiden's mouth back up to his, Skylar said, "I'm so overwhelmed right now, I can't take it. I have to stop for a second."

Aiden, who was feeling similar emotions, just started nuzzling Skylar's neck as he waited for Skylar to give him the signal to continue.

Once Skylar felt he could breathe again, he gently flipped Aiden over on his back. He started kissing down Aiden's body. He kissed his body as if he was worshiping it. Licking and nipping at each nipple, he reveled in the moans that were escaping his lover's mouth. Skylar felt as if his cock was going to explode from the hardness. He vaguely wondered if he had ever been this excited.

Maneuvering himself between Aiden's legs, he made his way down to Aiden's cock. When he took it all in with one lunge, Aiden came up off the bed in pleasure. "Baby… please. I need you."

Skylar made his way back up to face Aiden. "I want you to take me this time. I want you inside me."

Aiden was shocked. Skylar was always a top—he had never wanted to bottom before. "Are you sure that's what you want?"

Skylar held Aiden's face in his hands and said, "Yes. I want you in every way possible." Leaning down he gently kissed Aiden on the mouth.

Aiden gently rolled Skylar over on his back. "I promise I'll be slow and easy."

"I know you will. Just make love to me."

Aiden's heart swelled. Skylar had never referred to their lovemaking in such a way before. Looking at Skylar with a smoldering gaze, Aiden started kissing down Skylar's chest again but stopped right before taking his cock into his mouth. He leaned over and reached inside the nightstand for a condom and some lube. He applied some of the lube to his fingers and started to prepare Skylar. Since Skylar had never bottomed before, Aiden knew it would take quite a bit of lube and preparation.

As he gently inserted one finger, he could feel that Skylar was uncomfortable. "Are you sure, baby? We can do this another time."

"Yes, I'm totally sure. This is what I want." As he felt Aiden place a second finger and try to loosen him up, Skylar was trying hard to not think about anything except how much he loved Aiden, but damn this was burning.

"Relax, baby," whispered Aiden.

As he prepared Skylar with his fingers, Aiden moved down to position himself between Skylar's legs. Slowly, he lifted Skylar's hips up and slid a pillow underneath him. Gently, he took Skylar's cock in his mouth. As he moved his mouth up and down, he did the same with his fingers. The double sensation was working its magic. Skylar was feeling things he had never felt before. It was like fireworks exploding inside him, zinging him with pleasure over and over. Aiden continued to stretch Skylar until he felt that he was ready.

Removing his mouth from Skylar's cock, he leaned back to put on the condom. Skylar reached down and took the condom out of Aiden's hand and started to roll it down on Aiden's cock. The touch of Skylar's hand on his cock sent Aiden reeling. He loved this man so much.

Once the condom was in place, Aiden stretched Skylar a bit more before positioning himself at Skylar's entrance. Holding Skylar's face in his hand and never moving his gaze away from his, Aiden slowly started to enter him.

"Ohhhh…," Skylar groaned, half out of pain, half out of the sensation this was causing.

"Look at me, baby… just keep looking at me. I'll stop when you say to stop."

"Don't stop," whispered Skylar. The pain was intense but not in a bad way. Skylar kept gazing into Aiden's eyes and trying to relax.

Aiden kept pushing slowly inside Skylar. The tightness was almost unbearable for Aiden, but he tried to focus on Skylar's face. When he saw a look of pain, he stopped and waited for the pain to ease. Once it felt right, he would begin again. Very carefully, Aiden kept pressing forward until he was all the way inside.

Never had Skylar felt such sensations. He felt completely full and loved by Aiden. Looking up at him with pure love in his eyes, Skylar whispered, "I love you."

Tears filled Aiden's eyes as he heard those words as he was inside Skylar. "I love you too, so very much," he whispered back. Leaning down, he captured Skylar's lips with his and passionately started to kiss him. Reaching between them, Aiden took Skylar's hardening cock and started stroking it while he remained still inside Skylar.

Groaning at all the sensations—the kiss, the stroke, and the feeling of Aiden inside him—Skylar wanted to come that very second. "Baby, please move. I need you. I need to feel you making love to me."

Aiden, who was practically coming himself, started to move gently. Skylar was so tight and hot; Aiden forced himself to think of something, anything to delay his orgasm. Moving in and out, Aiden started to pick up speed as Skylar loosened up enough so that he was not hurting.

"Ahhh… fuck! What was that?" asked Skylar.

"That, my darling, is the best part about bottoming," Aiden panted out as he maintained the same angle to hit that prostate gland every time. At this point, Skylar was able to take Aiden pounding into him, and the intensity was more than they could stand.

"*Damn*…. Holy fuck…. Stop, baby… I'm really going to come."

"Come for me, baby," Aiden said. "Show me… give it to me… all of you…."

Skylar was gasping for breath. "You have all of me. *Fuck...* I love you!" he shouted as he came like he had never come in his life, all over Aiden and himself. It was the most intense orgasm he had ever felt.

"I   really"—*thrust*—"really"—*thrust*—"really"—"*Love   you.* Ahh." Aiden pounded one last time inside Skylar as he came with a force that could be felt all through his body. He captured Skylar's mouth and just kept his open mouth over his as they both struggled to come back to reality and get their breathing back to normal.

Later, as they snuggled in each other's arms. Skylar buried his head against Aiden's neck as he said, "Never let me do anything to mess us up again."

"Not a chance, baby... not a chance. You're mine forever, and I'm never leaving you again."

Hugging each other tightly, they almost didn't hear the cell phone buzzing. Skylar reached over and pulled it out of his pants. It was a text message from the production company for *Illusions*: *Skylar, give us a call tomorrow morning. Want to talk to you about* Illusions. *We want you for our starring role. Call us.*

Skylar beamed as he read the text message. After placing the cell phone back down, he gathered Aiden into his arms.

"Who was that?" asked Aiden.

"The producers for *Illusions*. They want me for the starring role in their new feature."

Smiling, Aiden hugged his boyfriend. "I'm so proud of you."

As Skylar hugged Aiden back, for once in his life, he felt safe and at home in someone's arms. He knew, without a doubt, that he and Aiden would be hanging photos together in no time. He was home.

S.A. OZMENT was born and raised in North Carolina. From day one, she had stars in her eyes and by the time she hit high school she wanted to move to NYC and sing on Broadway. The fates (her parents) had other ideas, so she was hustled off to college and four years later, she was an accountant and had pushed those dreams aside.

For many years, in her time off, S.A. worked with different actors and singers in various roles such as a fan club president for a country music band and as a forum manager/social media promoter. Today, she is again an accountant by day but still finds time to promote a few actors (some officially, some not so officially) at night.

In 2013, she was laid off from her accounting job of twenty years. While looking for another job, she had free time to do other things. She had always loved to tell stories and therefore, she decided to use some of her experiences and write a book. Once the writing bug hit her, there was no stopping it. She has just finished her second book and is beginning a third.

Most nights, you can find her curled up in the recliner with her laptop either writing or working on some type of promotion. Unless *The Walking Dead* or *Criminal Minds* is on, then she will be captivated by the television.

You can reach S.A. Ozment at saozment@gmail.com.

Facebook: https://www.facebook.com/saozment

Twitter: https://twitter.com/saozment

Blog: http://saozment.wordpress.com

FIRE AND Water

ANDREW GREY

A WEDDING TO DIE FOR

XAVIER MAYNE

A BRANDT & DONNELLY CAPER

CASE FILE THREE

http://www.dreamspinnerpress.com

www.ingramcontent.com/pod-product-compliance
Lightning Source LLC
Chambersburg PA
CBHW070122260626
47160CB00004B/1579